THE EDGE

Briana Beijo

Amazon KDP

PROLOGUE:

I sit on the couch across from him and wonder if I have made the wrong decision. Surely, there will be consequences for doing what I'm about to do. Divulging my deepest, darkest secrets and desires feels like a betrayal to myself. What am I hoping to accomplish? I fidget uncomfortably on the sofa as I gaze at the clock hanging on the wall above him and wonder if it's too late to turn back. He leans forward in his chair and studies me as I try and come up with an excuse to leave.

"Why are you here, Dorothea?" he asks.

I clear my throat, looking up into his dark brown eyes. The weight of his question crushes me, but I feel the words bubbling in my throat like a steaming hot kettle of water ready to overflow.

"I think I'm a psychopath," I tell him – holding my breath as I watch my words sink in.

His reaction is unexpected. He doesn't seem surprised; he doesn't seem moved. He nods his head, acknowledging me as I wait for him to make the next move.

"And why do you think you're a psychopath?" he asks – seeming genuine in his want to know.

But only a fool would tell the truth now and so I stare at him blankly - wishing I could tell him that I've planned on killing my partner for weeks now, but that I just can't bring myself to do it. I wonder if he could help me. I wonder if he could change my mind. I wonder if I'm beyond saving. I wonder if I'm out of my mind. But mostly, I wonder if he notices the new perfume I'm wearing and wonder if it turns him on. I look back up at the clock and instantly regret coming. I know we both have better things to do on a Friday anyway.

CHAPTER 1

Week 1

I didn't used to be this way. I feel like I had a pretty normal childhood and everything in my life was pretty good in comparison to everyone else's around me. I mean, there were a few exceptions. My dad was an asshole. My mom was wonderful. From as early on as I can remember, I was always disappointing my dad though. I would come home from kindergarten and be grilled on why my coloring didn't stay all the way within the lines. I was screamed at in the second grade for not smiling big enough in my school photo. I would be grounded for getting anything below a B+ on homework assignments. I was expected to get A's. I couldn't even make my own friends in peace without worrying about the constant barrage of questions on how much money their parents made and what they did for a living.

"You're lucky you were even born, Thea," he'd say to me under his breath. "I didn't want kids and I was hoping that if we *did* have them, they would grow up to be smart and successful. Not this disappointing mess you're becoming. Do you want to be white trash? You need to set higher standards for yourself. You are the company you keep."

It's no surprise that I had pretty low self-esteem and by the time I graduated high school, I was ready to move as far away from him as possible. I felt bad about leaving my mom and my sister behind with him, but the second I was able to leave, I got on the first plane to California to follow my high school sweetheart, Bobby, to follow his dreams.

Bobby was going to be a rapper. He was 22 when I started dating him (I was 15) and the second I turned 18, I was off to start my happily ever after with him. Those first few months of living on my own were really hard. We lived in a studio apartment in LA and paid $2000.00 a month for rent. It wasn't long after we arrived, that we figured out we were in *way* over our heads. Bobby was doing gigs for practically *nothing* and working part-time at the corner store and I was working 60 hours a week in retail just to make ends meet. The thought of having to go back home and tell my father that I had *failed* to make it out on my own, was simply not an option for me. Something had to give, but Bobby was hell bent on becoming the next Eminem and who was I to stand in the way of his ambitions?

"You might have to get a second job, Babe," he'd said to me one night before crawling into bed after one of his shows. "I have an idea, but you have to have an open mind."

He pulled out his phone and started recording as I stared up at him, dumbfounded, as he started unzipping his pants.

That was my introduction into sex work. Apparently being freshly 18 and looking as young as I did with such an older looking boyfriend, would make me a hot commodity on porn sites. I didn't want to do it. I never in a million years imagined I would make any type of porn, but Bobby told me that I was being selfish and that if I loved him, this was the way I could help financially support our family. When I told him no, he accused me of not loving him enough - and said that maybe I *was* too young for him after all - and that maybe I wasn't confident enough to be his girlfriend. These bullshit manipulation tactics worked because I was young and stupid and hopelessly in love with him.

I was surprised how much money we were making. And I was even more surprised how much I enjoyed doing it. I had grown up such a shy and well-behaved girl that I got off on being naughty on camera for others to see. I didn't see the harm. I was making love to my boyfriend – it wasn't like I was whoring myself out to strangers or anything. Sure, I'd do weird things like call him "Daddy" and let him choke me and pull my hair on camera, but other than that, it all felt pretty natural to me. After a few months, Bobby was able to quit his job and focus on his career full-time, while I spent my days working retail and nights sucking his dick.

I really did love Bobby and had all of the confidence in the world that he was "the one". I really did think that we would be one of the few high school sweethearts who would make it. I didn't care how unlikely it would be for him to hit the big time – I was his number one fan. You can imagine my surprise when I walked in on him fucking some random 16-year-old when I left work early one day.

"I'm sorry," he said. "I didn't mean to hurt you."

Apparently, having a porn star for a girlfriend was unattractive to him and he wanted someone more wholesome whom his friends couldn't brag about wanking off to on their free time. Did it matter to him that he was the one who got me into the industry to begin with? No. Did he care that he was breaking my heart? No. And so, I did what I thought any rational person would do in that situation. I called the police and turned him in for sexually abusing a child.

That girl was 16 and still living at home with her parents. He was almost ten years older than her. Was it consensual? Sure. Did she want it? Probably. Did I give a fuck? No. I wasn't turning him in to be a good person or do the right thing. I was 15 years old myself when I started seeing him. No,

I turned him in because he hurt me and I thought he deserved to pay. And pay, he did. I'm pretty sure he's still a sex offender to this day - and it's been 17 years.

I had several strings of disastrous relationships after him. I guess you could call me a serial monogamist, I always wanted to be in love. I wanted to find that special person (man or woman) I could grow old with and start a family with.

Bad relationship after bad relationship left me questioning whether there were any good people out there at all! I could seriously write a book about each relationship – they were *that* bad. But I really did think things were going to be different this time. This was the first time in my entire life that I was one hundred percent sure. I had never in my entire life loved anyone more than I loved Lira.

After Bobby and I broke up, I moved back home to Salina, Kansas. Lira and I met in high school, reconnected a few years back, and had been living blissfully together for the last six years.

I didn't know it was possible to be this happy. I didn't know it was possible to get to spend the rest of my life with my best friend. Being in so many bad relationships had left me jaded, but being with her was effortless. It was easy. It felt right and good and pure. Our relationship was something I coveted. It was by far the best thing to have ever happened to me. But a few weeks ago, my entire life changed.

Lira has been cheating on me. She has been having an affair with some personal trainer named Tess. I can't even begin to tell you how this has destroyed me. To put the pain into words would be impossible. We never fight. Our relationship was seemingly perfect. There had been no indications whatsoever that she was unhappy or wanted to be with someone else.

But this affair was very real and, apparently, so was her love for this other woman, Tess. Hence, I have been thinking.

6

Lira has to die.

I don't know how and I don't know when . . . but I'm not going to let her get away with this.

CHAPTER 2

I woke up to soft kisses scattered across my face. I smelled the sweet, sugary scent of her vanilla perfume as she nuzzled into me - draping her arm across my chest as she trailed her lips up the nape of my neck to my earlobe. Something deep in the pit of my stomach twinged as she moved her hand slowly up my shirt.

"Good morning, beautiful," Lira whispered as she delicately ran her fingers across my stomach.

I smiled as I opened my eyes to look at her. Her long, dark chocolate hair was messy. Her brown eyes burned into me as she bit that perfectly pouted lip. She lingered momentarily before pulling me in to kiss her. I ran my fingers through her hair – careful not to pull too hard when I coiled tufts of it in my fist. She moaned into my mouth before rolling on top of me. I felt how wet she was as she straddled my thigh. This was where I mentally checked out to go through the motions.

I never had to worry about trust with Lira. Trusting her was second nature to me. Imagining I lived in a world where she would be capable of hurting me was impossible. It simply was something that never seemed like a possibility. You can imagine my complete and utter surprise and disappointment when I stumbled across our old iPad and charged it up to listen to music, only to discover she was betraying me. Because she had logged into this iPad in the past, it was completely synched up to her iCloud account – enabling me to have access to all of her text messages and phone calls. I wasn't even looking for anything! I had no *idea* that she was capable of such an atrocity. But there I was – getting ready to vacuum our living room on a normal Sunday, only to see incoming text messages from some slut named Tess telling her how she couldn't wait to sit on her face again.

"Mmm," Lira moaned as I slid two fingers inside of her.

She sat up, rocking softly back and forth on my hand as I looked up at her. She was beautiful.

But it's hard to act like nothing is wrong when you know that she does this same thing with someone else. I spent hours going through all of her messages. She never had to worry about me going through her phone before because it wasn't something I would ever do. She had a secret passcode and I honestly didn't care. Even so, she was smart. She was clearly deleting things periodically as her text thread was only from that day. But they were texting nonstop. And when I say nonstop, I mean nonstop. How the fuck was she able to text this much and get things done during the day?

"Thea," she exhaled as I rubbed my palm into her clit.

This entire situation made me sick. It had been almost two weeks now that I had been acting like nothing was wrong while reading her harlot text conversations between her and Tess. I kept telling myself that surely there was a logical explanation for this. Was I being punk'd? Was this some kind of elaborate prank she was pulling on me? Sadly, no. Each day, I learned more and felt worse. And with each passing second, the anger inside of me was taking over like some kind of living and breathing monster that had a life of its own.

I flipped her on her back and watched as her breasts bounced beneath her sheer, white t-shirt. I wasn't in the mood to take my time with it today. This bitch needed to get off so she could get off of me and go about her business. She gasped as I gripped her thighs before pulling her into me. She moaned out, loudly as I made laps around her clit with my tongue.

What I had learned from tireless hours of virtually stalking my girlfriend was that she met Tess through "work". Tess didn't work with her though. Lira made a bold move, resigning from her day job about three months ago or so to become a full time influencer and Instagram model. She was constantly creating content of her photoshoots, collaborations, brand partnerships, and events. Tess was a personal trainer for several of Lira's peers. How it escalated from them meeting to becoming full-fledged lovers was something I still hadn't figured out yet, but I was nothing if not determined to find out. Judging from their conversations, I guessed that they met right around the time Lira started her new job because big words like "love" were already being thrown around.

Tess was athletic, toned, strong – almost masculine with her muscles. She was a personal trainer and often sent selfies of herself to Lira from the gym. She had strawberry blond hair that she always wore up in a ponytail, big blue eyes, and big white teeth. Thank goodness she always wore headbands or hats though because without them, she'd look stupid as fuck with her unfortunately large forehead.

"Baby, I'm close," Lira crooned as I sucked on her clit – steadying her legs as I felt them begin to shake.

How the fuck could this happen to me? She was completely lying to me about her schedule. She would "work long hours" or "meet up with friends" almost every night. She even joined some imaginary book club so that she could sneak around with this slut! I never saw her read!

"Tell her one of your brand ambassadors is having a nervous breakdown," Tess would say. *"Tell her you forgot your friend has an extra ticket for The Chiefs!"*

And the worst part of it all was that when she was done and when she'd come home, she would wear that pretty smile and kiss me with those same lips that were just on somebody else and act like absolutely nothing was going on. She'd act like everything was peaches and cream and look at me with those eyes full of love and tell me how badly she missed me all day . . . then turn around and text Tess, "I love you, Babe. Goodnight."

"Fuck!" Lira cried as she came.

I felt her relax as she tried to catch her breath. I kissed her inner thigh before crawling up to lay beside her – smiling before I held her close.

"Jesus, Babe – you're too good at that!" she laughed, squeezing me tight.

Fucking sociopath. How had I spent six years of my life with this? I longed to smother her with the pillow. I imagined what would happen if I grabbed the pillow out from under her and tried. I wondered how long it would take her to realize I was actually trying to suffocate her and that I wasn't just playing around.

"You taste so good," I replied – smirking as she looked back up at me.

"No, seriously Thea . . . that was amazing. How am I supposed to get anything done now?"

She sat up and swiveled her hair over her left shoulder, trying her best to look innocently sexy. Oh, how I used to love that look in her eyes after I made her come undone. Now I tried my hardest to hold in the laughter building inside – she was just ridiculous to me now.

Dorothea May. I used to practice my signature using her last name. It sounded so much better to me than Dorothea Duckworth. What kind of last name was Duckworth anyway? I had to act like I wasn't completely devastated that I would have to spend the rest of my days with a hideous last name while Tess what's her forehead could potentially get Lira's last name.

"I love you," Lira smiled before leaning in for a kiss.

"I love you too," I whispered as she pulled away.

"I've been thinking a lot about the living room and I think we really should go pick out paint colors this weekend."

Lira had been wanting to redecorate and up until recently, I was excited to pick out new furniture and paint colors with her. I wondered how she could possibly be thinking about redecorating at all.

I watched her shuffle through the paint swatches that were sitting on our nightstand and was surprised how horrifyingly normal she seemed. She looked over at me and lifted up a slate-colored square – searching for my approval.

"Whatever you want, Babe," I shrugged.

She frowned, rolling her eyes as she set the square aside.

"I was thinking something neutral, modern, but sexy. Do you have an opinion? I want you to help."

"I feel like that color's too dark, Lira. We should probably pick something brighter."

"Good point," she nodded before lifting up a nearly identical swatch of a barely lighter grey.

"Oh, that one's nice!" I lied.

"I think so, too!" she smiled, lifting it up against the wall. "And I think it will look really pretty behind that cream-colored couch I told you I wanted to buy."

I thought about how easily that cream-colored couch would stain. I wouldn't be able to kill her in the living room after we got that couch. It would be too risky. I needed to do it somewhere without light colored couches and carpet. I needed to do it somewhere where I could clean up the blood.

"Do you want to order pizza and watch a movie tonight?" I asked as she turned on the shower.

"Oh, I would, but I have book club tonight – remember?" she pouted – jutting out her lip in pathetic exaggeration.

"That's right, I forgot," I replied. "What book are you reading?"

She walked back to the bed and leaned down to kiss me – holding my chin between her fingers as she pressed her lips against me. I sensed her tense as she pulled away.

"I forget what it's called! To be honest with you, I didn't like this book very much. We'll hang out tomorrow night," she whispered, gazing at me with fake sincerity. "I hate that I've made all of these commitments. You know I'm so bad at saying no to people! Why do I have to be such an overachiever?"

"It's okay, I understand," I smiled. "But you better make time for me tomorrow."

"I promise," she grinned, before stepping into the shower and shutting the shower curtain.

I grimaced – glaring at the bathroom ahead of me. She honestly didn't deserve to live. Why should I have to suffer and be heartbroken and alone while she got to jump from our relationship into another? Why should I have to deal with the humiliation of answering everyone's questions? People would pity me. People would talk and I would have to live with knowing that everyone else knew what happened.

Because Lira was loud. Lira was unapologetically open. When she loved someone, she loved them very publicly and proudly. I dreaded the day she decided to replace me with Tess for the world to see. No. That was *not* going to happen. Over my dead body.

I reached under the mattress and pulled out the iPad. I leaned over to make sure she was still in the shower before opening up the text thread. Thirty minutes ago. Only thirty minutes ago, she was talking to Tess before waking me up to fuck.

Tess: Good morning my love *winky emoji*

Lira: Good morning!!! *heart emoji*

Tess: Did you sleep good?

Lira: Would have slept better if I was next to you *sad emoji*

Tess: Well one of these days we have to change that *winky emoji*

Lira: I agree.

Tess: What time do I get to see you tonight?

Lira: Probably around 6:00. I need to remind Thea that I have book club.

Tess: Tell her not to wait up! *tongue out emoji* *water emoji*

Lira: I love you, Tess. I really hate that I can't wake up next to you.

Tess: I know, Love. Someday things will be different.

Lira: I'll text you later. Can't wait for tonight!

Tess: Ok. Have a good morning, Lira. I love you too.

I turned off the iPad and stuck it back under the mattress. I felt my cheeks warm as the blood rushed to my face. It was just the brazenness of it all. It was borderline scary. How could she have conversations like that and then have the morning she had just had with me? It was gross. I hated her. I couldn't believe this was going on.

I wondered if I could smash her head against the wall of the shower. Maybe if I tripped her, she would at least get knocked out and stay out long enough for me to drown her. Accidents happen every day. It could happen to anyone.

I frowned, feeling tears sting my eyes as I looked away. I didn't want to risk her screaming and the neighbors hearing. They would wonder why I didn't call for help, since my car was parked in the driveway and I was clearly inside.

Maybe I could smother her first with the shower curtain . . . muffle the screams?

But she might fight back and that could get messy. I wasn't confident I could overpower her. And she had long nails. I didn't know if I could get away unscathed.

I sighed before looking up at the wall ahead of me. Our picture hung above the dresser. Her arms were wrapped around me. Her long hair tumbled in curled waves. Her eyes almost seemed to sparkle. We both had ridiculously cheesy grins on our faces.

She was so beautiful to me. I always felt like she was too good for me. I was overweight. I had a pretty face, but nothing like hers. Don't get me wrong – I was smoking hot! Even for a plus sized girl, I knew I was hot shit. But Lira was hotter, which was annoying. I had mousy brown hair – stick straight. Brown eyes. But she made me feel beautiful. She made me feel loved. She made me feel special. And now she made me wish I'd never met her.

I had never seriously wanted anyone to die before. This was a first. Lira was hurting me so badly that it was all I could think about! I heard the creaking of the pipes as she shut the water to the shower off. I listened intently, hoping she would slip and save me the trouble of finding a better way.

CHAPTER 3

I remember the first time I showed crazy tendencies. I was your normal geeky kid of the 90's, but was generally liked by everyone. I wasn't popular by any stretch of the imagination though. I was just nice. I wore glasses and t-shirts that were several sizes too big and jeans that were embarrassingly too baggy. I sat in the front of class, always turned my homework in on time and always packed my lunches in my oh so super trendy Backstreet Boys lunchbox. I had two best friends. Growing up, the three of us were inseparable. We had the kind of friendship that people envied and based movies off of. The Three Amigos. Those two were all I needed.

Grace was shy. She was tall, skinny, funny, and smart. She loved to play Four Square, Dodgeball, and Tetherball on recess and gossip with me about boys during lunch. I was jealous of her thick, shiny brown hair that always looked perfectly styled - and I was envious of her baby blue eyes. She was the sweetest human on the planet and I felt like I could tell her any secret, no matter how big. She was fiercely loyal and kind.

Raymond was easy to talk to. He was chubby, short, and quiet. When you got him talking though, my GOD was he funny. He loved rock and roll and played the guitar. He had curly blond hair, wore a leather jacket, and had friendly green eyes. He didn't care that his two best friends were girls. He would be our sounding board – providing us with the much-needed male perspective on things. He never made us feel awkward or judged.

I was devastated to learn that I would be spending my fifth-grade year in a different class than them. How could our teachers be so cruel? They knew that the three of us were a package deal, but didn't take our bond into consideration when they ripped us apart; placing Grace and Raymond into Mrs. Jones' class and leaving me in Mrs. Coolidge's class to fend for myself. I was mortified.

For years, the three of us shared the same classroom. We would walk to school together, go to class together, eat lunch together, walk home together . . . we would even spend all of our free time on weekends together, too! This was a crime.

I didn't know what to do with myself. At this point – this far into elementary school – it was too late to make new friends. Everybody already had their little groups. I was placed into a mixed class of fifth and sixth graders. The fifth and sixth graders ruled the school. We were the big kids.

And the sixth graders were super intimidating. The older girls wore tighter clothes and heavy coats of mascara and the older boys had strange voices that cracked and deepened with age. For the first time in years, I hid in the back of the classroom, not knowing where I belonged or who even noticed me. All of that changed when I met Logan.

Logan was one of the most popular boys in school. He was a sixth grader. He had a large group of friends and a long line of potential girlfriends who dreamed of getting his time of day. He had blond hair he slicked back with gel, blue eyes with unusually long eyelashes, and a smile that made all of the girls in the school weak in the knees. I was intimidated by him.

Apparently, Logan was on a similar boat as me and was separated from his main group of friends – finding himself flustered on the first day of school as he tried to scope out where he should sit. He decided the back of the class was the safest bet while he suss'd out the cliques to figure out where he would best fit in. Not that it would be hard. Everyone knew who he was and everyone seemed to like him. But on this fateful first day of school, Logan picked the seat next to mine. And things for me would never be the same.

Logan had no idea who I was. Why would he? I was nice, but I was a nobody. Invisible. I didn't have cool friends or stick out in a crowd. I was shocked when he started talking to me – bitching about how awful it was that he was put in *this* class. I could empathize. I, too, didn't want to be there and longed to be reunited with my better halves. Other than Raymond, I hadn't had any male friends before. I was surprised how quickly Logan became my friend and how quickly the two of us became inseparable.

It was odd. I felt like I was living in some kind of twilight zone where I would spend my lunches and free time with Raymond and Grace – then return to class and live in some kind of fantasy world where I was close friends with one of the most popular boys in school. We talked about *everything*. He was obsessed with Bone Thugs in Harmony and secretly enjoyed my favorite movie, The Princess Bride. He would tell me all of the hot gossip about who was dating who in his grade and bragged about all of the cool stuff that the older cool kids would do after school.

He showed genuine interest in my life, too. He wanted to know all about my likes and interests, my hopes and my dreams. He wanted to know about my friends and family. He wanted to know what kind of music I listened to, what my favorite movie was, what I wanted to be when I grew up. We would talk all night on the phone before going to bed – helping one another with homework questions and giggling over anything and everything because we both thought we were *so* funny. I was happy. And I developed a *serious* crush on him.

Logan liked me too. I can't remember how it happened, but one day we got together after school and he kissed me by the monkey bars. I felt like I could fly.

I don't know who saw us or how it got out, but the next day at school, kids were laughing.

"Oh my God, you and *Dorothea Duckworth*?"

"What are you *thinking*? She's such a *nerd!*"

"Man, talk about low standards."

"Are you really *that* desperate?"

The comments went on and on. Kids could be so mean. I was hurt, but I tried not to let it get to me. Those kids didn't know the bond that Logan and I shared. They didn't even really know who he was. They didn't spend hours learning what his favorite sandwich was, the name of his dog, what made him feel better when his parents were fighting, or what made him laugh or cry. They could laugh at me all they wanted, but what Logan and I had was special. We cared about each other. Nothing could make that change.

Or so I thought.

It was shocking how swiftly it happened. He changed seats, moving to the center of the class with a couple other popular kids who I had overheard laughing at me in the hall. As soon as the bell rang, he was *gone*. He didn't call me after school like he always would. He wouldn't answer my calls. His mom said he had a headache. She told me to wait for his call.

The next day at school, he was colder. He acted like I didn't exist – avoiding eye contact with me altogether. I received silence in return when I said hi to him in the halls. I could hear everyone laughing. I didn't understand what I had done that was so wrong. I was nice to everyone and no one ever noticed me, but suddenly I was hated and I had no explanation for why - other than that I was nerdy and unworthy of the attention I was receiving from him. I tried not to let it bother me, but I openly cried when I heard him laughing with the other kids about how nerdy and pathetic I was for thinking I had a chance with him.

After that, things only got worse. Raymond and Grace almost didn't believe me, but the only break I got from the torture was my lunch hour spent with them. I would return to class and be mercilessly ridiculed. Over the weeks, it got worse and the kids got meaner. It escalated from whispers and giggles to full blown verbal abuse.

"Ugly bitch," someone would say before tripping me as I walked to my seat.

"Fat, desperate, wannabe," someone would laugh before launching a spit ball in my hair.

"Pathetic loser," Logan would sneer before knocking over all of my books and belongings from on top of my desk.

"Why are you doing this to me?" I would ask him, with tears in my eyes as I crouched down on the floor to pick up my things. "I thought you were my friend."

"Why would I ever be friends with someone like *you*?" he'd snicker – surrounding me with several others as they looked down on me from where they stood. "Oh, are you going to cry again? What kind of baby cries over someone they barely even knew?"

My cheeks would turn red as I'd sit back at my desk, pleading silently at Mrs. Coolidge for relief.

I'd get sent to the Principal's office daily because I was so depressed. I'd tell her they were bullying me and they'd always get in trouble. This seemed to only make them meaner and no matter what I would do or say, nothing would work.

"So, you're a tattle tale now?" Logan would say before pushing me on the ground. "Stop being such a crybaby, Thea! Nobody cares!"

I'd sob as I stared up into his once familiar blue eyes – trying to understand who this monster was that made it their mission to ruin my life.

"Stupid Bitch," he'd laugh before dumping water on my head at recess.

"Loser," he'd mumble under his breath as he'd trip me in the hall.

I didn't know what depression was until the fifth grade. It's amazing what months of bullying can do to a young, impressionable psyche. I never thought about things like suicide before. What kind of child ever would? But I cried myself to sleep every night and dreaded waking up to go to school.

"Please don't make me go, Mom," I'd wail. "I can't deal with it any longer!"

My mom tried talking to his parents. They said I was obsessed with him and that I was the one causing the problems.

"Logan would never do what you're describing," they'd say. "Your daughter just wants attention."

My dad got sick of me crying every night. He said I was weak and that it was no wonder they kept harassing me. I made it easy, he said. I needed to have a backbone.

Raymond and Grace tried their best to comfort me. Because we were in different classes, there wasn't much they could do. The teachers and principal were getting sick of me. I think they felt just as helpless as I did. These kids were freakishly relentless and no punishment seemed to deter them. Detention was like a cool hangout for them. They would only get together and plot new and cruel ways to punish me for getting them in trouble.

I felt like a shell of myself. I was heartbroken that I lost someone I considered a good friend . . . someone I cared about deeply – my first real crush. I was tired of being bullied. My self-esteem was nonexistent. I was only ten years old and I wanted to die. Something had to change. I couldn't go on much longer.

It started as a white lie. I never meant for it to get so out of control. Looking back, this was the first sign that there was probably something wrong with me – but at the time, it seemed completely justified.

I was about to walk home from school one day. Raymond and Grace couldn't walk with me for some reason, so I was alone. I heard Logan calling my name, but I ignored him. Maybe if I walked fast enough, I wouldn't be able to hear the mean things he was saying. Maybe if I ignored him, he'd go away. But, no. He ran up to me and pushed me as hard as he could from behind.

I went down, staining my jeans in the grass as I skid on my knees. He laughed so hard; he made an asthmatic honking noise. He hovered over me as I got up, wiping the dirt off my hands.

"God you're fun to fuck with," he laughed, shoving me again.

I felt my eyes burn as I tried to hold back my tears. I looked up at him, hoping to find some humanity in his gaze. There was none.

"Oh, are you going to cry again, Thea?" he pouted. "Are you going to run to your friend, the principal, and tell on me again?"

He *spit* on me, glaring at me with disgust.

"Run home, Thea. You better run before I catch you."

My heart was pounding as I got ready to listen to him and make a run for it, before I heard a woman's voice yelling at him from my side.

"HEY YOU!" she screamed – pointing at Logan. "I SAW YOU SPIT ON THAT GIRL! COME HERE! WHAT'S YOUR NAME?"

His eyes got wide before he turned and bolted in the opposite direction. The woman approached me, seeing that I clearly needed help. I burst into tears.

"Oh my God, sweetie, are you okay?" she asked, leaning down as she wiped the tears from my eyes.

I don't know what compelled me to say this. Maybe it was the culmination of many little things. Maybe pieces of my soul had been slowly chipped away. But I was over Logan's bullshit. I wanted him to pay.

"Did you see that?" I asked, staring up at her with a look of fear that made the color in her cheeks fade. "Did you see the knife?"

"The knife?" she asked, listening intently.

"He had a knife!" I sobbed, cradling myself as I stared at the ground. "He said if I told on him one more time, he would kill me!"

"He said, WHAT?" she asked – her tone painted with shock.

"I'm scared!" I cried – launching myself into her arms. "Please help me! I want to go home!"

"Okay, honey, don't worry – I'll get you home!" she said.

I could see my house from where we were standing. She walked with me across the field as she followed me home. I told her all about the kids and how they would bully me. Everything I said was true. I didn't think I would see this woman again. I was hoping she would tell the teachers and that he would finally get in some real trouble. I didn't realize how serious my accusation was.

The next day at school, I got pulled into the principal's

office. The door opened and Logan stepped out with tears in his eyes as two police officers escorted him out of the room. He made eye contact with me and screamed.

"YOU LYING BITCH!" he howled. "TELL THEM THE TRUTH, THEA! I NEVER THREATENED YOU!"

"That's enough!" one of the cops warned before jerking him away.

He sobbed uncontrollably as they ushered me into the principal's office, before shutting the door.

"I'm so sorry, Dorothea," the principal said to me as I took a seat next to another police officer. "You will never have to worry about him again."

"Tell us what happened," the officer said kindly, placing her hand on my shoulder as I prayed that they couldn't see the deception in my eyes.

"This doesn't surprise me," Mrs. Coolidge interjected. "He and his friends have been bullying her relentlessly for months."

I repeated the same story to them as I had the day prior. I made sure to keep every part of the story the same. I learned that Logan was being expelled and sent to a place called juvenile hall. It was basically a prison for kids.

"He'll never hurt you again," the officer assured me. "It's over, Dorothea. You're safe."

To this day, I still think about that lie I told. It was the first thing I ever did that I knew deep down was wrong. Logan never threatened to kill me. He never had a knife. But I was tired of being bullied. I was tired of crying myself to sleep. He needed to pay.

I had a wonderful rest of my fifth-grade year. None of those kids dared to mess with me anymore. I think they were all afraid. They had underestimated me. They didn't want to end up in juvie. Something my teacher said still haunts me. When kids told her I was lying, she'd defend me and say:

"Good things happen to good people, Thea. You're a *good person*. So good things will come back to you, but bad things also happen to bad people like Logan. He got what was coming to him."

I still wait for Karma to come back at me for that one.

CHAPTER 4

Over the years, my friendships with Raymond and Grace remained as strong as ever. We went to the same middle school and high school. I was active in theater and arts, while Grace went on to become head cheerleader. Raymond focused more on his studies. When we graduated high school, Grace received a full ride scholarship for cheer – leaving Raymond and I behind while she left the state.

After Bobby and I broke up, I returned home and moved in with Raymond while I took courses online to study sociology. Over time, Raymond and Grace drifted apart, but she and I remained close while Raymond and I maintained our own friendship. I ended up living with Raymond for almost four years.

I seemed to have terrible luck in relationships. No – seriously. *Terrible luck.* It meant everything to me that I had Ray by my side. I didn't exactly have the most positive male influences around me growing up. My father seemed to always be annoyed with me and I always seemed to fall in love with cheating assholes who were incapable of keeping it in their pants. Ray was different. I didn't *have* to worry about anything with him because there were no ulterior motives. He was my best friend. He was my brother. I felt protected by him. I felt safe. I could confide in him . . . I could tell him anything.

When I was sad, he was always there to lift my spirits. When I was angry, he was the voice of reason. When I needed someone in my corner, he was my biggest supporter. Grace was there for me too, but she lived far away for several years. It's difficult to describe the brother/sister bond you develop when you become roommates with one of your best friends.

One of my more meaningful relationships had been with a guy named Peter. Peter had gone to high school with us and ended up moving in with Ray and me after I moved back from California. It wasn't awkward that Peter lived with us. Ray never felt like the third wheel. He and Peter had become best friends as well - and we felt like one happy little family.

Peter was funny and nice. He was extremely smart. He was tall, scrawny, nerdy and awkwardly charming. I was surprised I fell in love with him. Peter and I ended up dating for four years and one summer night, he proposed to me beneath the stars.

I was only 23. I had spent that autumn planning our wedding and was genuinely happy and excited to begin the next chapter of my life with Peter by my side. Things quickly took a turn for the worse when I walked in on Peter cheating on me. I had gone out of town for the weekend with my family and returned a day early. I didn't tell Peter or Ray. I wanted to surprise them. You could imagine how upsetting it was when I walked into our apartment to discover Peter balls deep in some big breasted blond he had bent over our dining room table. There really wasn't much he could say.

He had fallen in love with aforementioned bimbo and admitted he had been getting cold feet.

"I'm too young to settle down," he told me. "I'm not ready to get married. I want to break up."

I was crushed by this. Peter and I had never had any problems. We hardly ever even fought! I felt blindsided and heartbroken. I didn't want to believe it was true either. But upon discovering this treachery, I moved out of our apartment – and ended up moving into a new one with Grace, who had moved back home upon receiving her degree.

Peter ended up marrying the girl he cheated on me with, years later. It took me years to fully recover from that blow.

One of the things that bothered me the most about that situation was that Peter had confided in Ray that he was having an affair. Raymond was bothered by this – not wanting to be caught in the middle between two of his best friends. He continually told Peter to tell me, but never told me himself. I was hurt by this.

I knew that if the tables were turned and someone was hurting Ray, I wouldn't be able to stand by and turn a blind eye. I ended up forgiving him though, trying to be sympathetic of the awkward position he'd been placed in. Peter *was* one of his best friends, after all. But Peter's name became a point of contention and so Raymond and I agreed to never talk about him again.

Years passed and life carried on. I was enjoying my twenties – living with Grace and making new memories. Eventually, I got over the pain that Peter had caused. Raymond had made new friends of his own through work and told me he thought he found the "perfect guy for me". I was reluctant to become romantically involved with someone he was friends with again, but figured – what the heck.

Ray introduced me to his good friend, Westly and I was instantly smitten with him. It was almost creepy how similar Westly and Peter were. I made a mental note that clearly Raymond had a "type" when it came to friends – and that type also happened to be one that I was fond of myself.

I was 26 and ready for something serious. Westly had all of the qualities I wanted in a man. He was intelligent, loyal, funny, and true. By true, I mean that he was a genuinely good person. I felt like there wasn't a bad bone in his body.

One of the most attractive qualities about him was that I was confident he would never hurt me. And that was something that was *very* important to me after the last few breakups I had been through. When Westly and I began to get serious, Ray pulled us aside and told us that it was *imperative* that we were good to one another.

"I won't go through what I went through with you and Peter again," he told me. "If Westly ever cheats on you, I'm never speaking to him again. And same goes to you, Dorothea. If you ever cheat on him, I won't ever speak to you again either. I love you both too much to deal with one of you getting hurt like that."

"I would never!" I assured him.

There was no way I would ever cheat on someone I loved. I had been hurt too many times to do that to somebody else. I was better than that. I was a good person. Or at least, that's what I told myself in the beginning.

A few years into my relationship with Westly, things went south. We were *completely* wrong for one another. I don't know why I convinced myself otherwise. What I had with Westly was a glorified friendship. There was no passion between us. There was no spark. After six months of no sex from him and refusal on his part to go to couple's therapy, he dropped a bomb on me that I'll never forget.

"Thea, I need to talk to you," he said. "I'm not sure how to tell you this, but I've given it a lot of thought. I don't think I want us to be intimate anymore."

I stared at him, not knowing what to say.

"I think I'm asexual," he said, taking a deep breath.

"What the fuck does that mean?" I replied.

"It means I have no desire to be sexual in any way, shape or form. I get that expecting you to be abstinent is out of the question. If sex is something you need in your life to be happy, then go get it elsewhere. Just make sure I *never* find out about it."

I should have left him right then and there. I should have packed my bags and hit the road. But adulting is hard - and I felt trapped in many ways. I couldn't afford my own place. I had nowhere to go. I didn't want to move back in with my parents and Ray had his own place. Grace had gotten married. I didn't want to barge in on their lives. I told myself I would give it a genuine shot and tried to accept that I would likely spend the majority of my life lonely.

Sex was a big deal to me and living without it was something I wasn't sure I could do. But for a while, I tried. I didn't go into it with intentions of fucking other people, as he so blatantly suggested. I didn't want to be intimate with anyone else.

This is where Lira came in. Lira had been my friend for years and I had always had an unrequited crush on her. She was a lesbian and I was bisexual. I never imagined anything would ever happen between us. I never dared to make a move for fear of ruining the friendship we had. But one drunken night, I vented to her about my frustrations with Westly and told her all about his asexuality and the struggles I had been dealing with. She was nonjudgmental and concerned. She listened to me and was there for emotional support. I didn't mean to fall in love with her. I never expected I would be put in such a crazy situation, but there I was.

"You wouldn't have to deal with this if you were with me," she whispered. "I love you, Thea. I always have. Leave him. Be with me. I'll show you how love is supposed to be."

This launched me into one of the most scandalous chapters of my life. Lira and I had a secret relationship for three months while I tried to figure out what to do about Westly.

I didn't want to hurt him, but what he wanted from me

was not something I could give. I didn't want to have *half* a relationship with someone. I didn't want to fuck other people and come home to him for the companionship. I wanted someone who was more than just my best friend. I wanted it all. I found that in Lira. When I finally got the courage to leave Westly, he was crushed.

"I love you," he sobbed as I packed my bags. "Please don't do this to me. I'll do anything. I'll go to therapy with you. I'll force myself to have sex with you – I'll do whatever you want!"

"That's the problem right there," I said, not wanting to hurt him, but needing him to understand. "I don't want someone that feels like they have to *force* themselves to have sex with me. I just," I shrugged, "need more."

Westly poisoned my name to all of our mutual friends. I didn't tell any of them that he was asexual because it wasn't my secret to share. I accepted the consequences, cutting my losses as people gradually stopped talking to me. I knew deep down in my heart that Lira was the right one for me.

I wasn't expecting this to happen. It wasn't my fault. But there was one person who was angrier than anyone else. This person was the *only* one I cared about in the fallout of this breakup. Ray.

"Did you cheat on him?" he asked me.

"No," I lied. "I had feelings for her, but I didn't cheat. I left him for her, Ray."

"You're lying."

I always planned on telling him, but I didn't know how. I needed to let the dust settle. Westly was too hurt. Things were too fresh. I didn't want to add insult to injury by telling Westly that I had cheated on him with Lira in addition to leaving him for her too . . . even though he told me I could as long as I made sure he never found out about it.

"You're not ready to admit it and that's fine," Ray said – his voice ice cold. "But I told you that if you ever cheated on him, I'd never speak to you again."

That was six years ago. And that was the last time Ray ever spoke to me.

Grace and I got together weekly to share a few glasses of wine, catch up, and talk about anything new that was going on in our lives. Her eyes widened as I told her about my discovery of the iPad and filled her in on everything that had been going on with Lira's deceit. She was unprepared for this.

"Jesus Christ, Thea!" she gasped, covering her mouth in shock. "What are you going to do?"

I drummed my fingers on the table before raising my glass to my lips. Grace was by far the most stand-up human I had ever met in my life. I didn't know how to respond to her question without lying so I took another drink.

"I can't believe she's doing this to you!" Grace said, shaking her head in disbelief. "You and Lira are soulmates! How could she do this to you?"

I laughed – the wine tasting bitter as I took another sip.

"Thea, talk to me," she pleaded – reaching across the table and resting her hand on mine.

I pursed my lips, trying to hold back the anger that was bubbling up inside.

"I think I'm just gonna wait it out," I said, avoiding eye contact with her. "It's probably just a stupid fling she needs to get out of her system."

Grace laughed incredulously, shaking her head in wonder at me.

"You can't keep up this act forever," she spat. "Eventually, this is going to eat you alive."

"I'm fine for now," I said, looking into her blue eyes.

"Dorothea, come *on*," she said, not bothering to mask the concern in her tone. "The love of your life is cheating on you. How do you expect to walk around acting like everything is ok?"

"I need to let this play out some more," I said, raising the glass to my lips. "I haven't figured out what I want to do yet."

I was lying of course. I knew *what* I was going to do – I just couldn't decide *how* I wanted to do it yet.

"Baby girl," Grace said as tears filled her eyes. "I don't even know what to say."

"It makes me sick," I said, shaking my head. "And dealing with this - while I deal with the Ray thing has been a challenge. As if I'm not already hurting enough."

Grace sighed, shaking her head at me.

"Dorothea, what do you mean?" she groaned – penetrating me with her worried gaze. "You and Ray haven't been friends for *years*. What were you expecting, hun?"

A few weeks prior, I had sent Raymond a hand written letter. It was the most beautifully tragic message ever conveyed. I poured my heart out to him. I told him the pain of being erased from his life was too much to take. I told him that no amount of years could dull the ache of his absence and that I just wanted him to talk to me to provide me with closure on *why* and *how* he could throw our friendship away like it was nothing. I had tried talking to him countless times throughout the years with no answer. He never responded. He blocked my phone number and blocked me on all social media outlets. He completely ghosted me after I got with Lira.

It was the worst thing that had ever happened to me in my life. I cherished my friendship with Ray. I had been friends with him since I was a little kid and couldn't wrap my mind around how he could end our friendship because I had cheated on my asexual boyfriend when he was still best friends with another ex-boyfriend of mine who had cheated on *me.*

I sent him this letter – *begging* him to at least talk to me. It had been six years. I thought that a handwritten letter would for sure tug at his heartstrings. Why couldn't he at least give me the compassion of a conversation? I needed it to heal.

"What he did to me was unfair," I said – feeling tears well up in my eyes. "I deserve an explanation."

"Honey, you're never going to get one," Grace whispered. "Raymond's stubborn. Remember, I used to be friends with him too. Sometimes no answer *is* the answer, Thea. He doesn't care. I know that's hard to hear, but he's moved on with his life. I think it's time you try to move on too."

A single tear dropped from my eye as I took another sip of my drink.

"Seriously, to hell with Raymond right now!" Grace lamented. "The real issue is Lira cheating on you. *That* is what you should be focusing on right now!"

"Nobody fucking stays with me," I whispered. "Everyone abandons me. Everybody leaves."

"Um, hello . . ." Grace waved. "What am I? Chopped liver?"

"You know what I mean," I replied. "I feel like I can't trust anyone. I can give my whole heart to someone and they just turn around and step on it."

"You need to break up with her," Grace insisted. "You can stay with Greg and me. We have a spare room you can stay in until you get back on your feet."

"I'm good for now," I said, shaking my head at her. "Like I said, I don't know what I want to do yet."

"You're just going to torture yourself," she replied. "What she's doing is fucked. You don't deserve this. You shouldn't have to stand by and watch as someone lies to you day by day."

Oh, Grace. Soon it wouldn't matter because Lira was going to get taken care of. She was a lost cause. Now, what to do about Ray . . .

"Thea," Grace said, pulling my attention back to her. "I love you. You know I love you, right?"

"For now," I sighed, pouring myself another drink.

"I resent that," she said, glaring at me as I filled my glass. "But I'll let it slide because I know you're hurt."

"I love you, too," I replied to her.

And I really did love Grace more than anything. She would never understand what I was going through. Aside from her, loving people never did anything but hurt me. And I was done letting people hurt me. The only thing that mattered to me now was coming up with a plan.

CHAPTER 5

Week 2

Sometimes Lira would snore when she was in a deep sleep. It wasn't one of those loud and obnoxious snores that kept you up at night, but one of those tiny – almost inaudible – snores that seemed cute. I used to find it endearing, but now... I waited patiently as I lied in bed next to her – making sure not to move or disturb her in any way until I heard the familiar pops and crackles of her little breaths.

Finally.

I quietly and carefully crept out of bed, staring down at her cautiously to ensure that she was, in fact, fast asleep. She looked so peaceful and vulnerable just lying there . . . incapable of the crimes she had committed against our relationship.

I glared down at her before reaching under the bed to pull out the little bag I had waiting for me there - ready to go. I tiptoed across the bedroom, taking care to open the door as silently as possible as I made my way out into the hall. I wanted to get this done quickly. I also didn't want to rush it and make a mistake by running into something or knocking something over. No. I had to be smart about this. I had to be patient.

I descended the stairs, slinking down the hall and

through the kitchen before delicately and carefully slipping out of the sliding glass door that led to the back yard. I caught myself holding my breath as I opened the gate that led to the side of the house – hoping the familiar creak of the rusty hinge wouldn't disturb Lira from her slumbers.

I looked up at our bedroom window when I reached the front of the house – watching intently to make sure she hadn't awoken. I saw no evidence of movement and smiled to myself before opening the little bag. I pulled out the car key and looked around at the other houses around me. It was 3:17 AM in the morning. The street was quiet. All lights in the surrounding neighbors' homes were off. I turned the key to the car door and slid inside.

I had spent a lot of time over the past few weeks on some shady websites – deep in search of ways to continue my observations of Lira's behavior. I couldn't break up with her until I knew why she cheating on me with Tess. I also didn't want to break up with her until I knew how I was going to kill her.

Some friendly internet sleuth I met in one of the forums I frequented, pointed me in the right direction of the tiny device I now pulled out of my bag. I smiled smugly to myself as I admired it in the palm of my hand.

This tiny, black device would be my new best friend – enabling me to hear any and every conversation that took place inside of Lira's car. I pulled out the flat headed screwdriver in my bag and carefully and quietly popped a panel off of her dashboard before delicately inserting this little device inside. I replaced the panel and pulled out my phone, opening up the software I had installed to monitor the recordings.

"Test, test, test," I whispered before a red notification popped up on my screen.

I listened back and smiled to myself. This microphone was strong. I took a deep breath, feeling satisfied as I carefully exited the car. Slowly and stealthily, I crept back to the bedroom. Phase one was now complete. The bitch's car was now officially bugged.

I slept like a baby for the next few hours before meeting Lira downstairs for breakfast. I turned the corner into the kitchen and paused as she looked up at me from across the island as she poured herself a to-go cup of coffee.

She was wearing faded blue jeans and a low-cut red V neck tee that left almost no room for imagination with the way it expertly hugged her curves. Her chocolate hair tumbled in curled waves and her lips curved into a smile – coated appropriately in blood red lipstick. Where was she going so early in the morning on a weekend? And who was she all dolled up for? Obviously, Tess, but it blew my mind that she thought she wasn't making it obvious.

"Good morning, Babe!" she smiled as I made my way over to her.

I pulled her in for a hug, nuzzling into her neck as I breathed her in. She smelled so good. She smelled like candy. I felt a pang of resentment as I imagined Tess thinking the same thing.

"You're up early," I said, looking down into her eyes as I wrapped my arms around her waist. "Where are you going, looking so damn beautiful?"

She flushed, looking down as she tucked a strand of hair behind her ears.

"You're sweet," she said, biting her lip. "Don't you remember? I'm having brunch with the girls from work today!"

I nodded my head – certain she had never made mention of this alleged brunch.

"Must have slipped my mind," I sighed, leaning into the counter. "I'm bummed. I was hoping we could spend the morning together."

"Aw, I'm sorry, Babe," she pouted, looking disappointed. "I'm free later tonight, if you want to hang out?"

"Well," I paused, pretending to think, "ok, good! I can whip up something for us to eat and grab a bottle of wine. Or I could come with you!"

Lira's eyes widened ever so slightly as I watched her internally panic.

"That's so sweet of you, Thea, but the other girls aren't bringing their significant others. I hope you understand!"

"Yeah," I frowned. "I just feel needy today. You look too good to leave the house."

She laughed out loud, shaking her head at me.

I wondered if flattery and loving words would eat at her conscience. Did she care at all that she was lying to me? Did it hurt her to know that I was so wonderful while she was so conniving?

"Oh stop," she said, waving her hand bashfully. "I wish I could stay with you today, too. But, I can't – I promise I'll get home early tonight so we can spend some time together!"

I smiled, clenching my jaw.

She stepped closer, gazing into my eyes before pulling me in for another hug.

"I'd kiss you, but I'd smudge my lipstick," she said.

"Wouldn't want to mess up that pretty face," I agreed.

She pulled away and smiled again before grabbing her purse and mug off of the counter. She kissed the air before turning to head for the door.

"Love you bunches, Thea!"

"Love you more!" I called after her.

Fucking bitch.

I watched out the window as she started up her car. I fired up the application on my phone to the bug I had planted hours prior. I fumed as it opened up and began to play – filling the kitchen with her songlike voice.

"Good morning, Love," she said – holding the phone up to her ear as she put the car into reverse. "I'm good and you?"

I watched her back out of the driveway – oblivious to me watching her from the window. She couldn't even wait long enough to get out of the driveway before calling this bitch!

"Yeah, I like that place too. I'm starving! I did tell her I was having brunch with some friends... What do you want to do today?"

She disappeared from view as she took off down the street. She laughed – clearly amused by whatever Tess was saying to her on the other end of the phone.

"Mmm. That sounds nice," she chuckled. "Don't talk like that, not here, not now. You're making me wet."

I laughed an audible, "HA!" as I opened the fridge to pull out the gallon of milk for my cereal.

She was silent for a while as she drove. The clicks of her turn signal and passing cars exited the speaker.

"Tess, I know," she sighed. "It's just not a good time."

A good time for what, I wondered? *To tell me the truth? To leave me?* I rolled my eyes as I sat at the table.

"It's not like that," she replied. "Let's not fight about this today, please. I want to have a good day."

Oh cute, they fight.

I chewed my cereal – annoyed that I couldn't hear what Tess was talking about on her end of the call.

"I love you, Babe," Lira insisted. "I know this isn't ideal, but it's complicated."

What's complicated, Lira? – I was fuming. *You're fucking around with a personal trainer and lying mercilessly to your girlfriend of six years. Sounds pretty straightforward to me.*

"Okay, well I'm excited for that," she laughed – her tone lighter again. "I'll see you in ten."

She hung up the phone and sighed.

"Fuck," she whispered.

Yeah, Lira. Fuck. My sentiments, too.

I turned off the app, feeling annoyed as I finished my food. Who the fuck did she think she was? Why did she love somebody else? I had given *everything* to this girl. I had devoted myself to her – heart and soul! I never gave her a reason to stray. My family adored her. Her family adored me. We had the same likes, interests and goals. We had a vision for our future. She was my *friend.*

I sighed as I made my way up to the bedroom to pull out the iPad. I didn't understand why I still let this get under my skin. It's not like she could do anything to fix this. She showed zero remorse. That was why I wanted to kill her. Maybe if she had a shred of empathy, things would be different. But she was evil. She was hollow inside. She wasn't the good person I thought she was.

I powered up the iPad and pulled up her messages for the day. Tess had texted her at 6:52 AM.

Tess: Come get it

I stared in shock as the text was followed up by a pic of her vag.

Lovely, I muttered – clicking on it to zoom in.

There was a landing strip of light blond pubes and her fingers reached down, parting her labia – snapping the pic up close and personal for Lira to see.

Gross, I whispered, shaking my head. It wasn't even a sexy photo. It was just a desperate thirst trap. If I was going to send photos of my lady bits to someone, I'd at least make the photo beautiful. This was worse than your standard dick pic.

What an amateur.

I closed the photo and continued reading the conversation.

Lira: Oh my, hi!

Tess: Hi!

Lira: Damn, Baby – YUM *tongue out emoji* What are you doing?

Tess: Waiting for you

Lira: I can't today. Thea's off.

Tess: Well, tell her you're busy. Make something up. I want to see you.

Lira: I don't want her to get suspicious *Sad face emoji*

Tess: Just make her think you told her you had plans and she forgot.

So you're the culprit, I sighed.

Lira: That's fucked up!

Oh, she has a soul after all! My eyes widened as I shook my head.

Tess: Lira, I told you, I can't be with someone that doesn't prioritize me. It feels a lot like you're prioritizing her.

Well I'm her girlfriend, you stupid bitch. I kept reading.

Lira: That's not fair. Thea and I are still together.

Tess: Sounds like a personal problem. *Shrugging emoji*

Lira: Fine. Let me take a shower.

Tess: Really? Thank GOD! *Smiley emoji*I miss you so much! I've been thinking about you all morning.

Lira: I love you!

Tess: I love you more!

I shut off the screen. I really hated Tess. I couldn't wait to confront her one day. What would I even say? I'd think of something clever, no doubt. For now, I just had to deal with her desperate attempts to ruin my life.

I shut off the iPad and got ready to take a shower. I wanted to wash off the smell of Lira's lingering perfume.

Lira returned home around 6:00 PM. She had messaged me after "brunch" saying she had to do some photo shoot she forgot to tell me about. I had salmon baking in the oven and was finishing up my garlic herb rice pilaf and salad for the sides. Her favorite. She smiled as she took a deep breath – basking in the scent as she made her way into the kitchen.

"That smells freaking *amazing*," she said as she set her purse down and walked up behind me – hugging me as I chopped the carrots.

"I hope you're hungry," I smiled before turning my face to kiss her – making a mental note that her red lipstick was no longer anywhere to be found.

"Starved!" she crooned, rubbing my lower back as she moved beside me. "Thank you so much for this! You didn't have to cook. We could have ordered in."

"I felt like spoiling you," I replied as I scraped the cut up carrots off of the cutting board and into the salad bowl. "It's been a while since we've had a decent date night. I just want you to know how much I love you, Lira."

I turned to face her, reaching for her hand as I gazed into her big, brown eyes. Her eyes flickered momentarily as she looked at her feet and back up at me. What did she think about in that nanosecond? What did she feel? *Guilt?*

"This is really nice," Lira whispered, smiling briefly before pulling me into her arms. "I don't deserve this."

Well that's for sure, I silently agreed.

"What do you mean?" I laughed, kissing her forehead. "You've been so busy with your new job and juggling all of these new activities. I'm proud of you! I guess I've just been craving more quality time."

"Yeah," she agreed, looking away. "My schedule has been pretty busy. I'm sorry about that, Thea. I hope you understand."

Sure, Lira. I understand you're a manipulative slut. I understand you don't value our relationship. I understand you don't give a shit about me.

"Of course I understand. Sorry, Babe. I just want to spend more time with you. Can we maybe work on that?"

Lira was quiet for a moment before returning my gaze.

"Definitely," she said, nodding her head. "Things will be slowing down soon. I miss you a lot too."

She leaned in and kissed me – her lips sending flutters to my stomach as she ran her fingers through my hair. *Damn, she was good.* I wondered why I wasn't enough for her. I wondered if she even felt anything when she kissed me anymore.

"I'm going to go get changed into something more comfortable," she sighed – smiling at me as she pulled away.

I grinned as she turned her back and headed for the stairs.

I hoped she felt terrible. I hoped it made her sick to think about what she had done and what she continued to do. I hoped she would reach the bedroom and text Tess that this craziness had to end and that she couldn't go on hurting the love of her life. I really, really wanted that.

But I knew better. I knew that she wouldn't stop. So I also hoped she would accidentally trip and fall down the stairs.

Relationships could be so exhausting. I needed to keep my head on straight.

CHAPTER 6

I remember knowing there could possibly be something wrong with me at a young age. There were certain things I would do that I knew wouldn't be classified as "normal". I was a people pleaser. I wanted so desperately to make everyone happy and for everyone to like me. Other people's opinions of me mattered. I was able to play into other people's unique personalities – molding myself into a version of myself I thought they would want me to be.

Some people would call this manipulative. I felt it was necessary. Getting along with people was so simple. I was such an extremely empathetic person – I knew that I could connect with anyone. The problem was trying to get people to connect with *me*.

If I could tell someone didn't like me, I would observe the people they *did* like and try to emulate *that*. I was very submissive and amiable. People found me to be irresistibly charming.

In my adult life, this has done wonders for my career. But the reality is, you can't make everyone like you. And I always took it unusually hard when I failed to win someone over.

Most people . . . *normal* people, wouldn't care. They would simply accept that said person didn't like them and move on with their lives. But there was something dark in me.

I harbored a lot of resentment and hatred toward people who were cruel. And I thought it was cruel if someone didn't like me back.

"Fine," I would think to myself. *"If we aren't friends, we can be enemies."*

And then I would make it my mission to make them miserable in some kind of way.

I wondered where this behavior stemmed from. I had seen many therapists over the years and received many different diagnoses. Anxiety Disorder, Depression, Borderline Personality Disorder, Histrionic Personality Disorder, Bipolar Disorder, and PTSD were a few. I never felt like any of these labels *fit*. Labels were for soup cans, anyway.

I was so much more than just one thing. What I didn't lack was emotion. One thing I knew about myself was that I felt things *too* much. But the flip side to that coin was that if someone hurt me, I felt an unimaginable sadness followed by an unimaginable rage. This part of myself was getting worse with age.

I always wanted my father's approval. I never got it. My father didn't see anything wrong with his behavior. He showed favoritism to my sister, Shelly, but only because she was someone he wanted her to be. I was something he couldn't understand and this caused him great disappointment.

My father was the type of person who liked to control everyone and everything around him. I could not be controlled. This pissed him off. And it pissed me off that he wanted me to be someone I couldn't be.

I felt like narcissistic people were attracted to me. I had dated a couple of them and realized they were like magnets to me and I fueled their narcissistic needs. I craved attention. I lived for drama. I didn't feel alive unless things were passionate and exciting. Unfortunately, that energy was usually provided by unhealthy relationships that fanned the flames of my mental illness. I no longer pretend not to know and accept that I am mentally ill.

Another weird thing about myself, was that from a young age, I was very sexual. When I was a kid – as young as 11 or 12 – I used to masturbate with my friends. I loved it.

This behavior continued well into my teens. I loved seeing the looks in my friends' eyes when they would cum with me and I didn't think it was weird. I thought all friends should do it! This unexplained want to explore my own body and share that part of myself with other people was just a part of who I was. Obviously, this made a lot of the people closest to me question my motives.

Was I doing this because I was a closeted lesbian? Did I want attention? Was I just a pervert? Maybe a little bit of everything.

I never cared if it was a male or female – I was capable of wanting and loving someone regardless of gender.

As I got older, the masturbating with friends turned into sex with friends. I couldn't seduce all of my female friends into fucking me, but I definitely tried. I was more successful with the guys. There was a strange power in knowing I could get anyone I wanted to fuck me.

I felt like friendship became so much more *intimate* once I had watched one of my friends cum. While I knew that my friends were doing it for other reasons – because they wanted attention, were just curious, or fantasizing about someone else . . . I was *in* it with them. I *wanted* them to feel good. I *wanted* them to moan for me. I don't know. This earned me a reputation of being a slut, but the older I got, the more I was able to keep this part of me in check.

Once I fell in love . . . and I fell in love easily . . . I was a very loyal and loving partner. But I thrived on knowing people thought I was pretty. I didn't just want people to think I was pretty. I wanted men to go home with their wives and think of me while they jacked off before bed. I wanted to be *wanted*. It gave me great joy. I prided myself on my ability to eye fuck and come across as effortlessly innocent and hopelessly seductive to any person I would meet. I exuded sexuality. I was the most sensual being I knew! But I didn't talk about this with anyone other than my doctors. I didn't want people to think I was a freak. I just let them think I was a giant flirt. A giant flirt is a much easier pill to swallow than sexual deviant.

I was turned on by anything taboo. I had dated a bisexual man once and it *thrilled* me that he wanted to have his first male experience with me. I remember watching him get his dick sucked as I stared into his eyes – watching him love it and need it – as I encouraged him to give into all of his deepest desires.

"You love it," I would whisper in his ear as he trembled – looking down to watch as his dick hit the back of the guy's throat. *"It feels so good to you."*

"So good," he whimpered, letting his eyes roll into the back of his head.

"I want you to cum in his mouth," I whispered – feeling wetter than I had ever been in my entire life. *"I want you to look into my eyes as he swallows every last drop."*

He came right then and there – staring at me as he did what I asked of him. He moaned helplessly as the guy sucked him dry. I knew he felt so good and that I was giving him such a gift by letting him live out this fantasy. It was so hot. Possibly the most erotic thing to have ever happened to me. I felt like I owned his soul. There was something so vulnerable about watching him give into his forbidden desires. This was the type of shit that got me off.

Sometimes when I was alone, I'd get really bored and touch myself. Sometimes I felt numb and like no matter what

I did or what porn I watched, nothing would get me there. I would have to think of the most fucked up scenarios to get off. In my mind, I'd be fucking Grace's husband – or maybe even Grace. I'd picture myself giving Ray a blow job or going down on his mom. Sometimes I'd think about watching my sister and her husband. Sometimes I'd think of my dad. I'd feel disgusted with myself the whole time, but the *wrongness* of it all, got me off. Then afterwards, I would feel the need to shower and wash away the shame I felt from having such a sick mind.

I didn't *want* to do any of those things in real life. I just occasionally thought about them to get me there.

Another weird thing about myself was my weird fascination with the macabre. I would watch horror movies and true crime – throwing myself into the psyches of various psychopaths to try and figure out what made them tick. I frequented gory websites – finding the most messed up videos and photos of real bodies and gore. Who does that? Why did I need to see that?

I had watched horrible accidents and even seen suicide footage before. It gave me anxiety and made my heart beat faster. But it made me feel alive.

When people would hurt me, I would have fantastical scenarios play out in my mind – like a movie that only I could see. I would imagine myself getting revenge on them. I would wish for awful things. But I never acted on these thoughts. They were just fantasies. But now, something was different. Something deep inside of me had changed.

Lira broke a part of my soul and I felt like I could never get it back. I swore to myself after getting with her that she was the one. I risked my friendship with Raymond to be with her. Losing her would mean I lost everything for nothing. That was simply not something I could live with. If I *had* to live with it, then someone had to pay. She crushed my heart. She ruined my friendship with my best friend. She ruined my life. So now . . . she needed to die.

I was desensitized to gore – this much I knew was true because I had seen a lot of fucked up shit on the internet. I was good at lying. I knew I could manipulate anyone if I really tried. It was like an evil power I had that I never wanted to abuse unless I absolutely *had* to. I knew I wouldn't be alone forever. I knew I was lovable and lusted after - and that Lira would eventually be replaced. What I *didn't* know was how to get rid of a body. I didn't know if I actually had what it took. The motivation was there . . . but the follow through was still lacking. Deep down, I wanted to do it, but I also knew I was afraid. My mind had been made up. I knew I wanted to kill her. But I also didn't want to get caught. I needed to figure out a way to not only do it, but get away with it. This, I knew, would take time.

Lira had really hurt me. I pushed those feelings aside whenever I thought about what she did. When I first found out, I cried inconsolably for hours. I hyperventilated, feeling like my heart had been physically ripped from my chest.

The old Dorothea would have broken up with her, then tried to get back with her – begging her to love her more than Tess. The old Dorothea would have done whatever it takes to make the relationship work – no matter how hurt she got in the process.

But this new Dorothea simply could not. Not after losing Ray. Losing Raymond was something that I would never get over. Losing Ray was something I could never forgive or forget. And I knew that if Lira went on with her life, I wouldn't be able to live knowing she was happy and thriving. I needed her miserable and in pain. Worse than the pain she caused me. And since I knew I wouldn't be able to torture her forever, I knew that there would be no happy ending to this story.

I wonder what my life would have been like if I had been loved by my father. I wonder what it would have been like if I wasn't bullied to the point of wanting to die at a young age. I wonder what it would have been like if the people I gave my heart to hadn't destroyed it over and over again until there was nothing left but scar tissue. I wonder what my life would have been like had I gotten help for the dark thoughts in my brain.

There is a quote that really resonates with me. I think about it every day and wonder if I could be saved.

"If you gaze into the abyss, the abyss gazes also into you."

Knowing this, I wonder . . . why do I keep looking out into the dark?

CHAPTER 7

Week 3

I sat at my vanity and glanced at Lira in the reflection behind me. She was frantically texting between curling sections of her hair. I wondered what she and Tess could be talking about. Were they making plans to meet up? Were they professing their love for one another? Were they talking shit about me? Were they arguing? The possibilities were endless.

No matter, I thought. *I'll find out soon enough.*

I coated my lips in a raspberry colored lip gloss, tasting the sugary and fruity notes of the balm on my lips. I used to love kissing Lira – never minding if it messed up my makeup. Now, I cringed at the thought of her lips on mine as I knew they had likely, very recently been on somebody else. I had read a message that Tess hated kissing Lira when she wore lip gloss. I would make it a point to make out with Lira as hard as I could in hopes that some sticky fragments of my gloss would ruin Tess's day. *Fucking cunt.*

"Should we bring anything to your parents' house?" Lira asked me – pulling me from my vengeful thoughts.

My parents had invited us over for dinner. My sister, Shelly and her boyfriend Nathan were going to come too. I had been avoiding visiting my parents since my last argument with my father – not too long ago.

My dad was disgusted with me because I didn't want to finish my college education. I saw no point in finishing at this point, as it had been *years* since I'd dropped out. I had recently quit my job at a publishing house because I hated my boss. It was never difficult for me to find work. This didn't sit well with him though because "the Duckworth's aren't quitters". My mom never did anything to deserve my abandonment though, so I decided to grin and bear it for her sake.

"We can bring a bottle of wine," I replied, turning to face her. "I have a few bottles of Riesling in the chiller."

"Ok, great," Lira smiled, turning her back on me. "So, are you nervous to see your dad? Have you talked to him at all since your last fight?"

"No," I shrugged as I sprayed my wrists with perfume before rubbing them against the sides of my neck. "I don't really care if we talk anymore or not. Nothing I say is ever going to make him happy – so I might as well just accept defeat."

"He's an ass," Lira sighed, twirling the curling iron cautiously up to the crown of her head. "I don't know why he judges you so harshly. Correct me if I'm wrong, but didn't he drop out of college too? What makes him think he has any legs to stand on when it comes to finishing what he started?"

I laughed, nodding my head at this. It was true. My father had dropped out a semester short of graduating with his bachelor's degree when my mother got pregnant with Shelly. He had always planned to go back, but started working and fell into a pretty good career.

"It's different," he said to me when I had pointed out the same thing. "I paid for my own school. You didn't. I paid for your education and you didn't finish. You essentially stole from me."

"I'll pay you back then," I said. "I don't want to be guilted into finishing a degree for a career I no longer have an interest in starting."

"You're such an ungrateful and lazy piece of work," he said, wrinkling his nose in disgust. "You've had every opportunity handed to you and you don't appreciate a thing. You don't even make six figures like your sister. You're settling for pennies because you're too stupid to finish your degree."

"He's a hypocrite," I sighed as I stared into my reflection. "He just has unrealistic expectations of me."

"Well don't let him get to you, Baby," Lira replied. "Just remember, you have me. Fuck what he thinks."

My eyes darted back to her as she continued curling her hair.

That's a pretty bold statement, Lira, I thought – feeling my hands clutch into fists.

This bitch really had no shame, did she? She really didn't have one single fuck to give! If I was horribly unhappy and cheating on my girlfriend, I wouldn't continue letting that girlfriend think that I would always be there for her, no matter what. I found her behavior to be chilling. Did she even want to break up with me, or did she just want to be with both me *and* Tess? I laughed.

"What's so funny?" she asked, turning around to face me.

Shit.

"Just my life in general," I sighed as I put the finishing touches on my hair. "It just sucks having a father who hates you."

Lira frowned before walking over to me. I mentally winced as she wrapped her arms around me from behind – resting her cheek against mine as she looked into our reflection in the mirror.

"I can't imagine what that feels like," she whispered before exhaling dramatically through her nose. "I know it hurts your feelings, but you *have* to know that his opinion doesn't matter, Thea. He's been cruel to you since you were a kid. You shouldn't punish yourself. You've never done anything to deserve this from him. It's just the way he is. He wasn't hugged enough as a child or something."

I laughed, looking down as she kissed me on the cheek.

"When we have kids, we will make *sure* they always feel loved. We won't make the same mistakes he has made."

I smiled . . . internally wishing I could bash her face into the mirror.

"Anyway, I'll grab that Riesling," she chirped – squeezing my shoulders before turning for the door. "We can drown out his negativity with wine!"

"Not a bad idea," I laughed as I watched her disappear into the hall.

My parents lived in an oversized and very beautiful home on the outskirts of Salina. Mom was a retired choir teacher and Dad still worked full time as the Director of Purchasing for a well-known oil company. My father was popular in the town and they had many friends they schmoozed on the regular. They had one of those crazy and exaggerated wrap around porches that you would see in movies – like the movies based on books by Nicholas Sparks.

Everything was a pissing contest with my father. He had money and wanted people to *know* he had money. He was all about stature.

My mother wasn't like that at all. She was funny and sweet. I honestly had no idea why she married my father or what she saw in him to begin with, but they had been married since they were in their early twenties. I always dreamt of a world without my dad where my sister and I could have been raised alone with our mom. I truly feel that I would have had the happiest childhood *ever* with her.

But unfortunately, that wasn't our reality and she and my father were a package deal. Dad was very controlling and had high expectations of her. I am sure that being married to him was exhausting.

We pulled up to the house and parked in the driveway. Lira drove separately in case there was an emergency with work, since there was apparently a "very important photoshoot" she had been working on. This of course was code for Tess Time. We got out of our cars and made our way up the walkway toward the west side of the porch where my mother waived enthusiastically to us as she set the outdoor table.

"Dorothea and Lira are here!" she exclaimed – yelling into the house to alert the rest of the family.

Shelly stepped outside, lighting a cigarette as she nodded in acknowledgement in my direction. Her brown hair had been recently chopped into a blunt bob that made her already intimidating presence more formidable.

She was a county judge and her reputation and prestige in the community had made my father extremely proud – often resulting in constant comparisons and questions like, "Why can't you be more like your sister?" She was three years older than me and one of the people I loved most in the world.

Nathan stepped out behind her, raising a glass of scotch on ice to his lips before waving politely. He was shorter than Shelly, but what he lacked in height, he more than made up for in humor and charm. I thought he was the perfect match for her, balancing out her more serious personality with his lightheartedness.

My father stepped out and glanced in our direction. He didn't wave. He didn't nod. He didn't say hi. He simply looked momentarily before taking a seat at the table beside my mom.

"Oh hi, Girls!" my mom crooned as she pulled us in for a group hug.

I smiled, feeling her squeeze us tight before planting a motherly kiss on the both of our cheeks. She was wonderful. Lira didn't deserve her affection. Thinking about how hurt my mother would be if she knew the truth, made me want to punch her in the face.

"Dinner's almost ready. I made ribs!"

"Ohhhhh, that sounds amazing!" Lira groaned as she moved passed my mom to greet my sister.

"Hey Shelly! Hey Nate!" Lira grinned – pulling Shelly in for a hug as she puffed out a plume of smoke.

"Hi," Shelly said as Nathan smacked Lira on the back.

"Hey, Kiddo! Long time no see!" he barked.

Shelly smiled at me as I walked up, reaching out to gently squeeze my hand as I took a seat at the table.

"You're looking good, Dorothea," Nathan said, nudging me in the arm. "Did you do something new to your hair?"

"I brushed it," I replied – smirking.

"She does look good tonight, doesn't she?" Lira agreed, as she pulled up a chair next to mine.

I looked up at my dad who nodded cordially at me as everyone else took their seats.

"Hi Mr. Duckworth," Lira said, smiling politely at him.

"Greetings," he replied, his tone a mixture of forced politeness and boredom.

"How have you been?" Lira asked as she poured herself a drink.

"Still old and grumpy," my mother interjected, winking

at us as she brought out a bowl of salad, setting it in the middle of the table.

My dad rolled his eyes. "Your mother says that, but she hasn't aged as gracefully as me."

"OOHHHH, *burn*," Nathan laughed, covering his mouth with his fist.

My mother frowned before heading back to the kitchen.

This was the type of shit my father did that really got under my skin. My mom – or anyone for that matter – could say something in fun and he would respond with something meaner. He didn't handle criticism well and he loved making others feel like the brunt of the joke. Shelly kicked the leg of his chair – giving him a "be nice" type of look that prompted him to smile.

"I've been doing well," Dad sighed. "Same old, same old. How about you girls? Anything new and exciting in your lives?"

I looked over at Lira, wondering what went through her head when asked such a question.

Go on and tell them, I thought. *I'm sure my father would be thrilled to hear about your infidelity. Anything to make me look stupid.*

"Nothing too crazy," Lira sighed as she wrapped her arm around the back of my chair. "Just working a lot! I joined a book club and got a gym membership! Been keeping myself pretty busy. And you know Thea – she's always busy! She's still trying to find a better job."

"Ha," my dad said before taking another sip of his scotch.

My mom returned with a platter of ribs, staring proudly at them as she set them down on the table.

"This looks delicious, Mrs. D.," Nathan said – practically

drooling. "You always make the best ribs."

"They're okay," my dad sighed as he passed the salad. "My mother's were better."

"Not even close," I snickered, rolling my eyes.

My mom smiled at me as she loaded her plate.

"Yeah, at least she cooks," my father continued – looking at me momentarily with contempt, "which is more than anyone can say for you."

"Thea *does* cook," Lira said, trying hard to sound polite. "She just made me a wonderful dinner the other night."

"Real women cook every day," my dad said – avoiding eye contact with her.

I clenched my jaw, trying to ignore him as Shelly chimed in.

"So Nathan and I have news," she said, looking mysterious as everyone stopped to look up at her.

"No, we aren't having a baby! God damn!" Nathan laughed.

"We got a dog," Shelly finished.

"Oh how lovely!" Lira exclaimed. "What kind of dog?"

"It's a Shiba Inu," Shelly smiled. "We rescued her from the pound. Her name is Daisy."

"That's wonderful," my mother crooned, clapping her hands.

I smiled, trying to imagine my sister with a dog. She wasn't exactly the active and energetic type. I wondered if she fully realized what she was getting herself into.

"Dogs are a big responsibility," my dad said, smiling at her. "I'm happy you guys are taking that next step in your relationship."

"When we get a dog, I want us to rescue also," Lira said.

My dad stared at her in quiet surprise, raising his eyebrows as he forked his salad.

"That's very noble, Lira," he replied. "When you're ready for that kind of responsibility, of course."

Lira stared at him, biting her tongue. Before she had a chance to respond, my mother started telling a story – pulling everyone's attention back to her. I fumed, trying to mentally tune him out. He was being an asshole just for the purpose of being an asshole. He *wanted* to get under our skin. I stayed mostly quiet for the remainder of dinner – taking care to only laugh at my mother's jokes or smile when Shelly would chime in. I had to remind myself that I did these sorts of things for *them.* If I had it my way, I would have disowned my father long ago.

Lira excused herself early, stating she had an important photoshoot they needed her for. I did my best to look bummed and supportive – waiting twenty minutes or so before leaving, myself.

I went to my car and launched the application, taking a deep breath as the red notification blinked in my face. I pressed play and froze as their voices filled my car.

"Fuck," Tess moaned. There were sounds of kissing and sucking and slurping and rustling around. "Don't stop," she panted. "Right there, Lira . . . God . . . right there!"

I closed my eyes, shaking my head as I continued to listen. Tess sounded like a dying cat. I really hoped they were parked in a public place and that someone would give them a ticket. I hoped Tess started her period on Lira's face. I hoped Lira caught an STD. But mostly . . . I *really* hoped I'd figure out a way to kill this bitch soon, so I wouldn't have to hope for any of this anymore at all.

CHAPTER 8

It was wine night with Grace and she pulled me into the living room, staring at me with anticipation as she poured us our first round of drinks. I laughed to myself as she waited for me to spill the tea – clearly living vicariously through the scandal that was my so called life.

"Well?!" she asked, her blue eyes huge with impatience. "What's been going on this week? Have you talked to Lira yet? Does she know you know?"

"Of course not," I chortled, rolling my eyes as I crossed my arms across my chest. "I already told you, Grace. I don't plan on talking to her any time soon. I am still figuring out exactly what I'm dealing with."

"You're dealing with a hussy!" Grace responded, squinting her eyes into judgmental slits. "What on Earth is the purpose of allowing this to continue? She's cheating on you, Dorothea."

"I'm aware," I sighed, taking a sip of my wine. "I put a bug in her car."

"YOU DID WHAT?!" she gasped – her mouth hanging open in shock.

I laughed, looking guilty before looking away from her.

"You're a fucking psycho!" she laughed incredulously. "You put a *bug* in her *car*?!"

"You make it sound worse than it is," I sighed, looking back up at her. "And besides – she's *cheating* on me! How else am I supposed to find out what all is going on?"

"What more is there to find?" she asked, still gaping at me. "I mean, Jesus, Thea . . . she's having an affair. What good will it do to listen to her private conversations?"

"I'm just curious, that's all," I sighed. "I want to learn more about this Tess bitch and the dynamic of their relationship. They seem pretty serious. It's extremely annoying."

"Annoying?" Grace asked – her voice squeaking in disbelief. "Stubbing your toe is annoying. Learning your girlfriend is seeing someone else is way beyond that. Are you okay? How have you been coping?"

I sighed, drumming my fingers on the table. "Well, what really irritates me is Lira seems super happy with me. You would *think* that she would show signs of wanting to leave me - or at least give hints that she's unsatisfied in this relationship. I don't know what to make of it, Grace."

Grace stared at me, looking sad as she thought about what to say.

"Maybe she isn't necessarily unhappy in your relationship," she responded. "Maybe this has nothing to do with you and she wants her cake and wants to eat it too. But that isn't fair of her to do and it's not something you should have to put up with. Dump her ass."

A dump would be a good place to hide a body, I thought.

Surely, I could look up some landfills nearby. But how would I be able to search anonymously? Once she goes missing, I can't have the cops seeing, "Where is the closest landfill?" in my search history.

"I'm working on it," I sighed. "It's just not the right time."

"What are you waiting for?" Grace asked.

I pursed my lips. Grace wasn't going to give up that easily. I had to play into emotions she *would* be able to understand.

"I don't know if I want to leave her," I said – trying to look as sad as possible. "We have been together such a long time . . . what if she really *does* love me and this is a giant mistake? Maybe she wants to get this out of her system before settling down with me and getting married or something."

Grace laughed, rolling her eyes at me. "Oh Thea, come on, Babe. You're smarter than that."

I smiled.

"Even if that is true, you need to talk to her. Relationships are based on trust and she clearly has no respect for you."

"That's the truth," I sighed. "She's in a full blown relationship with this woman as far as I can tell. She's juggling her relationship with her and her relationship with me. She must be so tired."

Grace sat back in her chair, taking a contemplative sip of her wine. "Well then maybe you need to make it harder for her."

I raised my eyebrow, intrigued.

"Clearly, you're not going to listen to a damn thing I say, so if you insist on spying on your girlfriend and torturing yourself with this knowledge for longer than you need to, then I would make her life miserable."

I tilted my head to the side – my curiosity peaked.

"Guilt trip her, Dorothea. Become super needy. Shower her in attention and affection. She won't have time for another relationship if she's super busy with yours."

Boring, I thought. But she was onto something with the

misery thing.

"Yeah, I should," I agreed.

"I still think you're making a terrible mistake. You need to have open dialogue with her. Even if this fizzles out, what is to say she won't do this to you again?"

Oh trust me, Grace, she won't. I won't let it happen. She'll be six feet under, soon enough.

"Don't worry," I lied. "I am going to talk to her eventually – I *am*. I just am not ready for it yet."

"You're in denial, I get it," Grace sighed, looking sympathetically at me. "You've been together a long time. You love her. It's going to take a long time to get over this."

I bit my lip, tasting blood before taking another sip of my drink. "I just can't believe she did this to me," I whispered. "I never thought she would hurt me like this."

"I know, honey," Grace replied. "I'm happy you're at least opening up to me."

I wanted to tell Grace everything – I did. But I recognized that my thoughts weren't exactly . . . rational. I didn't want to cause her unneeded stress and grief. And I didn't want my best friend to think I was crazy. So what if I wanted vengeance? I was sick and tired of letting the people closest to me get away with breaking my heart. People needed to be held accountable for their actions. I wasn't some toy people could discard. I was a *human being.* I didn't understand why this was so fucking hard for some people to understand. You break it, you bought it. Period.

"I still haven't heard anything from Ray," I said, changing the subject and feeling knots in my stomach at the sound of his name.

Just thinking about him felt like squeezing citrus on an open wound. It made me feel hopeless and overcome with grief. Grace was quiet as I fought to hold back the tears in my eyes.

"Dorothea, I think you should talk to someone," she said cautiously. "I love you very much and I hate seeing you this way. I know this has been something that's really affected you for a long time. It might help to talk to someone about it."

"Like a shrink?" I asked, feeling offended.

"Well, yes," she sighed. "There's no shame in needing therapy. I have gone to a therapist for years." She admitted.

"Since when?" I asked, feeling confused as she stared at me. Since when did Grace need a therapist?

"Off and on since finishing college," she sighed. "I *like* therapy. It's such a release for me."

"You don't need a therapist," I huffed, smiling at her in amusement. "What could you possibly have to talk about? Your life is great."

Grace shrugged her shoulders, holding eye contact with me. Why was she keeping secrets from me? I was her best friend. *I* should be her therapist!

"Sometimes I get really depressed and anxious," she said, tapping her wine glass pensively. "It's not like my life is perfect, Thea. No one's is! And getting a fresh perspective from someone who doesn't know you is just different. It makes you look at things differently."

I glowered, feeling my cheeks warm at the thought of some random psychologist knowing more about Grace than I did.

"You should be able to talk to me about anything," I said, feeling uncomfortable. "Sorry if I've made you feel neglected in some way."

"Don't be ridiculous," she said, shaking her head. "I love you, Thea – you know this! I just like having that emotional outlet. And I think with everything that you are going through, you would like it too."

I chuckled, rolling my eyes at the stupidity of it all. I had seen therapists in the past. It was pointless. No amount of talking ever made me less . . . well, *me*.

"Ray's not your friend anymore," Grace said.

Her words felt like bullets, but her tone was tepid.

"In fact," she shrugged, "the two of you are strangers at this point."

"That's a fucking crazy thing to say," I laughed, taken aback by her statement. "We will *never* be strangers. He was my best friend for over twenty years!"

"Well, it's been six years since he's stopped talking to you," she said before taking a deep breath. "I just think there comes a point in time where you have to try and let it go."

"I'm not going to ever let it go," I said, gulping my wine in irritation.

"That's a problem, Thea," Grace replied.

I suddenly had the urge to leave. Who did she think she was to say things like that to me? Was she my real best friend or *not*? I would never abandon my best friend and I would never give up hope. What the fuck was wrong with people? I wasn't the one in the wrong, here – *he* was. *He* was the one who cut me out of his life for *no* fucking reason.

"I think you and I have really different views on friendship," I said, pushing my glass aside. "In fact, I kind of want to go home right now because I feel like you are the *one* person who is supposed to understand me and I feel like you really don't."

"Dorothea," she said with pain in her eyes. "I love you. You know that I do. I'm not going anywhere and I *do* care. You *can* talk to me. Always! But I feel like you're suffering. I feel like the longer you hold onto that dead friendship, the longer you'll continue to be sad. I don't know why he chose to end your friendship,"

"Abandon me," I corrected her.

"Okay, abandon you," she continued, "but, you can't sit around and be sad about it forever. What purpose does that serve you? What is the point of hurting yourself by refusing to let go? I can't force you to want to let go of him, Thea. That's something you have to want for yourself."

"And I don't," I snapped – feeling stung at the mere thought of it.

"Well, I know . . ." Grace sighed, reaching over to hold my hand. "But someday, I don't want you to look back and hate yourself for wasting so much time on someone who doesn't deserve it. And he doesn't deserve your tears, Thea. He doesn't deserve you."

I felt a wave of sadness hit me like a train. There was no preventing the knife of sorrow from twisting into my soul. I felt the tears rush over the brink of my eyelids – falling in rivers down my cheeks.

"Oh Thea," Grace whispered as she rose from her seat to walk over to me.

She held me in her arms as I sobbed into her chest. How could he have done this to me? He was my best friend. I loved him more than anyone in the entire world. He and Grace were a *part* of me. I felt like I had a hole in my heart where our friendship used to be. I didn't understand how people got over these types of things. It just wasn't possible for me. I needed to understand *why* he didn't care about me.

Why did he throw me away like I was nothing? Why? Why? *Why?*

"I'm sorry," I sobbed, wiping my snot on my sleeve as I pulled away from her. "I hate crying. This is stupid."

"It's not stupid," Grace said, combing my hair with her fingers lovingly as she stared down at my tear stained face. "People handle grief in many different ways. Your feelings are valid. I just want you to be *happy* again, Thea. I think therapy would really help you smile again."

I sighed, feeling annoyed at the thought of it. But I *did* hate feeling this way. I hated that I couldn't get over him like a normal person could. The thought of me being a stranger to him while he continued on with his life really horrified me. Imagining it to be true made me feel physically sick. Maybe talking to someone wouldn't be such a bad idea.

If I didn't love him as much as I did, I'd want him to die too. But I wanted us to be friends again. That's all I wanted.

"Maybe I will talk to someone," I sighed as I reached over and grabbed the bottle of wine to pour myself another drink. "Fuck it. I might as well talk to someone about all the bullshit going on in my life."

"It's a lot," Grace agreed, rubbing my back before moving slowly back to her seat. "And especially with everything that's happening with Lira. I mean, your heart is broken, Dorothea. You have every reason to fall apart."

"I'm not falling apart," I huffed, hoping she didn't see me as weak. "I'm just overwhelmed."

"Potato, potahto," Grace sighed. "I just think you'll feel better to have someone else to vent to."

"Maybe," I shrugged. "I'll look into it this week."

"Good," Grace replied as she took another sip of wine. "I really hate seeing you hurt, you know? You're one of the most kind-hearted people I have ever met and I would do anything for you. I just want to see you take the trash out of your life."

I laughed – envisioning Lira's body wrapped up in black trash bags. Grace made some pretty good points.

"I love you," I muttered – pushing thoughts of Ray aside as I looked back up to meet her gaze. "Thanks for talking to me. I appreciate you being my sounding board."

"That's what best friends are for!" Grace grinned as she raised her glass for a cheers.

Best friends were supposed to bring you happiness. They weren't supposed to break your heart. I wondered what any shrink would be able to say to make that hurt less. I'd humor Grace with her little therapy idea. What's the worst that could happen, after all?

CHAPTER 9

Week 4

When I was in my early twenties, I had briefly dated a girl named Tedra. She was tall and blond with a hot body. She played sports and worked out. She was funny and extremely smart, which I found to be extremely sexy. She was strong - so had no issues with throwing me around and overpowering me between the sheets. Our romance fizzled out though, when we realized we were better suited as friends. The sex was great and the friendship was great, but we just couldn't emotionally click in that way. Lira hated her. Actually, Lira hated everyone I'd ever been intimate with. Tedra was one of the few people I didn't have a messy break up with, so I was bummed when Lira told me she felt uncomfortable with Tedra and I remaining close.

"I'm not friends with any of my ex's," she said, pouting her lips. "They're your ex's for a reason."

"But it's not like that with her," I said, trying to reassure her. "We genuinely only want to be friends."

"I don't trust it," she said, getting visibly annoyed. "Obviously, do what you want to do. I won't ever give you an ultimatum, but I don't feel comfortable with it."

So, I had let my friendship with Tedra simmer on the

backburner – only occasionally liking things on social media once in a while and wishing her a happy birthday once a year. There was no reason to make my loved one uncomfortable. I would have *hoped* she would have shown me the same respect if the tables had been turned. But since *respect* was now a distant memory Lira had tossed out the window . . .

"Oh my God . . ." I gasped as Tedra lifted me against the shower door. I ran my fingers through her hair as water cascaded over our bodies. I felt her teeth on my neck as she pressed the shower massage over my clit – sending waves of pleasure through my body before she whispered in my ear.

"God I missed your body," she laughed – watching as my eyes began to roll in the back of my head. "You're so fucking beautiful . . ."

"Fuck, I missed this!" I trembled as Tedra opened the door to the shower – walking our soaking wet bodies to my bed where she flung me down like a ragdoll.

I was a bigger girl. That couldn't have been easy. My eyes burned on her as she propped herself over me, locking her hazel eyes with mine as she thrust two fingers in me.

"Tedra," I groaned, feeling a rush of excitement at the thought of moaning her name so loudly in the house I shared with Lira. "Don't stop!"

She took my lips into hers and kissed me with hungry need. Her hair dripped on my body with every thrust – strings of it tickling my nipples as she grinded back and forth. I gripped the sides of the sheets – clutching them in my fists as she went hard and deep, making me whimper helplessly as she possessed me.

"Bet she doesn't fuck you like this," Tedra growled as she took a nipple between her teeth.

I cried out, coiling my fingers in her hair as she sucked on my breast – feeling overwhelmed with the sensations overpowering me. She trailed kisses down my chest and to my stomach – nibbling me softly in the side as she moved down to my pelvic bone and inner thigh. I bit my lip – laughing as she began to lick me. I pressed my wet sex into her face and felt her taste all I had to offer.

"*Eat it*," I said, feeling dizzy as her hot breath encompassed me – her tongue lapping it up as I let myself get wetter than ever for her.

Lira and I never had hot sex like this. There was so much emotion with Lira. Our connection had always been so vulnerable and sweet. Because there were no feelings between Tedra and me, our connection was more primal.

I had always been able to lose my inhibitions with her and submit to the lust and heat that resulted from the undeniable sexual chemistry between us. She had my number. She knew what my body craved and how to deliver. I panted as I felt her suck on my clit, sending pulses of electricity into the deepest and most sensual parts of me.

"I'm going to cum," I cried, feeling her hands grip my thighs to steady them as they began to shake. "Tedra!"

She moaned as I came on her tongue – writhing and thrusting into her face with each wave of pleasure that flowed over me. *God, she was good at that.* I had really missed those classic Tedra orgasms.

I tried to slow my breathing as she crawled up to my side, laying down beside me as she steadied her own breaths. She laughed out loud, biting her lip as she looked up at me. I felt my cheeks start to turn pink.

"Well, when you said revenge sex, I didn't know what to expect," she chuckled. "But that was . . . wow, Thea. God damn."

"That's *exactly* what I needed," I smiled. "I wanted to make sure to cum on her side of the bed. I hope she smells it when she goes to sleep."

"You're awful," Tedra laughed – her eyes widening in awe. "Things are that bad, eh?"

"God awful," I sighed, turning to face her. "She's been cheating on me for weeks with some personal trainer. She doesn't know I know yet."

"Oh my God, Thea, I'm sorry," Tedra replied – her brows furrowing with sympathy. "That's so messed up. Why haven't you confronted her yet?"

"I don't know," I sighed, looking back up at the ceiling. "I just don't know what to do about anything these days."

Tedra sighed as she traced her fingertips up and down my arm.

"I thought you two were happy," she whispered. "I never pegged Lira for the cheating type."

"That makes two of us," I agreed. "She's a wolf in sheep's clothing. You should see how freakishly normal she is around me. It's sociopathic."

"Geez," Tedra cringed.

"Can you keep a secret?" I asked, smiling guiltily at her as I waited for her to reply.

"Um, yeah . . ." Tedra laughed, looking intrigued.

"I've been spying on her," I whispered, biting my lip. "Her iCloud account is logged into my iPad and I put a bug in her car."

"Shut the fuck up," Tedra gasped – her hazel eyes like giant saucers on her face.

Tedra worked in IT and had experience with home security. Part of the reason I had wanted to meet up with her was to pick her brain on other ways I could spy on Lira. I was hoping she would be willing to help me set up hidden cameras.

I didn't want to throw too much at her on our first meeting, though.

"You're wild!" she said, shaking her head in disbelief. "Remind me never to piss you off!"

"I mean, she deserves it," I huffed. "She's the one who's cheating!"

"Well, what kind of dirt have you discovered?" she asked, curious.

"She met this girl through mutual model friends because she is a personal trainer. They fell in love and talk about eventually being together down the road – though she still hasn't made any kind of plan to leave me. They have a lot of sex and do a lot of lying and sneaking around. That's basically it."

"And she has no idea you're onto her?" Tedra asked, shocked by the nonchalance of my tone.

"Not a fucking clue," I responded.

"Well, when do you plan on telling her?" she asked.

"I have no idea."

"Thea, you need to break up with her!" Tedra pushed the damp hair out of her eyes.

"I know, but I'm not ready to yet."

Tedra took a deep breath before rising to her feet and walking over to the bathroom to grab a towel off the hook.

"Use the pink one," I said – watching her hesitate before grabbing it. "It's Lira's."

"Oh boy," Tedra laughed as she dried off with Lira's towel.

"It's honestly so hypocritical that she wouldn't even let me be friends with you all of these years because she didn't trust us together. I mean, *she's* the one who turned out to be the total slut."

Tedra sighed, pursing her lips as she looked down on me. I was fuming.

"I gave that bitch everything. I was the best girlfriend on the planet. What's even worse is we were friends before we started dating! The disrespect is just out of this world!"

"It's pretty messed up," Tedra agreed. "Which is why you probably should leave her. Why keep dragging it out? What's your endgame? You're just going to cheat on her back until she finds out?"

I laughed, shaking my head at her. "I don't know. I'm not really thinking about that right now. I'm just so angry."

"I don't want to see you get hurt," Tedra sighed, taking a seat on the corner of the bed as she towel dried her long, blond hair. "I care about you. I want you to be happy."

"I'm gonna start seeing a shrink," I mumbled, wincing at the thought. "Grace thinks it will help."

"I think that's great," Tedra said. "I think therapy is good for everyone. I've seen a therapist before. Sometimes it's nice to just have someone neutral to talk to."

"That's what they say," I sighed. "But my needs aren't being met with Lira right now. I obviously don't want to be intimate with her, so do you think we can keep doing this for a while? Obviously no strings attached?"

Tedra chuckled, crawling over me with a look of mischievousness in her eyes.

"Watching those breasts bounce again is like living in a wet dream," she crooned. "As long as you promise not to catch feelings, I'm totally down."

"Oh Tedra, that ship has sailed," I rolled my eyes. "I mean, don't get me wrong – you're wonderful. But I'm too complicated for you."

"I just don't want any lovey dovey bullshit right now," Tedra smiled. "I'm really enjoying the single life. But yes, I'll fuck you whenever you want, Thea. Just name the time and place."

I smiled, satisfied with this answer. Tedra was always reliable. I was looking forward to having my way with her in every room of our house. I'd have her bend me over Lira's vanity next time. I'd make sure to use her makeup brushes as titty tassels. Anything to further taint the things she loved.

"Just promise me you plan on leaving her eventually," Tedra said, staring down at me with intensity as she tucked a strand of hair behind my ear.

"I promise," I said, smiling up at her.

She technically didn't ask for the definition of *leave*. Lira was going to have to leave the Earth eventually. My hatred for her was growing with each passing day. Unless my therapist was a miracle worker, nothing was going to get in my way.

"In that case, roll over," Tedra said, grazing her lips against my earlobe as she whispered in my ear.

"Roll over?" I asked, raising my brow.

"If memory serves me correctly, you love it from behind," she teased me – her words sending warmth between my legs. "So be a good girl and roll over before I make you do it, myself."

Everyone needs a friend like Tedra. I made a mental note to buy her an extra special Christmas gift. She was definitely on my nice list.

CHAPTER 10

I had spent a few days scrolling through various websites in search of a therapist to start seeing. I would read their profiles and specialties, trying to determine if they would be a good fit for somebody as potentially crazy as me.

I found that I had very picky tastes – not liking someone if I didn't like their photo, or passing if their website was too boring, or moving on if I read something that got on my nerves.

She's too old, I'd think. *He looks like he has a stick up his ass. This guy reminds me of my Dad, so he can fuck right off. This lady's wearing a turtle neck. This guy misspelled 'your'.*

I would become frustrated and slam my laptop shut, cursing myself for telling Grace I would talk to someone. What could a therapist know that I already didn't? I was already well aware that I was two steps shy of diving off of the deep end. What was talking about my feelings to a stranger going to do? I had more productive ways to spend my time. But, I begrudgingly kept looking and finally settled on a photo of a *very* attractive young psychologist who specialized in patients with BPD.

Dr. Douglas Griffin, PsyD, I stared at the smiling face on my screen.

He was hot . . . arguably the hottest doctor I had seen

on any of the websites I had been on, thus far. He looked Italian or something with his warm, olive toned skin and welcoming brown eyes. But he couldn't be Italian with a name like Douglas! He had curly brown hair that was long enough to day dream running my fingers through and a smile so big and bright he could have modeled for a Crest commercial. I smirked to myself as I googled his name.

He was a young doctor. 38 years old. He specialized in Borderline Personality Disorder, Trauma and PTSD, and Domestic Abuse. He handled various issues like addiction, anxiety, chronic illness, chronic pain, codependency, depression, divorce, domestic violence, drug abuse, eating disorders, family conflict, infidelity, marital and premarital, narcissistic abuse syndrome, narcissistic personality, parenting, relationship issues, self-harming, sexual abuse, spirituality, substance use, suicidal ideation, transgender, and women's issues. He was friendly to LGBTQ + and had experience in dissociative disorders and personality disorders.

This man was *qualified.*

I reluctantly sent him a message asking if he accepted new patients and was surprised with the quick response. He asked if I had availability to come in later that very day. I started sweating and immediately looked for something to wear. If I was going to spend my time opening myself up to a sexy doctor, I at *least* had to make myself look presentable! I didn't just want to look *presentable* to this man, though. No. I wanted him to think I was *cute.*

I fished through my wardrobe, trying to find something professional and sexy to wear to make a good impression. I settled on a simple, black dress shirt and nice, dark jeans. I put my hair in a side swept pony and wore jangly bracelets that clinked with every move I made. I swiped a coat of strawberry colored lipstick over my lips and smiled at myself in the mirror before heading to my appointment.

I was still completely skeptical about whether or not seeing a therapist would make a difference in my life, but felt jittery with excitement at the thought of being in a room alone with *that man.*

Dr. Daddy Griffin, I crooned, licking my lips as I started my car. I couldn't wait to see that face in person!

It was a weekend, so I was surprised he took patients at all. I pulled up to the office building and noticed the few number of cars parked in the parking lot. He had provided me with a code to access the building and directions to find his office on the second floor. My heart thumped in my chest with anticipation as I made my way to the waiting room – standing awkwardly alone at the front desk as I waited to be greeted. I heard a door around the corner open and held my breath as Dr. Griffin appeared before me.

Shit, I thought as he smiled down at me. *He was even more perfect in person.*

"You must be Dorothea," he said, extending his hand to me. "Thanks for coming on such short notice. My name is Dr. Griffin."

I smiled shyly as I took his hand in mine, locking eyes with him as he motioned for me to follow him to his office.

He shut the door behind me, gesturing for me to take a seat on the comfy black couch that sat across from his very well-organized desk. The room smelled like cinnamon apple candles and a hint of cologne. I set my purse down, taking a seat as he made himself comfortable across from me.

"It's very nice to meet you," he smiled, leaning forward in his seat. "I like to use the first session to get to know each other. We don't have to talk about anything too deep today if you don't want to. We can just relax, chat, and see if you feel I would be a good fit for you and vice versa. No pressure."

I nodded, feeling my shoulders relax as he penetrated me with his chocolate drop eyes. Oh, he was good. How the fuck did I manage to lock down *this* guy?

"Okay," I nodded, grabbing the arm of the couch to my left as I looked around his room with curiosity.

He had several plants and a humidifier. His degrees were hung on the wall and he also had several motivational posters. There was a white board with different techniques for breathing and relaxing also on display. The lighting was warm and perfect – not too bright, but not too dark. He had a small table with a Keurig and several bottles of water. I felt instantly at home.

"So tell me a little bit about yourself," he smiled. "What brings you into therapy today?"

I took a deep breath looking down into my lap. How to begin to talk to this guy?

"Well, my name is Dorothea," I said, avoiding eye contact with him. "You can call me Thea, though."

"You got it, Thea," he grinned.

"I told my best friend I would come see a therapist because she thinks I need someone to talk to about everything that's been going on in my life."

He nodded his head, concentrating as he listened to me.

"I have been dealing with a lot in my personal life, so figured you might be able to help me with it."

"So your best friend thought you should come in?" he clarified. "Did you want to come in yourself, or are you only coming in because you told your friend you would?"

I sighed, tapping my thumb on the arm of the couch. "I guess both," I replied.

"I see in your paperwork that you have been to therapy in the past. You were diagnosed with Generalized Anxiety

Disorder and Depression in 2004, PTSD in 2006, misdiagnosed with Bipolar Disorder in 2012 before determining it was a combination of Histrionic Personality Disorder and Borderline Personality Disorder in 2016. Did I miss anything?"

I shook my head, studying him as he looked through my paperwork. Did he already think I was crazy?

"So tell me something personal about yourself," he smiled, pushing the stack of papers aside. "What do you do for fun on your free time? What interests you?"

I fidgeted in my seat, not expecting the conversation to move in this direction.

"Well, I used to work for a small publishing house full-time, but I'm currently between jobs. I wasn't happy there. I like reading and watching true crime documentaries. I like drinking wine and spending time with my best friend. I like camping and road trips and traveling, though I haven't gone on vacation in a few years. I don't know . . . my life isn't very exciting."

There was the most miniscule furrow in his brow as he observed me, nodding his head as I completed my answer.

"I noticed you didn't mention your girlfriend," he said, stroking his beard. "You said you lived with your partner in your paperwork."

"Oh yeah, her," I said, nodding my head. "Yeah, we've been together for six years. Her name is Lira."

"Are you happy with Lira?" he asked, his voice curious, but calm.

"Not exactly," I replied. "She's been cheating on me for quite a while. I've known for about a month."

He raised his eyebrows. I fumbled with the strap of my purse on my lap, not knowing what to say.

"That's quite the story," he said, pulling my gaze back up

at him. "So you say you have known for about a month. How has that affected your relationship?"

"It hasn't yet," I said, pursing my lips. "She doesn't know that I know."

I watched his reaction – trying to measure whether or not I'd scared him off. I was going to give this guy a run for his money with the amount of drama I had in my life. I wondered if all of his patients were like me.

"You haven't told her?" he clarified.

"I have not," I responded. "I'm not sure when or if I ever plan to."

He nodded his head – his expression not revealing what was probably going on in his mind. He looked professional and understanding . . . not like someone who wondered if I was insane.

"We don't have to talk about this today if you don't want to," he said. "I am sure that this is probably very hard to deal with."

"No, it's okay," I sighed. "I might as well get this over with. It's why I'm here, I suppose."

Dr. Griffin smiled, leaning back in his chair.

"My girlfriend left my iPad logged into her iCloud account and forgot about it. Long story short, I saw a bunch of text messages between her and her girlfriend, Tess. They've been sneaking around and having sex behind my back and based on everything I've read between them, they seem pretty happy and in love."

I proceeded to tell him all about my discoveries and their relationship – revealing all I knew about them thus far. He nodded his head, listening intently as I explained her odd behavior and how she didn't seem unhappy in her relationship with me at all.

"I just don't get it," I shrugged. "She is either the cruelest and most evil bitch on this planet and plans to lead me on mercilessly for the unforeseeable future, or she is in love with us both. I can't really figure her out yet."

"And you feel you need to figure her out?" he asked. "It bothers you not knowing what her intentions are. You want to learn why she is having this affair before you confront her with it head on?"

"Maybe," I sighed. "Yes. Or no. I don't know. I'm really angry."

"That's understandable," he replied.

"She makes me feel crazy," I muttered. "I don't like being lied to. Especially when it's coming from someone I truly love. Loved," I corrected myself. "I *trusted* her, you know? I would have *never* imagined she would hurt me. I feel like I'm living in some kind of bad dream."

"Do you want to be with her?" he asked.

"How can I be with her now?" I responded. "She's a fucking liar."

"Do you think that if you talked with her about it and she admitted to you what she was doing, that you would be willing to stay with her if that was something she wanted too?"

I huffed, rolling my eyes at him.

"If I confronted her with it, I'm not sure what she would say. What could she possibly have to say?"

"I don't know. What do you think?" he asked.

This is why therapy was bullshit. They never give you the answers. They just ask a bunch of stupid questions in hopes you find the answers yourself. How the fuck was I supposed to know how she would react if I confronted her? I wasn't going to confront her . . . or at least I didn't plan to.

Maybe right before she took her last, dying breath.

"I don't think I would be willing to forgive her," I said, staring vacantly at him. "I would never be able to get over the way this has all played out. She really hurt me. She doesn't deserve a conversation."

Dr. Griffin breathed through his nose, nodding his head.

"So it sounds like you aren't interested in talking things out with her," he said, licking his lips. "You mentioned that you would never be able to forgive her and that she doesn't deserve a chance to talk to you about it. So if you don't plan on staying with her, then what is the purpose of maintaining your relationship?"

I stared at him in silence, not knowing what to say.

"Are you afraid of leaving her?"

"No," I replied, feeling annoyed. "I'm not afraid of anything."

"Okay," he said, submissively as he tilted his head to the side. "How are your finances? Do you have a lot of bills together? Shared equity, perhaps?"

I shook my head at him. "No," I sighed. "Nothing like that."

"So you don't feel financially obligated to stay with her. You aren't afraid to leave her. You mentioned you are unemployed. Does she financially support you?"

"No," I replied. "I have a lot in savings."

"That's good. Do you have any pets together?"

"No," I shook my head.

"Are you worried about what your family would think? Your friends?"

"Yes," I said, feeling grossed out at the thought. "I mean, it's embarrassing."

"It embarrasses you," he said, nodding his head as he tried to understand. "Perhaps you care so much about what other people think about your relationship, that you're afraid of letting people down? Could that be it?"

"I mean, that isn't *it*, but it definitely sucks to think about," I sighed. "Honestly, therapy is supposed to be confidential, right? What exactly am I allowed to tell you?"

He raised his eyebrows.

"You can talk to me about anything, Thea," he said. "As long as it doesn't have to do with hurting yourself or others, what you say will always stay in this room."

Well, shit.

"Well, basically, I'm really angry," I said, glaring back at him. "I am still figuring out how to properly get revenge."

"Oh, revenge," he said – his expression serious. "What kind of revenge did you have in mind?"

Slitting her throat, drowning her in the bathtub, hanging her from a tree, selling her into sex trafficking – how was I supposed to know? I just wanted it to be interesting and miserable. I didn't know how to kill a person or hide a body. How the fuck was I supposed to know what kind of revenge I had in mind?

"I don't know what to do yet," I said through tight lips. "I just know she shouldn't get to jump from my relationship into a new one with Tess and get away with it. I'm not going to let her just ruin my life and start a new one with the girl she left me for."

He nodded his head, seeming to try and understand me.

"You feel she ruined your life?" he asked.

"I mean, she's part of it," I replied. "I loved her and I thought I finally found someone who wouldn't hurt me. She knew what I had been through in my past relationships. Even worse, she knew what happened with Ray. Shit, she is the *reason* everything happened the way it did with Ray."

"With Ray?" Dr. Griffin asked.

"He was my best friend," I replied, feeling my eyes start to sting. "I would prefer it if we wouldn't talk about him today. It's really emotionally taxing for me to talk about what he did."

"Okay, we don't have to talk about it," Dr. Griffin replied.

"He abandoned me," I continued, biting my lip. "He and Grace are my best friends. We have been friends since we were little kids. I left my ex to be with Lira. That ex was one of Ray's closest friends and he didn't take it well that I cheated on him. But it's a whole story, Dr. Griffin. Raymond told me if I ever cheated on his friend, he would never talk to me again. But my ex was an asexual and told me to seek intimacy elsewhere. And so I did."

Dr. Griffin scribbled in his notebook, nodding as he looked back at me.

"So intimacy was a problem in your relationship with his friend?"

"Yes," I replied. "He just stopped fucking me. He said he had no desire to ever be intimate again and told me if I wanted to have sex, to cheat on him and make sure he would never find out."

"Well that isn't exactly fair," Dr. Griffin replied.

I stared at him, nodding my head. *No shit, it wasn't fair.* I was pleased he agreed with me.

"Did you enter your relationship with your ex knowing he was an asexual?"

"No," I replied.

"Was Raymond aware his friend was an asexual?"

"I tried to tell him after we broke up, but he didn't seem to care."

"You can't be expected to give up your own needs for someone else's. He gave you permission to cheat, you said?"

"He did!" I exclaimed.

"But only as long as he didn't find out about it?"

"Yes," I nodded.

"But you left him for your girlfriend?"

"I fell in love with her," I replied. "She gave me everything I wanted in a relationship. I was never going to be happy with Westly. I would have had to make so many sacrifices. It wouldn't have made sense."

"What was Raymond's reason for being so strongly opposed to you cheating on Westly?"

"Well, I had a fiancé before him named Peter who was *also* Raymond's friend. Peter cheated on me and broke my heart into a million pieces. Raymond didn't want to go through that again with one of his best friends. So when Westly and I started seeing one another, he told us both that we weren't allowed to cheat on one another. If we did, he would stop speaking to us forever."

"That's a pretty harsh ultimatum to give for a relationship he has nothing to do with," Dr. Griffin responded.

"But it gets even more fucked up," I laughed. "You see, Peter told Raymond he was cheating on me and Raymond never told me! So Raymond sat back and knew Peter was having an affair. And after Peter and I broke up, he CONTINUED being friends with both Peter and me! So tell me, WHY, *Dr.,* is it okay for Peter to cheat on me and *they* can continue being friends – but it's not okay for me to cheat on Westly? I'm not saying what I did was right. I'm just saying, Raymond's a fucking hypocrite! It makes ZERO sense to me!"

Dr. Griffin nodded his head, looking empathetic.

"I can understand why this is confusing, Thea," he

agreed. "So Raymond is no longer your friend?"

"He hasn't spoken to me in six years," I whispered, feeling a lump in my throat. "I have tried reaching out numerous times. I recently wrote him a heartfelt letter and he never replied to me. Maybe he never even read it, who knows. He seriously threw twenty years of friendship away like it was *nothing*. He won't even tell me why."

Dr. Griffin nodded his head, examining me.

"And this really has had a negative impact on your mental health," Dr. Griffin said.

I nodded my head at him.

"And now you have Lira who could potentially do the same thing. She could leave you with no explanation. She promised to always be there for you and that she would be honest, loyal and true. But you have been watching her deception play out for weeks. You are afraid she is capable of throwing your relationship away the same way Raymond did."

"Yes," I said, feeling breathless.

I started to cry, feeling anger at the thought of it. I trusted her. She knew what I had been through. *How could she?*

"Also, you have the potential to harbor resentment for Lira because loving her is what made you cheat on Westly. And cheating on Westly is what made Raymond end your friendship. Am I correct?"

"Yes," I whispered.

"Thea, your feelings are valid. You have every right to be angry and upset. You have every right to be sad. I think I can help you."

I wiped my eyes, staring back at him.

"My style of therapy can be a little brash sometimes, but I think we could be a good fit if you were interested in pursuing therapy with me. When you have Borderline Personality

Disorder, it can be challenging to deal with emotions like loss and betrayal. BPD can cause many black and white feelings. Do you know what that is?"

I nodded my head, having read numerous books on BPD.

"This kind of thinking can make you feel extreme emotions – flip flopping between hating someone and loving them. No in-between. This can also apply to yourself. You can think you're the most amazing person on the planet one day and the biggest failure the next. It can be exhausting. This 'all or nothing' point of view is something we can work on. Just because someone hurts you and does a bad thing, doesn't necessarily make them a bad person. Likewise, just because someone discards you, doesn't mean you are unworthy of love."

I clenched my jaw, feeling anxiety as he leaned forward in his seat. I felt very seen by this man. I didn't know if I liked it or if it made me afraid.

"I am confident I can provide you with several techniques to help cope with what you've been through and deal with your symptoms of BPD. We have only scratched the surface, and the surface is a lot. Lira and Raymond alone are traumatic topics we can talk about. Are you interested in meeting with me once a week?"

I took a deep breath, staring up at him with hesitation. Once a week? Was I really going to trust some stranger to help me with getting over Lira and Ray? I mean, was I actually going to be willing to give it a real shot? I wanted to kill Lira. But was there another way?

"It's up to you," Dr. Griffin said. "I would be more than happy to be your therapist."

"Cool, whatever, let's do this," I replied.

Dr. Griffin smiled, nodding as he relaxed into his seat.

"I look forward to working with you, Thea. Don't worry.

We will hit these issues head on, together."

CHAPTER 11

Week 5

I was surprised how pleased I had been with my first therapy session with Dr. Griffin. I felt like I was talking to someone who could really understand me. I didn't want to continue feeling this way. I was miserable day in and day out. With each passing day that Lira continued to cheat on me, I felt more and more mad. I wondered what made Tess so much better than me. Why was she so special? Why did Lira love her? Did Lira still love me?

I returned home from work a few hours early and stood in the living room, glaring at the collage of photos hanging on our wall. We looked so happy. I *was* so happy. I felt like for the first time in my life, I would be with someone who would never let me down. I picked up one of the pictures of us together and traced my fingers across her face. She looked so sweet and innocent. She was the devil in disguise.

I set the picture down and looked up at the fireplace mantle. The silver urn with her grandmother's ashes glistened beneath the light of the lowering sun that gleamed in through the window. I felt a rush of excitement as the wheels in my brain started turning.

Elsa was Lira's maternal grandmother. She had been Lira's favorite person in the whole wide world. I loved her so much too. She always baked the most delicious cookies and spoiled us with delicious leftovers. She was sassy and had the mouth of a sailor!

"Fuck the patriarchy," she told Lira when Lira came out to her. "Girls are prettier, anyway."

Elsa was funny. She was a ballerina back in her day and often pulled out photo albums to show us how delicate and beautiful she used to be. Even in her old age, I thought she was stunning. She loved to sing and dance and watch The Golden Girls and I Love Lucy. Lira would visit her multiple times a week. We were devastated when she was diagnosed with cancer.

You couldn't even talk about Elsa without sending Lira into a pit of sadness. I didn't blame her. Losing her was like losing a limb. You never got over a woman like that. She was a star that shone so brightly, even after death.

I unscrewed the urn and carried it to the table – my breaths deep and labored as I clutched at its sides.

"Elsa, your granddaughter isn't who you raised her to be," I whispered. "She's honestly trash. You would be beside yourself if you knew what she's been doing to me. I know that you're up in heaven right now and that your body can't contain you. I know you're not here. I know this is just what you left behind for us."

I took a deep breath as I carried the urn to the sink, turning the faucet on full blast.

"But since I know Lira doesn't feel that way and feels like she has a part of you . . ."

I started dumping the ashes down the sink. Clumps of mud formed as it swirled down the drain as a dusty cloud lingered by my face. I coughed, turning the garbage disposal on as I disposed of Elsa's ashes – watching them swirl down the drain like clumps of spoiled milk.

"Fuck you, Lira," I sang as I turned the water off, carrying the empty urn to the pantry.

I opened a bag of flour and poured it in the urn, laughing maniacally to myself as I screwed back on the lid. I carried it back to the fireplace and kissed my fingers, placing them lovingly on the inscription.

"Sorry, Elsa," I whispered. "I know you understand."

Well, I felt better.

I made my way up the stairs to the bedroom, still chuckling to myself as I looked around the room. I noticed Lira hadn't worn her favorite necklace today. It was sitting daintily in a coiled pattern on the corner of her dresser. I picked it up and went to my closet – hiding it in a plastic bag that I then put inside a black box that went into a larger bag, which was then hidden in the crawl space in the back of the closet. That bitch would never see her precious necklace again.

I took a deep breath, furrowing my brow as I made my way to the bathroom. I needed to take a shower and wash off some of the guilt I began to feel for washing Elsa into the sewer. I knew she wouldn't take it personal since she was up in heaven or whatever, but it was still a pretty fucked up thing for me to do. Regardless . . . it was totally worth it.

I turned on the shower, relaxing beneath the steamy water before reaching for the shampoo. I hesitated as I held the bottle in my hand before laughing out loud – shaking my head as I lathered my hair.

No, that'd be too fucked, I thought to myself. *I better not.*

But then after rinsing my hair, I questioned *why* I was hesitating. I mean if I was considering taking her life, then why was I reluctant to do something less drastic?

I turned to Lira's side of the shower and opened her bottle of shampoo, dumping half of the contents down the drain. I turned around and grabbed my bottle of Nair –

smirking to myself as I poured it into her shampoo. I screwed the lid back on and shook it vigorously – setting it carefully back in its place.

Lira had like four different types of shampoo. She wasn't going to use this one every day. But she would use it maybe a couple times a week. Who knows? I laughed when I thought about chunks of her hair falling out with every shower.

That's what you get, I chuckled.

Stupid bitch. Okay, I needed to calm down.

I got ready for the evening – wearing a t-shirt and jeans – throwing my hair up into a messy bun as I put my makeup on. I avoided eye contact with myself as I looked in the mirror, not wanting to fear the reflection looking back.

Why did I feel bad after everything she had done to me? She was cheating on me! I was the one getting hurt! I sighed as I heard the door downstairs open. Lira had come home.

"Hey, Babe!" she called up to me as I made my way downstairs.

She set her bag down before turning to face me – smiling tiredly at me as she made her way over to meet me at the base of the stairs. She wrapped her arms around me before squeezing me tight. Her hair smelled like apples and I winced at the thought of what it would smell like after Nair had had its way with her. She pulled away and looked up at me before kissing me softly on the chin.

"How was your day today?" she asked. "You look pretty."

"Thank you," I replied, pulling away from her. "My day was good, thanks. How was yours?"

"My photographer is a dick," she sighed, rolling her eyes as she moved to the sofa. "I got in trouble for texting too much."

"HA!" I blurt laughed – taking myself by surprise.

I shut my mouth, feeling stupid as she stared up at me with irritation.

"I mean, wow," I gasped, placing my hand on my heart. "You're an influencer. Isn't it literally your job to be on the phone? What did you say to him?"

Lira sighed, looking away. "Yeah, it was bullshit. I guess I have to be more careful when he's around so he doesn't catch me again. He was really on one today. He yelled at me in front of two other models!"

"I'm sorry," I lied, moving beside her on the sofa. "Don't take it personal, Babe. He sounds like an asshole."

Lira nodded before resting her head on my shoulder. "I just had a bad day."

I rubbed her back lovingly as I stared at the urn on the mantle ahead of us. She placed her hand on my cheek, turning me slowly to face her.

"I'm sorry I've been so busy," she whispered before looking away from me. "I know I haven't made you a priority lately and I feel really bad about that."

I tilted my head to the side, feeling puzzled as she looked back up at me with her dark brown eyes.

"I was feeling really overwhelmed today and all I could think about was coming home to *you*. I really just want to feel close to you right now, Thea. Do you think we could just watch a movie and cuddle on the couch?"

I gulped, feeling confused as she nuzzled into my chest. Did she get into a fight with her other girlfriend, or what?

"Of course," I responded, feeling her relax as she took a deep breath.

"I love you, Thea," she whispered.

I stared blankly ahead as I hugged her, not knowing what to think.

"I love you, too."

We didn't watch a movie for very long. I was content laying on the couch – trying to pay attention – when Lira started kissing my neck. I closed my eyes, feeling annoyed as she rolled on top of me, kissing me gently as she dry humped my leg.

I let her rub on me – fake moaning as she brought herself to climax, letting her think I was getting there with her at the same time. She kissed me softly as she rested her head on my chest. Her breathing slowed before she gradually fell asleep.

I finished the movie, feeling Lira's drool pool on my sleeve as she rested on me. I carefully and quietly slid out from under her before heading to the restroom. I waited for five minutes before peeking out to ensure she was still asleep before tiptoeing back up to our bedroom.

I pulled out the iPad and powered it on, locking myself in the bathroom as I pulled up their conversation. I wanted to know why Lira was so needy for me today. Something interesting must have happened.

I scrolled up and started reading their conversation. Same old boring and romantic bullshit. I kept scrolling, looking for something more interesting to explain her behavior.

Tess: Lira, enough is enough. *angry emoji*. I am sick of all of the excuses. What's taking you so long? When are you going to talk to Thea?

I raised my eyebrows, feeling my heartrate increase as I

took a seat on the toilet lid.

Lira: It's not a good time.

Tess: It's never a good time. You say you love me and that you want to be with me, but you're not doing anything to make it happen! It's like you want to stay with Thea! Is that what you want?

Oh fuck, I laughed as I kept reading.

Lira: I haven't even known you for very long! *Eye roll emoji*. I'm not going to throw my life away until I'm one hundred percent convinced I'm doing the right thing.

Tess: Bitch, what do you mean by that? *Red angry emoji*. You make it sound like it's a competition between Thea and me! I'm not competing with her, Lira! You either want to be with ME or you want to be with HER! Which one is it?

Lira: I don't know!

What the fuck, I whispered.

Tess: Well that's all the answer I need! *Middle finger emoji*. Don't fucking call me or text me ever again!

My eyes widened as I kept reading.

Lira: Tess, don't be like that – I'm sorry! *Crying emoji*. I've told you this already. Thea is my best friend. I've known her for years. We've been together for six years.

Tess: She sounds amazing, so what the fuck is your problem? Why did you start fucking with me if you are so happy with her?

No response from Lira.

Tess: I'll tell you why! You're still in love with her!

I felt strangely happy as I kept reading to see what Lira would say.

Lira: Tess, I love you! Thea's just so different than you! I feel an unexplainable pull to you. I told you when I met you – I feel like you're my twin flame.

Tess: Well what the fuck does that do for me if you have a girlfriend you refuse to leave? *Huffing emoji*. I don't want to be the other woman forever, Lira. It's not a good look. And I feel bad for Thea. I don't know her and I feel bad! Don't you? We aren't sister wives, Lira. This isn't the fucking Lira show!

Lira: If you're willing to do this to with me, Tess, then what's to say you won't do it with someone else once I'm officially with you?

Tess: Pot calling the kettle black, much? I could say the same thing to you! Am I supposed to believe you can be faithful after this?

Lira: I've never done something like this before! I don't want to ever do this again! The only reason this is happening is because it's *you.*

Tess: You need to tell Thea. I am not going to do this with you anymore. It's me or her. Take your pick.

Jesus, I whispered, biting my lip. I mean . . . she has a point, Lira.

Lira: I love Thea. *Crying emoji*. I'm sorry, but I do. I love you both.

Tess: That's really sad. I mean it's sad for you because you're probably going to lose both of us.

Lira: I'm not ready to make a decision.

Tess: I'm not a decision for you to make!

FFFFFFUUUUUUCK, I thought, shaking my head. Where was the popcorn when I needed it?

Lira: Tess, please! I love you! I never lied to you! I want to be with you! I am just confused.

Tess: Figure it the fuck out! I'm not going to be your second choice.

Lira: I don't want you to feel like you are! I am so sorry that I'm in this position. You don't know Thea. She's a good person!

Tess: I bet she is, which makes this even worse. Do you think I LIKE doing this?

Lira: Do you think I do? It makes me sick to my stomach, Tess. I know I'm hurting her. And I know I'm hurting you. And I know that whoever I leave is going to be hurt.

Tess: You should have thought about that before starting this affair with me.

Yes, Lira. You should have thought about this. Maybe this Tess bitch isn't as evil as I thought after all, and she's just a victim of your stupidity.

Lira: I love you, Tess. Please just give me more time.

Tess: Time for what? *Angry emoji*. Time for you to continue to string me along until you cut things off with me to stay in your fake ass relationship with Thea? No. I'm done.

Lira: I'm going to leave her! Tess, I don't want to lose you. Please just give me some time to figure out how to break it to her gently! I can't do it right now!

Wow, I thought – feeling let down and an unexplainable pain in my chest. She really was going to leave me.

Lira: If you love me the way you claim, you'll give me more time. *Broken heart emoji.* If not, then I'm done. I can't be forced into rushing this breakup, Tess. I've been with Thea a long time. We were friends before we dated. I need to be able to let her down gently and not just spring a fucking breakup on her out of nowhere. That wouldn't be fair. She has no idea that I'm cheating on her. She is going to be devastated.

I felt tears sting my eyes as I continued reading.

Lira: God damn it, Tess, please say something.

Tess: Fine. I'll give you more time. But if you are lying to me and you're just stringing me along, then you're going to be sorry. Just try and do that to me, Lira. I will tell Thea EVERYTHING.

I shook my head – imagining Lira having a panic attack as she read that one.

Tess: Go home to your happy little life with Thea and make the most of it while you can. Say your goodbyes. Make peace with it. Do whatever the fuck you have to do so that we can stop doing this to each other. I want a relationship with YOU, Lira. Not with half of you.

Lira: Ok. I'll talk to you later.

103

I turned off the iPad and wiped a tear from my cheek. I didn't know what to make of this conversation. Lira claimed to love me *and* Tess, but she had made her decision. She chose Tess. So . . . I still wasn't fully convinced I wasn't going to drown her yet. I really couldn't wait to tell my therapist about this conversation later in the week. I really needed to talk to someone about this bullshit.

CHAPTER 12

I had spent the last few days fuming over the conversation I had read between Lira and Tess, but tried to focus my energy on more positive things. I was a bigger person. I was seeking therapy. I could let my anger overwhelm me and make her really pay for what she had done, but I hadn't done that yet! Instead, I opted for less harsh options like petty revenge. It tickled me every day to see the urn on the mantle and I felt a fluttery feeling of excitement each time Lira got out of the shower. I would be patient. She would get hers eventually.

I was sitting at the dining room table enjoying my morning coffee when I heard a scream come from upstairs. I jolted – spilling coffee all over myself as I heard Lira running down the stairs.

"Thea," she sobbed, turning the corner into the kitchen.

I looked up and gaped at her as she held a handful of her long, brown hair.

Damn!

"Oh my GOD!" Lira sobbed, walking up to me with shaking hands.

I rose from my seat and rushed over to her – staring at her hands in terror.

"My hair is coming out in clumps!" she cried, trembling

as she held out her hand to me. "I got out of the shower and started combing my hair and noticed that more hair than normal was coming out! I dried my hair and huge pieces just started falling! I have a bald spot in the back of my head!"

"Holy shit," I whispered, staring at the fur ball in surprise.

It was a lot more hair than I had imagined. I figured she would shed a few patches out – but nothing like this. I looked up into her red face as she chocked on her tears.

"I don't know what's happening," she cried. "Am I dying?"

"Of course you're not dying," I said, pulling her into my arms. She cried uncontrollably as I tried to soothe her. "Let me see your head."

She lifted her hair up in the back and turned away from me – revealing a bald patch the size of a kiwi, of perfectly white skin beneath where her hair used to be. My eyes widened as she turned back to face me.

"What if it's cancer?" she gasped. "Cancer runs in my family! My grandma died of cancer. Oh God, Thea! Oh no!"

I shook my head, trying to keep a straight face as she stared at me. I couldn't have her rushing to the doctor to get tests for cancer. That would be crazy. I took a deep breath, reaching for her hands.

"Baby, please calm down," I said. "I've heard of this type of thing. I have seen it before. Have you heard of alopecia?"

She stared at me – blinking several times as she tried to remember what that word meant.

"It's a condition that makes your hair fall out in patches," I said to her. "Sometimes it can be triggered by stress. Are you stressed?"

Lira gaped at me, looking around in shock as she took in

what I was saying.

"Babe, you started a new career. It's a lot of pressure. You were just complaining about what a dick your photographer was a few days ago! You run around like a crazy person every day, never slowing down or taking time to focus on yourself! I think you might have burnt yourself out..."

Her eyes watered as she stared at the patch of hair in her hands.

"I'm going to stop at the store and get you some of those gummy vitamins for hair and nails. I'll pick up some bubble bath and hot chamomile tea too. You need to try and relax, Lira. The more you stress out, the worse this will get. If your hair keeps falling out, we can reassess. Don't jump to horrible conclusions yet."

She took tiny, little gasping breaths as she tried to slow her crying - nodding her head as she walked back into my arms.

"I *have* been really stressed out," she admitted. "I guess I didn't realize how much it was affecting me."

Being a whore will do that to ya, I thought.

"I can't believe this is happening," she said – her voice broken and hopeless. "I don't know what to do with my hair now."

"Just don't wear it up until it grows out," I replied. "You can't see it, Babe. I promise!"

She nodded her head as she ran her hand down the back of her scalp, petting herself as she tried to reassure herself that it could be covered. She sniffled before looking back up at me.

"What if all of my hair falls out?" she whispered. "My whole life revolves around me looking perfect! What if I go bald?! Will you still love me?"

"Oh my God, of *course* I will!" I responded. "Do you think

I'm so shallow as to care about something as stupid as hair? Come on, Lira. You're my *soulmate*! We're going to be together forever! Someday I'll be old and balding and I would hope you would always love me too."

She stared at me – frozen – before nodding her head in dismay.

"You're right," she whispered. "I can't believe that stress is affecting me this way."

"Yeah, you should really try and focus on positive things," I replied. "Just take it easy. Hair grows back! Don't worry, Lira. I'm here for you."

"Thank you," she sniffed before turning and slowly heading back for the stairs.

Holy shit, that was intense!

I took a deep breath as I walked over to the laundry basket, pulling out a new shirt as I pulled the coffee stained, wet one over my head. That had gone much better than I had expected. I wasn't sure if she would buy into the whole alopecia thing, but the more I thought about it, the more it made sense that she would. She and Tess had just had their first real fight and it was a bad one.

She was trying to figure out how to break up with me. That would be stressful for anybody who had the misfortune of having to deal with cheating on and lying to their significant other every day. I knew she was busy convincing herself that her slutty behavior was responsible for her hair falling out and possibly even blaming it on karma for the awful things she had done. *Good.* I hoped it shook her to her core.

I gave myself a final once over in the mirror before yelling up to Lira that I had to run errands. I had my second therapy session today and was excited to talk about everything that had been happening with Dr. Griffin. I sprayed myself with some perfume – checking myself out in the mirror before walking out the door.

I felt nervous as I walked into his lobby – ringing the little bell on the counter before hearing him walk down the hall. I felt my stomach do a summersault as he appeared before me – smiling widely as he peered at me through dark rimmed glasses.

My God, he was beautiful.

"Thea," he chirped as he reached out his hand to me. "So good to see you again! Right this way."

I followed him to his office, staring at his cute little ass as we made our way down the hall. He must workout. His legs and butt were thick with muscle and I felt myself salivating as I imagined what his body looked like beneath those clothes.

Get a grip, Dorothea! I told myself as I took a seat on his couch. He wasn't a sexual object. He was my freaking *psychologist.* I needed to have a little respect. But those legs . . .

"So, how was your week?" Dr. Griffin asked as he got comfortable in his seat.

I took a long dramatic breath as I laughed at this, looking down into my lap as I thought about where I could possibly begin.

"Well, there's a lot I want to tell you," I said, biting my lip. "But I'm really nervous about what you will think of me after."

He wrinkled his brows, holding my gaze as he watched me.

"There's no judgment here, Thea," he said. "This is a safe space."

"Okay . . ." I said, fidgeting nervously as I felt him searching my face. "Well, earlier in the week, I may or may not have done something bad."

"Define bad," Dr. Griffin replied.

"Well . . . I did a couple things. Okay, don't freak out. You know I have been wanting to get revenge on Lira for the shitty things she has done, so I started doing *that* this week."

He nodded his head, looking pensive as he waited for me to continue.

"I feel like I may have gotten carried away. I . . . may or may not have dumped her grandma's ashes down the sink and replaced it with flour before hiding her favorite necklace and putting a little Nair in her shampoo."

Dr. Griffin's eyes widened as he stared at me in shock. He was clearly trying to keep his face calm and professional as I smiled at him guiltily.

"Surprise . . ." I said before slumping lower into my seat.

Shit. Was he going to call the cops on me?

"Wow," Dr. Griffin replied. "And how did that make you feel?"

I took a deep breath, resting my head back on the cushion as I tried to think.

"Good," I said, before looking back at him. "I mean, I felt horribly guilty, but happy at the same time."

Dr. Griffin nodded his head. "You felt guilty because you know that doing these things are wrong. But it made you feel *good* because it gave you the control back. Since her affair makes you feel out of control and betrayed – hurting her without her knowledge is a way for you to get back that control and betray her in return. So what has happened since then? Has anything resulted from these deeds?"

I winced, looking away from him. "I don't want you calling the cops on me or anything, so maybe we shouldn't talk about that."

"I'm not going to call the cops on you for using the Nair," Dr. Griffin replied. "I strongly encourage you to never do that again though. But, I am more interested in what motivates you. Did anything happen as a result of this little prank?"

"She has a significant bald spot in the back of her head now," I chuckled, biting my lip. "Nothing too crazy. I told her it was probably alopecia caused by all of the stress she must be under from cheating on me – I mean, 'working' so much."

Dr. Griffin smiled slightly, nodding his head at me as he wrote in his notebook.

"You probably think I'm crazy, don't you?" I asked, pulling his attention back up at me.

"Why would you think that?" he asked. "Do you think I should think you're crazy?"

"Well what I did was pretty nuts," I shrugged. "I just don't want you to think I'm totally out there. I have reasons for doing what I do."

"Not that it matters what I think," Dr. Griffin replied, "but I don't think you're crazy. I think you're hurting. Hurt people can sometimes do out of character things."

I stared at him, feeling myself relax as he looked back at me.

"Your name's Douglas, right?" I asked. "Can I call you Doug?"

"Does it make you feel more comfortable to call me Doug?" he responded.

"Dr. Griffin is just so formal."

"You can call me Doug if you would like," he replied.

"*Doug*," I repeated, smiling before looking away from him. "Yeah, okay. I like that better."

"Very well," he replied.

"So anyway, she found the bald spot this morning," I sighed. "She was completely distraught about it. I did my best to comfort her, but I kind of gaslit her a little bit. She was concerned it might be cancer or something extreme, so I told her it was probably just stress induced alopecia. She asked me if I would still love her if all of her hair fell out and I promised her I would love her no matter what – since she was my *soulmate* after all, and since I *knew* we would always be together."

Dr. Griffin nodded, listening intently to everything I said.

"So, you hope that by reminding her that you are her soulmate, she will feel bad for cheating on you?" he asked, crossing his arms across his chest.

"Yeah, I mean *obviously*," I replied. "She should feel bad!"

"And do you think it worked?" he asked.

"I am not sure," I replied, furrowing my brow. "I think so. She looked guilty or ashamed or something. She's gotta know what she's doing is totally fucked. Maybe if she thinks it's making her hair fall out, she'll think about her actions."

"It won't change what she has already done though," Dr. Griffin replied. "Are you hoping that if you take care of her, she will love you more than Tess?"

"Oh, about that," I sighed – feeling annoyed again. "She and Tess had a horrible fight the other day. I read their conversation on the iPad. Tess wants her to break up with me. She's tired of sneaking around. Lira told Tess that she didn't know what she wanted to do and that she wasn't convinced she wanted to leave me. I guess she is nervous because she hasn't known Tess very long and fears Tess could turn around and do the same thing to her once they finally get together. Tess said basically the same thing. She doesn't know if she can trust Lira since Lira is cheating on me. They both are liars – so I get the conflict. Anyway, after going back and forth and back and forth over what they were going to do, Lira agreed to leave me for Tess. She told Tess she still loved me and that she loved us *both*, but that she didn't want to lose Tess and would need more time to let me down easily. As if *that* is something that she could *possibly* do. So Tess is giving her more time."

"I see," Dr. Griffin nodded. "Let's unpack that. Lira and Tess have trust issues with one another. You have never given Lira a reason not to trust you. She likely feels safe with you. How did it make you feel when she said she still loved you?"

"I was confused," I sighed. "How can she love me and do the things she is doing?"

"Sometimes infidelity has little to do with love," Dr. Griffin replied.

"Lira called Tess her 'twin flame'," I replied.

"Twin flame energy can be very intoxicating," Dr. Griffin said, taking a sip of his coffee. "It doesn't always make for the healthiest relationships. These types of relationships tend to be fleeting and full of passion."

"So, good sex," I rolled my eyes.

"Well, I can't say for certain, but in my experience, these relationships can be intense," he said.

"Well, she's fucking stupid if she thinks that Tess is going to be a better girlfriend than me. She's just going to hurt her the same way she hurt me and then she'll wish she never left me."

"That's a possibility," he agreed. "But there is also the possibility that they would be happy."

I glared at him, clenching my jaw at the thought.

"Have you considered the possibility that you could be happier without Lira?" Dr. Griffin asked me.

I took a deep breath as I thought about this. I honestly didn't know.

"I don't know," I muttered. "I don't think so. I gave up my friendship with Ray to be with her. If we broke up, I'd be left with nothing."

"So you hold onto her because of your loss of Ray," he said, leaning forward in his seat. "But do you *love* her, Thea? Does she bring you joy? Knowing that she wants to leave you for Tess and knowing that she has the ability to lie to you, can you ever be happy with her again? Could you ever fully trust her?"

"No," I said, feeling a sick feeling in my stomach. "But I can't reconcile what that means for me."

"You don't have to hold onto something that isn't right for you because it made you sacrifice something you loved. You're punishing yourself, Thea. I wonder if you feel like you deserve this treatment from her because you feel guilty for what you did to Ray."

I gaped at him, shaking my head as he thought about how to continue.

"You mentioned to me during our last session that you had promised Raymond you wouldn't cheat on Westly. When he confronted you about it, you lied to him. Could it be a possibility that his reason for not wanting to speak to you is *not* because you actually cheated on Westly, but because you *lied* to him about it?"

I felt queasy as I locked eyes with him. "I don't know," I whispered. "I apologized for lying to him in my letter and in several texts I had sent him before he blocked me. I had always planned to tell him, but it wasn't the right time."

"What if Lira said the same thing to you?" he asked. "I'm just playing devil's advocate. What if she said, 'Dorothea, I always planned on telling you I was unhappy in our relationship and that I wanted to be with Tess. I just didn't know how and it wasn't the right time.' How would that make you feel, Thea?"

"I'd laugh in her face," I said, incredulously. "But there's a huge difference between what Lira is doing to me and what I did to Ray. Lira is cheating on me. I didn't cheat on Ray. I cheated on his friend. And I had permission to."

"Sometimes people have very sensitive triggers," Dr. Griffin sighed. "Perhaps Raymond is triggered by dishonesty."

"Well I don't know what to fucking say to that!" I huffed. "It wasn't personal!"

"I'm just trying to make you think about things from different perspectives. We will never really know how Ray feels unless he eventually talks to you."

"Right," I agreed.

"But you can't wait around forever for him to talk to you, Thea. You have to accept the possibility that he won't and that you will never get those answers. That is what we have to work on and move towards. You have to be able to forgive yourself and forgive Ray. You have to be able to let him go."

"What the fuck," I shook my head, feeling tears sting my eyes.

"I'm not saying that will happen overnight," Dr. Griffin continued. "It will be very difficult. But, tell me, Thea. If Lira left you for Tess and you were completely alone . . . would you be able to forgive her and forgive yourself so that you could stop blaming her and yourself for what happened with you and Ray?"

"I just want my friend back," I cried, shaking my head as I looked back in my lap.

"I want you to imagine a world in which that doesn't happen, Thea. I want you to be able to cope with handling it by yourself."

"I don't know how," I gasped – feeling the tears come.

"And that's okay, Thea. I will help you."

CHAPTER 13

I stared at my computer screen, feeling anxiety overwhelm me as I read the Facebook event description. Raymond's coffee shop would be catering Janie Ardent's Book Reading today. Janie Ardent was one of my previous job's new first time authors, and they had just published her first book. She was going to be doing a Book Reading of her novel at 12:00 PM today at the Salina Public Library . . . and Raymond would be there.

I took a deep breath as I stared at the photo of his coffee truck on the web page. His profile picture and biography were highlighted underneath.

"Stop on by the Library to catch Janie Ardent read her new action packed novel, Into the Darkness! Ray of Sunshine Coffee Truck will be parked out front from 12:00-2:00. Enjoy your favorite cup of coffee while you dive into the incredible world of mystery and wonder, courtesy of Janie Ardent, herself!"

I shut the laptop, feeling overcome with nervousness as I paced back and forth around my office.

Shit, I whispered to myself. *Shit, shit, shit!*

I really liked this author and wanted to make an appearance, but there was *no* way in *hell* I would be caught dead anywhere near Raymond's coffee truck! I hadn't seen him in years and was certain he wouldn't want to see me. If he never took the time to respond to any of my messages, I could only imagine how awkward it would be to be faced with him in real life. No. There was no chance I would dare show my face. I was too afraid to see him. It was too dangerous. I was fragile. I didn't know if seeing him would prompt me to try to talk to him or if it would send me into a fit of tears. What if we got into a fight? What if he started yelling at me? What if he saw me and refused to cater – putting my previous employer in a tough position because of something involving me? I couldn't handle this.

I exhaled, flinging myself onto my mattress. What the fuck were they thinking?

I thought everybody knew that Ray's shop was off limits! Why on Earth were they supporting that bastard? Was it to spite me for leaving? The level of disrespect was *unreal!* I slowed my breathing as I stared at the ceiling. I had often fantasized what it would be like to see him again. It had been six years. I wondered what he would think of me. I had changed a lot over the years. My hair was longer. I had gained a lot of weight. Not in a bad way. I still knew I could get anyone I wanted to fuck me, but I didn't want to give him the satisfaction of talking shit about me to Peter or Westly. I wanted to remain invisible to him until I knew he cared about me again. I wondered if he looked the same. I wondered if he was happy.

It doesn't fucking matter, I reminded myself. *Remember what Dr. Griffin said. You have to accept that your friendship is done.*

I sat up, running my fingers through my hair as I stared at the clock. Maybe there would be no harm in making a secret visit. I could keep my distance and just scope things out from afar. I just wanted to know how he was doing and whether or not he seemed happy. I didn't want to talk or want him to see me. But . . . the curiosity was almost too much to take. I had to see him. What was the harm in taking just a little peek?

I ran to my closet, pulling out a black hoodie and black pants – throwing my hair up into a bun before pulling the hood over my head. I grabbed a pair of sunglasses and headed out the door.

The library was packed. I parked on the street to the east of the parking lot, grabbing a pair of binoculars as I peered toward the front of the building. A long line of people wrapped around in a zig zag pattern at the front of his shiny, yellow truck. I held my breath as I moved the binoculars up to the mouth of the truck's window – where I stopped upon landing on Raymond's smiling face.

My breath caught in my throat. I felt my stomach drop and my blood pressure spike as I looked at him. His blond curls hung loosely in his face as he leaned down to hand a little girl a cookie before sliding a cup of coffee across the counter to her mom. His green eyes sparkled as he smiled at them. I couldn't read his lips, but he looked animated and happy. He was still overweight, but he looked significantly smaller than the last time I had seen him. Other than the notable weight loss, he looked the same.

I pulled the binoculars away and frowned, taking a deep breath as tears filled my eyes. He looked so fucking *happy*. I became overwhelmed with bitter resentment as I looked back at his face.

Why did he abandon me?

I longed to run up behind him and hug him. I wanted to playfully tousle his curls and tease him about how good he looked and how I was sure all of the girls would want him now. I wanted to ask him how his mom and dad were doing and talk about all of the crazy documentaries I had seen that I was *sure* he was streaming too. I missed my best friend – my brother. I wanted more than anything for him to feel the same way.

But he doesn't feel the same way, I had to remind myself. *He doesn't give a fuck about you.*

I tossed the binoculars down as I clenched my steering wheel – watching as my knuckles began to turn white.

That mother fucker, I whispered.

He didn't deserve to be happy. He deserved misery for what he had put me through.

I stared at the coffee truck ahead, taking a giant breath before pulling the hood over my head and reaching into my glove box for my pocket knife. I exited my car.

I wasn't planning on doing anything bad. I initially thought it would be enough for me to do a drive by and just have a look. I wasn't anticipating the rage I felt when I saw his smiling face. He was responsible for countless hours of suicidal ideation and buckets upon buckets of tears. I pulled the knife out of my pocket and walked nonchalantly behind the truck – hovering only long enough to stab the tire with the blade. I heard a swish of air as I retracted it and made my way as swiftly as possible back to my car.

Jesus Christ, Thea, what if there are cameras? I thought to myself as I raced off into the distance. *No,* I assured myself. *I looked around beforehand. There weren't any cameras near me. And besides, I was wearing a disguise.*

I laughed maniacally at the thought of Ray's stupid yellow coffee truck and the thought of the look on his face when he realized his tire had been slashed at the public library. Would he wonder if it was me? Did he even think about me anymore at all?

A few hours went by and Lira was gone for work. I thought about how her day was going and wondered if anyone had noticed the bald patch on the back of her head. I really hoped so. I hope she fretted about it all day.

"Jesus, Thea," Tedra moaned as she straddled my face.

She ground gently onto me, throwing her head back as I tormented her clit with my tongue.

I moaned as she fucked me simultaneously with my vibrator. The electric pulses of the bunny ears on my clit combined with the rotating beads deep inside me made it very difficult to concentrate, but I was always up for a challenge.

"Ohhh," she groaned, as I gripped her thighs, pulling her deeper onto me.

Her pussy smelled like strawberries and she tasted like sugar, so I didn't have a problem really getting in there. I felt her tremble as I was brought closer to my own release.

"That feels so fucking good, Thea! Don't you *dare* fucking stop – I'm so fucking close, Thea, oh my God . . . oh my God . . . ohhh!"

I felt a rush of wetness as she came. I cried out – licking her passionately as I submitted to my own climax. Tedra was so freaking sexy. I was obsessed with her body. I panted as she pulled out the vibrator – tossing it on Lira's pillow as she collapsed onto my chest.

"Wow," I exhaled – feeling my heart thumping against her breasts. "That felt so good, Tedra. I needed that!"

"Ugh," she flirtatiously grabbed my ass, "You make me *shake*," she said. "I wish I could teach other people to fuck like you!"

"Same," I laughed – agreeing with her.

"So how are things between you and *Lira?*" she asked as she propped herself up on an elbow. "Have you spoken to her yet?"

"Oh hell no," I chortled. "Things are still the same. She's still cheating and I'm still watching her."

"That's not disturbing at all," Tedra said sarcastically, rolling off of me. "Don't get me wrong, Thea. I love hanging out with you and fooling around. I just worry about you, girl! I don't want you to have a broken heart."

"My heart's petrified at this point," I stared up at the ceiling. "I am seeing a shrink now. I'm going to leave her eventually. I just haven't figured out what I'm going to do yet."

"I get it," Tedra replied. "Getting cheated on is the worst. I can only imagine how sad you must be."

I swallowed hard, trying to mask the anger I felt inside. Sadness came sometimes. But the majority of the time, all I felt was rage.

"Do you at least like therapy?" Tedra asked.

I relaxed, nodding my head as I glanced over to her. "My therapist is smoking hot. I could talk to him all day just to look at him."

"Oh my God," Tedra laughed shaking her head. "You fucking bisexuals. You think everyone is hot!"

"Not *everyone*," I giggled, biting my lip. "I can just appreciate beauty, regardless of what's between someone's legs! And you should see this guy. I feel like I'm in someone's fantasy."

"So many porns start out with a sexy therapist," Tedra laughed.

"Yeah, but this guy is professional," I sighed. "I think he genuinely wants to help me."

"That's what you need, Thea," Tedra responded. "I think it's amazing you're seeing someone – honestly. It must feel nice to get it all off of your chest."

"It's nice," I replied. "I hate bottling everything up inside. I didn't even realize how pent up I had been until I started talking to him. Or until you started coming over to play."

"Ha!" Tedra chuckled.

"I'm just lost right now," I sighed. "I feel like whenever I really give my all to someone, they throw it away."

"You give your all to the wrong people," Tedra whispered, reaching over to hold my hand. "You have to kiss a lot of frogs before you find your princess. Or prince . . . or whatever you end up finding."

I squeezed her hand, feeling grateful to have her there for me in my time of need. Being vengeful was lonely. I needed to keep reminding myself that I had other people who were still there for me. I closed my eyes and tried not to think about Ray.

At least his tire is flat, I thought to myself.

There was a lot to be grateful for. It was the little things.

CHAPTER 14

Week 6

G race and I decided to meet up for lunch at The Olive Garden. We were both obsessed with their all you can eat soup, salad, and breadsticks deal. And splitting a bottle of wine wasn't too outrageously priced, either! They also had an all you can eat pasta promotion going on, but I was two sizes thicker than I wanted to be and knew I should probably behave myself when it came to the carbs. The people in my life insisted I wasn't fat, but I knew that I looked better a few years ago before I started eating my feelings. I wanted to get a gym membership and go on a diet, but everything went to shit after Covid and I became complicit with being lazy.

"Are you thinking red or white?" Grace asked, running her fingers through her shiny hair as she read the drink menu. "Personally, I'm in the mood for red, but I could go either way. It's up to you!"

"Red's fine," I replied as I stirred the ice in my water with my straw.

Grace set her menu down and clasped her hands together – staring at me as she waited for me to start spilling the beans.

"Ok, so what's new in the Lira/Tess/Thea saga?" she

whispered, biting her lip with anticipation. "Has anything else happened this week? Have you talked to her yet?"

"Still no," I sighed, looking up into her judgmental blue eyes. "Things are basically the same. She is still cheating on me with Tess, but now I know she is planning to leave me to be with her."

"She said that?" she asked – her eyes widening.

"Yep."

"I'm so sorry, Dorothea," Grace replied.

I nodded my head as the waiter greeted us and asked for our drink orders. Should I tell Grace everything that had been going on? How much would be too much information to divulge to her? I didn't want to lose my other best friend too.

"I started sleeping with Tedra," I said, watching Grace process what I had said before widening her eyes. "It's just casual. Just sex."

"Tedra – as in your ex-girlfriend, Tedra?"

"Yes," I smiled.

"Oh boy," Grace sighed as the waiter returned with our bottle of wine. "Are you sure that's a good idea, Thea? What if Lira catches you?"

"What if she does?" I rolled my eyes. "What the fuck is she going to say? 'Oh Thea, how could you do this to me? I love you . . . it's not like I'm having an affair with Tess or anything! You're a *terrible* person!'"

Grace laughed, shaking her head at me. "Where are you guys even meeting up to do this with each other?"

"My house," I grinned.

Grace gaped at me.

"I like to do it in our bed. It's thrilling."

"Dorothea!"

I giggled, raising the glass of wine to my lips. "I'm careful, Grace. I know Lira's schedule. I track her phone and her car. I'm not going to get caught."

"You're insane," Grace laughed in bewilderment. "But you *are* entertaining. I haven't been so swept up in drama since reading 50 Shades of Grey."

"It's pretty crazy," I sighed – hesitating as I took a deep breath to continue. "I hid her favorite necklace."

"Oh, that's mean," Grace laughed, "but shockingly tame for what I imagined you would be doing."

I internally laughed as she looked away from me.

"So, she said she's leaving you for Tess? When do you suspect that is going to happen? Are you making arrangements to find somewhere else to live?"

I nodded, biting my lip as I thought about it. "I have looked online at a few apartments," I lied, "but nothing has really caught my eye yet. I don't know. I'll probably ride it out until the end of our lease."

"I'm sorry," Grace sighed, shaking her head in disgust. "I still am shocked that this is even happening to you. I thought Lira loved you!"

"She told Tess she does," I laughed. "She said she loves us both."

"How convenient," Grace rolled her eyes. "She wants to be with you both then, or what?"

"Yeah, but Tess isn't having that."

"Neither should you!" Grace lectured me before taking another sip of her drink.

"It is what it is, Grace," I said, holding my hands up. "I have been seeing a therapist for a few weeks and I'm really working on dealing with all of this. Lira's a slut. I don't love her anymore. I'm just biding time before I get rid of her."

"I'm so happy you're going to therapy!" Grace smiled. "I *told you* I thought you'd like it!"

"I do," I smiled. "I think I just found the right guy. He isn't scared off by my crazy bullshit. He's easy to talk to."

"It's all about finding the right person," she agreed. "I had a terrible therapist once. She talked about her problems more than she listened to mine!"

"What?" I gasped, trying to imagine how awkward that would make Grace feel.

"Yeah, it was awful!" Grace nodded her head and laughed. "But yeah. I really am happy for you. Aside from all of that, how are you doing?"

I shrugged my shoulders, thinking about whether or not I should tell her I saw Ray. I definitely wasn't going to tell her I slashed his tire. I didn't want her to know I had gone full-blown basket case.

"Nothing really exciting with me other than all of that," I mumbled.

"Well, *I* have news," Grace said – catching my attention before ordering her food.

I felt impatient as we gave our order to the waiter, wondering why she was so cryptic in her tone. I was a sucker for drama.

"So the other night, I was at my neighbor's house and she is newly single," Grace began. "I was trying to convince her to make a dating profile, but she is so technologically challenged, you know? So we made a whole night out of it! I set up a whole profile for her on Tinder and Bumble. It was super fun!"

"Okay," I laughed, not seeing where this was going.

"Well, you won't *believe* whose profile I spotted while scrolling through potential suitors."

I raised my brow, intrigued.

"Raymond," Grace chuckled.

What?

"Raymond's on a dating app?" I asked, staring at her - dumbfounded.

"Yes! Isn't that crazy?" Grace replied. "I couldn't believe it. He always made fun of us for having profiles on those things! Anyway, I thought you would be amused to know that our ex friend is dipping his toes into the dating pool. I don't see that going well for him."

"Raymond doesn't date people," I said, shaking my head in disbelief. "He's never had a girlfriend in his life! He's terrified of girls."

"I know!" Grace chuckled. "I always secretly assumed he was gay."

"Me too," I laughed.

"So, whenever you are feeling sorry for yourself and feeling bad that Raymond isn't your friend anymore, you can take solace in knowing that he is trying to find his first love on *Tinder*." Grace burst out into a fit of giggles before taking another sip of her drink. "Poor guy. He doesn't know what he's getting himself into."

No he doesn't, I thought to myself as our food came. *But he was about to quickly find out.*

After I got home from work, I pulled up the application that tracked the vocal activity in Lira's car. I scrolled through each notification. A cough here and there. Some radio and music activity. Some podcasts. There hadn't been anything worthwhile in a few days.

When I approached the most recent notifications, I froze as I listened to a conversation from earlier this morning. Lira was supposed to be at work, but had apparently only worked a half day and was now hanging out with Tess.

You sneaky little bitch, I whispered, turning up the volume.

The turn signal clicked and there was some rustling around before Tess began to speak.

"It isn't noticeable, I promise," Tess said. "I'm so sorry this is happening to you, Babe. Have you changed anything in your diet recently? Started using any new hair products or soap?"

"No," Lira sniffled – sounding sad. "Thea thinks it's stress."

"It very well could be," Tess replied. "I wouldn't get up in arms over this unless it keeps falling out. I know it's scary, but I swear it doesn't look that bad."

"This is what happens when you get mad at me," Lira spat, her tone bitter.

"Excuse me?" Tess exclaimed. "I have been telling you for *weeks* to break up with your girlfriend. The reason why you're stressed out is because you are *choosing* to live a double life! That's on you, Lira, not me. Take some accountability."

"Whatever," Lira sighed. "I'm working on it, okay? I can't deal with this right now."

"You never want to deal with it," Tess laughed. "At least have the decency to start showing her you're unhappy. It will hurt her less if it doesn't come out of nowhere."

"I know, shut up!" Lira screamed.

"Don't fucking yell at me like that," Tess sneered.

Silence as they continued driving.

"Look, Tess, I'm sorry," Lira said. "I need to figure out how I can do this delicately. Losing Thea romantically is one thing. But I don't want to lose my best friend."

"Are you fucking insane?" Tess laughed. "You think that Thea's going to want to be friends with you after what you've done to her? You'll be lucky if she ever talks to you again."

"Maybe not," Lira responded.

What the fuck?

"Why does she need to know about us?"

There was silence momentarily before Tess responded. "What do you mean by that, Lira?"

"Well, Thea would be devastated if she knew I was cheating on her. I don't think there's any reason for her to know that. Why hurt her like that? None of this is her fault!"

"You're not going to tell her about me?" Tess exclaimed.

"Baby, calm down," Lira responded. "I think we should just lay low for the first several months of our relationship. I can work on my friendship with Thea before throwing a relationship in her face."

"I am NOT going to be your SECRET!" Tess yelled. "What the hell is the matter with you?"

"You're getting what you wanted," Lira huffed. "I'm breaking up with her, aren't I? I'm going to move in with you! I'm going to be your girlfriend – we are finally going to get to be together!"

"But not publicly!" Tess laughed. "You are high as a kite if you think that's ever going to happen, Lira! I'm not going back in the closet!"

"Well then get the fuck out of my car!" Lira yelled. Screeching tires.

"Are you serious right now?" Tess' voice was shaking.

"Dead serious, Tess. I told you from day *one* that Thea was one of my best friends! In what universe do you think I want to throw that away with her? I'm not going to! I may not want to be her girlfriend anymore, but she has been one of my closest friends for *years.* You either accept that or you don't. That is never going to change."

"You're choosing your friendship with Thea over your relationship with me?" Tess asked.

"A *real* girlfriend wouldn't make me choose!" Lira replied. "If you loved me the way I thought you did, then you would *understand* – and – dare I even say – *support* me through this!"

"Wow," Tess replied. "Let me make myself perfectly clear to you, Lira. A *real* girlfriend wouldn't give her girlfriend ultimatums involving her soon to be ex-girlfriend. A *real* girlfriend wouldn't keep her relationship a secret. A *real* girlfriend wouldn't make threats – choosing her ex over her significant other! Let me tell you what's going to happen. If I get out of this car, we are done. Okay? Done. And as soon as I get out of this car, I'm going to call Thea and tell her everything."

"Are you fucking serious?" Lira replied. "You're going to blackmail me into being with you?"

"Go fuck yourself," Tess replied.

"Jesus, Tess, wait!"

There was more silence. My heart was racing as I waited for them to continue.

"Why are we doing this to each other? It's not a good sign that we are already fighting so badly and being so cruel to one another before we're even official."

"We obviously don't want the same thing," Tess replied. "I wanted to be with you. I love you, Lira. But you can't have your cake and eat it too."

"I'm just asking you to chill the fuck out so that Thea and I can be friends!"

"You're a terrible girlfriend and a terrible friend," Tess replied. "At least to Thea, I mean."

I raised my eyebrows as I wondered what Lira was going to say next.

"If you want to tell Thea everything, then go ahead," Lira replied. "I won't stop you. But I will *never* have any warm feelings toward you, *ever* again. Thea and I have been friends for years. She'll be livid, but guess what – she'll forgive me. Why? Because she loves me, Tess. Thea and I will *always* be friends, but if you do this – you will be dead to me."

I wouldn't forgive you, you delirious bitch! I said, shaking my head in disbelief. *She's bluffing, Tess. I won't be forgiving shit. She's lucky she's even still breathing.*

"I need someone who will put me first," Tess hissed.

"I *am* putting you first," Lira groaned. "I am breaking up with her! But relationships are about *compromise*. My friendship with Thea is important to me! Please, just support me in this!"

"This is fucking ridiculous," Tess' voice shook. "You get one month, Lira. If after one month, you want to keep our relationship a secret, then I'm done."

"Fine," Lira replied.

"Fine," Tess repeated.

There was momentary silence before the car started up again. I stared ahead in a stupor as I tried to put everything together in my head. These bitches were so toxic! There was no way their relationship was going to last! HA! Lira was leaving me for *this*? For a moment, I pitied her.

You guys deserve one another, I whispered – shutting down the application. *Just thinking about being in a relationship with either one of you is exhausting! Hard pass.*

I took a deep breath as I thought about everything that

was said. Lira had a plan. A very manipulative and stupid plan. But what she didn't know, was that I was ten steps ahead of her and there was no shot in hell that I would ever have anything to do with her again.

CHAPTER 15

I stared at my phone, feeling my heart fluttering in my chest like a bird trapped in a cage. Was I really going to allow myself to be this level of crazy? Was I really going to do this? I took a deep breath, exhaling before finally clicking on "Save Profile".

Margot was 34 years old and lived in Aspen, Colorado. She was 5'5, 130 lbs. and loved to cook and go hiking. She was a dog person. She enjoyed reading books and drinking coffee. She was incredibly pretty. She had blue/green eyes, a megawatt smile, and dimples when she laughed. She had freckles and long, silky blond hair. She loved the outdoors. She was witty and fun. Her hobbies included bike riding, snowboarding, rock climbing, reading, writing, singing, and going to breweries. She loved to travel and hang out with friends. She loved watching true crime documentaries and horror movies. She was a natural beauty. She was smart. She was everything Raymond would ever possibly need.

Of course, Margot was wasn't real. I had spent hours searching Instagram for the *perfect* person to fit my description. Hannah Baldwin was the real name behind the face. She lived in Canada and didn't have many followers. But she had pictures for *days*. I created a folder and downloaded every one. I concocted a profile based on all of Raymond's likes and interests. I knew what kind of girl was his *type*. If someone like Margot showed interest in Raymond in real life, I was certain he would believe he'd struck gold. It was like she was *made* for him. I knew he wouldn't be able to resist. I looked over her profile, smiling from ear to ear as I admired my work. Margot was ready. I had never seen something more beautifully executed in my entire life.

Thanks once again to my friend, the internet sleuth, I now had software downloaded on my phone capable of changing my voice. I could have telephone conversations with anyone and would sound like a completely different person. I browsed my options before stopping on the *perfect* voice. It was airy and almost songlike. It was high and sultry, but sounded innocent and young. If I had a voice like that, I would be able to get anything I wanted! I smiled to myself as I began my search.

It took a while, but after searching through countless profiles in the Salina area, I froze. I laughed out loud as I stared into the photo of Raymond's smiling face.

There you are, I snickered to myself as I clicked on his profile.

Ray's photo was of him and his golden retriever. I giggled profusely to myself as I reminded myself that Hannah Baldwin had a golden retriever too. There were several pictures of them together. Margot was going to even have the same taste in *dogs* as him!

I chuckled as I swiped right. Now it was just a waiting game. I made myself a cup of coffee as I waited patiently for Ray and Margot to match. It didn't take long.

After I had lunch with Grace a few days prior, something incredible dawned on me. It was like the fog had risen and for the first time in a long time, I could finally think straight. Ray was never going to forgive me. He was never going to respond. His actions had shown me how little I meant to him and I was wasting my life waiting for him to feel the same way as me. Suddenly, it became so clear!

He was incapable of understanding the pain he had caused me because he had never been hurt himself before! He needed to feel what I felt. He needed to know what it was like to be tossed out like yesterday's garbage. When I was done with him . . . he would understand.

My heart raced as I received a message from Ray. I bounced in my seat with excitement as I pulled up the message.

Ray: Well hello there! *Smiley face emoji*. I saw we matched and had to check my eyes to make sure I wasn't making a mistake! It says here you live in Colorado.

Margot: I do! *Smiley face emoji* But my sister lives in Kansas and I plan on moving there later this year!

Ray: Wow, that's amazing! My name is Ray.

Margot: I saw on your profile!

I rolled my eyes at the screen as I laughed to myself.

Margot: *Smiley emoji*. My name is Margot. I guess it's nice to virtually meet you!

Ray sent laughing emoji's as I took another sip of my drink.

Margot: Your dog is so cute! What is her name?

Ray: Ruby! She's the best! I've had her for seven years – she's

my best friend. Do you have a dog?

Margot: I do! *Heart emoji*. Her name is Sunshine.

I sent him a photo of Margot and her golden retriever, chuckling as I waited for him to respond.

Ray: Wow, she's beautiful! She looks so much like Ruby! Her name is Sunshine, you say?

Margot: Yes!

Ray: That's pretty serendipitous. My business is called Ray of Sunshine.

I laughed out loud, slapping my thigh in amusement as I got ready to respond to him.

Margot: Oh that's amazing! What kind of business do you run?

Ray: I own a coffee shop and coffee truck. *Sunglasses emoji*. If you ever come to Kansas, you'll have to stop by. I'll give you the best cup of joe you've ever had in your life.

Margot: So sure of yourself *Winky emoji*. Don't tempt me with a good time.

Ray: LOL!

I waited excitedly – imagining how excited he must be. What an idiot. I felt sorry for him.

Ray: So what brings you onto this site? *Detective emoji*. You seem entirely too amazing to be single.

Margot: That's sweet of you. I've been single for a very long time, actually. Modern dating is so annoying. I always wished I could meet someone the old fashioned way, but it seems nobody does that anymore.

Ray: I know exactly what you mean. That's one of the reasons I finally caved and made a profile, myself. I want to make a sincere connection. I'm ready to settle down and find something serious.

This was too good to be true. He was making it too easy for me. I laughed hysterically to myself as I gaped at the screen. Baby Raymond was finally spreading his wings and getting ready to fly. Into a storm. Into a hurricane. Into a brick wall.

Margot: Me too. I know a lot of people use these apps for fun or just for hooking up, but I'm looking for so much more. So tell me about yourself, Ray. What are you looking for in someone?

I tried to imagine what Ray would say. He had never had a girlfriend before. I wasn't even sure he knew what he wanted. I always pictured him being a wonderful boyfriend to whoever he would end up with, but he seemed like an all or nothing type of guy. He was either going to fall head over heels in love, or run at the first sign of trouble.

Ray: I'll be straight up with you. I haven't been in many relationships. I'm really picky about what I want. I know that sounds bad, but let me explain. I grew up with amazing parents. They have been together for almost forty years. That's the kind of relationship I want. People are too messy, these days. What happened to marrying your best friend and growing old with them? Maybe it's stupid, but that's what I'm looking for in someone. I want to meet my best friend.

Well she's here, Bitch, I whispered, glaring at the screen.

Margot: That's amazing! *Heart emoji*. That's exactly what I want too. I haven't had a serious relationship in years. My last boyfriend cheated on me. It's really nerve wracking when I think about opening up again, but I totally would for the right person. I'm not wanting something casual or looking for some fling. I want to find *my person*, Ray. I know he's out there somewhere, waiting for me.

I cackled, feeling my stomach hurt as I laughed with maniacal glee. You couldn't make this shit up! I should write hallmark cards – this was just too easy! I knew Raymond was a hopeless romantic and he was eating this shit up like ice cream. My eyes danced across the screen as he typed.

Ray: I'm sorry you had to go through that, Margot. I promise you not *all* guys are douchebags.

You just happen to be one of the biggest ones, I sneered as I started typing back.

Margot: Well, if you're interested in getting to know me and talking until I move out to Kansas in a few months, I would love to keep talking to you. *Smiley Emoji*.

Ray: Definitely! *Smiley emoji*. So what do you like to do for fun?

Margot: Oh gosh, let me think. I'm not really a girly girl. Hope that's okay with you. I love camping, hiking, and exploring the outdoors with my dog.

Ray: Shut up, no way? I love all of those things too! I'm so jealous you get to do it in Colorado, though! The Rocky Mountains are beautiful! Were you born there?

Margot: Born and raised! The mountains are stunning! You experience all four seasons here! You and Ruby will definitely have to visit someday.

Ray: Noted *Smiley emoji*.

Margot: What about you? What do you do for fun?

Ray: I like to hike and camp too! I like to play Frisbee Golf and hang out with friends. I have a Jeep, so I love to go off roading.

Margot: Hell yeah, that's rad! *Gasp emoji*. I wish I had a Jeep!

Ray: It's definitely fun to play around in. Are you a beer girl or a wine girl?

Margot: Oh beer, all the way! I go brewery hopping every weekend!

Ray: You're blowing my mind! Most girls prefer wine. I love breweries. I'm working on creating my own coffee beer.

Margot: I bet it will be amazing. So tell me what got you into coffee to begin with!

Ray: My dad. His dad had a coffee shop when he was a kid and I always loved hearing stories about it. So many memories were made in my Pop's shop. I wanted his legacy to live on. He shared all of his recipes with me before he died and I've been cracking away with it ever since. I wasn't expecting it to be as successful as it is. I feel blessed. I love coffee and love meeting new people. My parents are very involved – so it's very family oriented. It feels good to keep my Pop's memory alive.

Margot: That's a beautiful story. *Blushing emoji*. I will definitely have to stop by your shop when I visit.

Ray: Yes, I would love that. What do you do for work?

Margot: I work in a little café. I'm going to culinary school. I really want to be a cook someday. My dream is open up a little bakery of my own. I'm such a foodie.

Lol.

Ray: That's incredible. What's your favorite thing to cook?

Margot: Cookies!

Ray's favorite thing in the entire world was cookies. I knew I had probably just shot cupid's arrow through his black little heart. I laughed out loud as he sent a cookie monster gif.

Ray: I LOVE COOKIES! Seriously, you don't understand how much I love cookies. It's my one weakness in this world!

Margot: Well that's good to know! *Smiley emoji*. You'll have to tell me what your favorite kinds are and I can make you a batch from scratch.

Ray: Who are you LOL?

Margot: *Angel emoji*.

Ray: Do you like horror movies?

Margot: Love them! I love anything dark. Unsolved Mysteries, True Crime Documentaries, Murder Mysteries, Paranormal Stuff . . . I binge watch a lot of shows! *Laughing cry emoji*.

Ray: Oh my God, me too! Margot, we have a lot in common!

Margot: It's crazy! So tell me about your family. Do you have any siblings?

Ray: No, I'm an only child. It's just me and my parents! I wish I had a sibling. I have always been envious of people who do. Do you have any?

Margot: I have two sisters. I have an older sister named Hope and a younger sister named Annie. My parents are divorced.

Ray: I'm sorry to hear that. Are you and your family close?

Margot: Oh we have a great relationship! My family is kind of a bunch of hippies. They smoke a lot of pot and love the outdoors as much as I do.

Ray: Do you smoke?

Margot: Guilty! *Teeth face emoji*. I hope that isn't a problem for you.

Ray: I love to smoke weed. It really calms me down.

Margot: Do you have anxiety?

Ray: I do.

Margot: My younger sister gets panic attacks, so I know all about how horrible it is. You don't have to ever feel ashamed of having anxiety. It's a lot more common than you think.

Ray: Thanks, Margot. It's embarrassing to deal with, but pot really helps.

Margot: So, how do you see yourself being in a relationship?

I bit my lip as I waited for his answer. I felt so weird talking to Ray like this and knew I would eventually have to get to some flirting. I tried to hold back laughter at the thought of it.

Ray: Very affectionate. I'm loyal and honest and want the same. When I give my heart to someone, that's it. They will have me.

Margot: Wow. That's good to know.

Ray: I know people have different love languages, but I think they're all important. I am all about communication and quality time, but I I'm obsessed with physical touch.

Margot: Me too, Ray. I am very touchy feely and all about that communication. I don't just want a boyfriend, you know? I want someone that's going to be more at the end of the day. Someone who will also be my best friend.

Ray: *Heart emoji*. I'm really happy you swiped on me today. I was getting ready to delete my profile. No one had caught my interest until you, Margot.

Margot: You really mean that? *Crying eyes emoji.*

Ray: I really do.

Well I got you right in the nick of time, I mumbled to myself as I smiled at the screen.

Margot: I have a feeling this is going to be the start of something really special.

Ray: You took the words right out of my mouth!

Ray was going to pay for hurting me. I didn't care how long it took or what I had to do, but one thing was very clear to me. Margot was the key. Phase one was complete and there was nothing anyone could do to stop me.

CHAPTER 16

I woke up to feeling Lira's fingers running through my hair. I felt her lips trail kisses from my neck down to my collar bone. I opened my eyes and looked down at her. Her brown eyes sparkled as she gazed up at me with a look of longing and love. I stared into her, trying to mentally make sense of what could possibly be going on in her head.

For the first time in our relationship, I felt a genuine chill to the bone when I looked down at her. I wondered if she could sense that this was the moment I realized I must be dating a sociopath.

"Good morning," she whispered as she kissed my stomach below my bellybutton.

"Good morning," I whispered, feeling like a fly trapped in a web.

Lira slid my panties down while trailing more treacherous kisses down my inner thigh. I stared down at the bald spot on the back of her head.

"I want you," She whispered as she looked up at me.

"Okay," I replied, feeling disturbed as she started going down on me.

I stared at the ceiling, trying to wrap my mind around the game Lira was playing. Her intentions to Tess had been made very clear. She wanted to be with her. She was planning on breaking up with me. She said she wanted to let me down easily - and keep me in the dark about her whoring ways, until she felt comfortable I wouldn't be suspicious of her leaving me for another woman. She didn't plan on telling me about her and Tess. She planned on staying friends with me. She didn't want to be with me romantically anymore. *So why then,* I wondered as she went to town on my pussy, *was she continuing to act normal with me? Was she a psychopath? Was she just horny? Was she lying to Tess and still in love with me?* I moaned – faking my rise to climax as I contemplated how insane this entire situation was.

After she finished having her way with me, I laid there – closing my eyes to mask the revulsion I felt inside. She kissed me softly on the lips before getting up from the bed, whistling as she made her way to the shower.

What the fuck was the matter with her?

After I got ready for the day, I made my way down to the kitchen where Lira was packing up her lunch. She looked up at me and smiled as I made my way to the counter behind her. I listened to the sound of her knife spreading butter on the burnt side of her toast as I poured myself a cup of coffee. I took a deep breath, counting the seconds until she'd be leaving for work, when I spotted her coffee mug to the right of me. I looked behind me to make sure she wasn't looking and smiled smugly to myself before spitting into her drink.

"I'm taking time off for our trip to Colorado," Lira said as she assembled her peanut butter and jelly.

"Colorado?" I asked, staring at the back of her head in confusion.

"The cabin . . ." Lira said, throwing grapes into a Ziploc bag as she looked back at me. "We were going to visit my aunt and go camping, remember?"

She couldn't be serious. I assumed we would be broken

up long before that. Any day now, I assumed. We weren't supposed to leave to Colorado for a few *weeks*.

"Oh yeah, sorry," I said, feeling confused as she smiled back at me. "It's early. I'm not fully awake yet."

"Well, wake up!" she giggled.

I felt a mixture of anger and despair as I tried to understand what was happening.

"Here you go, Babe," I smiled, as I handed her the tainted coffee, after screwing the lid on tight.

"Oh, thanks!" she replied before kissing me on the cheek as she walked passed me. "Sorry, gotta run! I'm late for a brand deal! That's what I get for playing with you this morning!"

"Drive safe," I responded.

"It was worth it," she grinned, before rushing out the door.

She was a crazy person. I genuinely didn't know what to make of it.

I felt like a shell of a person as I walked into Dr. Griffin's office. I was so shocked by the revelation that this was going to continue on for several weeks longer – I didn't even know what to think. I stood in silence at the front desk, staring off into space as Dr. Griffin turned the corner into the lobby.

"Thea," he said, pulling me out of the dark thoughts that had taken over me.

I looked up and nodded before following him down the hallway to his office. I sat down on the couch, gripping the arm of the sofa as he made himself comfortable at his desk across from me. Lira's cheery voice echoed in my mind as I wondered how I was going to continue the charade much longer. I felt like the walls were closing in on me and felt a rush of heat and dizziness as I stared down at my feet in shock.

"Thea, are you alright?" Dr. Griffin asked – his voice

bringing me back to reality.

I stared up at him, feeling light headed and nauseous as I met his gaze.

He got up and grabbed a bottle of water, handing it to me as I sunk lower into the couch.

"Drink this," he said, unscrewing the lid.

I grabbed the bottle and felt my hands tremble as I brought the plastic to my lips.

Dr. Griffin stared at me with concern as I took a sip of my drink – exhaling heavily after swallowing. I looked up at him in embarrassment before taking another drink.

"Sorry, I think I'm having a panic attack," I said, feeling myself shake as I looked back up at him.

"That's okay, don't be sorry," Dr. Griffin replied. "Please feel free to lay down. Here." He opened the closet and pulled out a blanket, draping it over me as I slid my shoes off to lay on the couch.

This was humiliating. I hadn't had a panic attack like this in a long time and felt suffocated and exposed as I curled myself up into a ball on the couch. Dr. Griffin made his way back to the desk and watched me as I tried to slow my breathing. Lira was going to have to answer for this. There was no reason anyone should have to put up with this bullshit. I couldn't believe she was doing this to me and planned to continue doing it to me for *weeks* longer.

"Talk to me, Thea," Dr. Griffin said, pulling my attention back to him. "How are you feeling? Is there anything else I can get you?"

"I'm fine, thank you," I sighed as I steadied my breathing. "I used to get panic attacks all of the time. It's just been a while. I'm sorry you have to see this."

"Please, don't be sorry," he responded. "And I have seen

plenty of panic attacks – trust me. It's perfectly fine. You're safe here. I just want to make sure you are doing ok."

"Thank you," I sighed, still feeling dizzy, but much more comfortable now that I had wrapped myself up into a cocoon.

"So what's bothering you today?" he asked.

I took a deep breath, grimacing as I stared back at him. "I don't even know where to begin. Lira's a fucking sociopath! She continues to cheat on me and continues to act like everything is fine. This morning, she reminded me about this camping trip we go to every year in Colorado. This trip is a few weeks away! Like, what planet is she living on? Why is she telling Tess she is going to break up with me and move in with her and then turning around and trying to plan a camping trip with me? I don't understand!"

I took a deep breath, feeling lightheaded as Dr. Griffin watched me with intensity.

"That's a lot," he nodded.

"I'm fucking over it!" I replied.

I closed my eyes and took deep breaths in my nose and exhaled out of my mouth as I focused on slowing my heartrate. I was at my limit. I was *beyond* enraged. I couldn't make sense of anything anymore.

"Talk to me about how you're feeling," Dr. Griffin said. "What about this particular conversation has pushed you over the edge?"

"I just don't freaking *get it*," I responded. "So, the other day I listened to a conversation from the bug I planted in Lira's car and she and Tess were arguing about how and when she was going to tell me. Lira basically told Tess that she has no intention of telling me she is cheating on me and wants to hide her relationship with Tess from me so that there will be a chance that she and I can remain friends! Tess said they can maintain this little charade for a month – but that's it.

So, I'm sitting here just waiting for Lira to break up with me and it *isn't happening*! She straight up isn't showing any signs whatsoever that she's going to leave me!"

"And what is stopping you from leaving her?" Dr. Griffin replied.

I took a deep breath, shaking my head at him.

"I don't know," I sighed. "Honestly, I have been wanting to get some kind of grand revenge and ruin her life before leaving her. But staying with her in the meantime is driving me insane!"

"You've already hidden a necklace, dumped her grandmother's ashes down the drain and put Nair in her shampoo," Dr. Griffin said, raising his brow at me. "You've bugged her car and read her private conversations too. What type of revenge is the kind you're looking for? At what point will you feel satisfied that you have done enough?"

I huffed as I pushed myself up to sit in an upright position. "I don't know," I mumbled. "I feel like she hasn't suffered enough."

"It's important for you that she suffers," he said, looking through me.

"I'm having sex with my ex-girlfriend," I said, looking away from him. "Her name is Tedra and she's been coming over and fucking me in our bed. I thought it would make me feel better. And I guess it does to a certain extent, but I'm just so fucking annoyed. I would feel so much better if I could rationalize *why* Lira is behaving the way that she is. If we were unhappy or fighting – fine. I'd get it. But we're not."

"It's a betrayal," Dr. Griffin nodded, leaning forward in his chair. "You could not imagine someone you love is capable of such an atrocity. You want to understand the *why* of it. The reason she wants to leave. You want to know what's taking her so long. What is the reason she stays?"

"Exactly, Doug," I sighed. "Like what is her endgame? Does she want to be with Tess or does she want to be with me?"

"Why does it matter?" Dr. Griffin asked.

I shifted uncomfortably in my seat.

"No seriously, Thea . . . why?"

"I don't know," I shrugged, staring back at him.

"Would you stay with her if she loved you?"

"No," I muttered.

"But you want to know if she wants to be with Tess or if she wants to be with you. Is that just so that you could feel better about yourself if she loves you more, or feel sorry for yourself if she doesn't?"

I glared at him, pursing my lips.

"Regardless of what Lira does or does not feel, it doesn't change her actions. She is having an affair with another woman, Thea. Let's talk about Raymond for a moment."

"What about Ray?" I asked, feeling confused.

"Raymond abandoned you," he continued. "Judging from our last few conversations, it seems the thing that bothers you the most about the loss of your friendship is not understanding *why*. Perhaps if he wasn't still friends with Peter, it would make sense to you. You would be able to tell yourself, 'Ok. He's just on a high horse of morality. He isn't friends with people who cheat,' but that isn't it, is it? Because he stayed friends with Peter, but ended his friendship with you, you have been devastated by this. It doesn't make sense to you. You can't wrap your mind around it."

I nodded my head as Dr. Griffin looked through me – seeming to pull the thoughts right out of my head.

"Same goes for Lira. She's cheating on you. You're already pissed off about that. She's responsible for ruining your friendship with Raymond, in your eyes. How could she do this to you after what you sacrificed to be with her, am I right? But now there is this element of *betrayal* that has you feeling dizzy. She's gotten completely under your skin. It's not as simple as her fucking someone else, now is it? Now, she's telling Tess one thing and acting the complete opposite way when she's alone with you. So what exactly is it? Is she cheating on you because she's in love with Tess or is it something else you haven't discovered yet? If she was unhappy with you, she wouldn't behave this way, right? So there must be a reason *why*."

"Yes," I whispered, feeling tears sting my eyes.

"I understand you, Thea. I understand why you're confused and why you're hurting. I understand why you're reluctant to leave. You want answers."

"I'm really confused," I nodded.

"But I have something to tell you that you aren't going to like," he replied.

I stared at him as he took the glasses off of his face and really stared at me. I held my breath as I wondered what he had to say.

"Sometimes you will never get the answers," he said, exhaling as he leaned back in his seat.

I furrowed my brow, wiping the tears from my face as I waited for him to speak. He didn't. I waited in silence for several seconds before shaking my head in bewilderment.

"What do you mean by that?" I asked.

"Sometimes life sucks and you don't get the answers you need," he replied. "It's terrible and it's unfair. Life isn't fair, Thea. Why did Raymond do that to you? Maybe he doesn't even know why, himself! Why is Lira doing this to you? Maybe she loves you, maybe she doesn't! Maybe she's indecisive. Maybe she's just a manipulative human being. The point is, you will drive yourself insane if you expect for everything to have a rational explanation. Sometimes life is just straight up *unfair*. Instead of focusing on understanding what other people are doing, why don't you try and focus on yourself? I know that sounds harsh and I apologize. I told you I can be brash sometimes, but what I am trying to say is *try*, Thea. Remove their motives from the equation for just a moment. Their motives do not matter, ok? Focus on *Thea*. Pretend Thea is someone else and you're like a ghost looking in."

"A ghost?" I asked.

"A ghost," he nodded with an ever so slight grin on the corner of his lips. "So you're hanging out and watching Thea because you're haunting her house or whatever. You have grown quite fond of her and feel protective of her, even. How would you help Thea cope with what people have done to her? If ghosts could speak and you could help her, how would you make her understand?"

"I don't know," I shrugged.

"Humor me, Thea."

"I'd tell her it's going to be okay," I mumbled.

"And why would you tell her it would be okay?" he asked.

"Because they are assholes and don't deserve her," I responded. "Because she'll be sad forever if she doesn't let them go."

"So you admit you will be sad forever if you don't let them go," he continued. "You also acknowledge that they are assholes and don't deserve you and that everything will be okay."

I felt my lip tremble as I looked away from him.

"Sometimes it's hard to love ourselves, Thea. It helps if you look at yourself as another person. Even better if you look at yourself as another person you care about that you want to help. You wouldn't want someone you love to be sad forever - over some idiot that threw their friendship away with no explanation - or some ex that cheated on them with a personal trainer with an unusually large forehead."

I laughed out loud as I wiped the tears from my face.

"Sometimes people's actions don't make sense," he sighed. "You have to focus on the things you *can* control. You can control this situation. You have the power to leave Lira. You don't have to stick around to learn the why. Fuck her reasons. She may not even understand them, herself. You can walk away and focus on healing yourself. You don't have to let her have this power over you."

I sniffled, nodding my head.

"But, for whatever reason, you're not ready and that's ok. I just want to empower you and show you that there can be light at the end of the tunnel. I want to encourage you to start focusing on the things you can control instead of obsessing over the things you can't."

"I slashed Ray's tire," I said, biting my lip as his eyes widened ever so slightly. "I started a dating profile with a fake identity with the intentions of leading him on mercilessly for fun."

"I see," Dr. Griffin replied.

Was my mind playing tricks on me or was he holding back a smile?

"I know it's ridiculous, but I want to hurt him," I sighed. "I want revenge."

"While this may be true, I encourage you to reconsider," Dr. Griffin responded. "It's a slippery slope you're skiing on, Thea. You are hiding behind a computer and a fake face, but your feelings are very real. You still *love* Raymond. You still fantasize about living in a world where he is still your friend.

Could this be a way for you to feel close to him again?"

"No," I replied, feeling uneasy as he penetrated me with his stare.

"For now," he continued. "But what happens when feelings become real for one or both of you?"

"He needs to understand what it's like to be abandoned by someone he loves."

"You've gone six years without talking to him, Thea," Dr. Griffin replied. "You're already ahead of the game. Taking a step back now could end up backfiring."

"Backfiring how?" I asked, feeling annoyed.

"You could get hurt," he said furrowing his brow. "Regardless of if you think you're going to hurt him or not, you'll be creating this fake relationship with him. You'll be talking to him every day. You don't have a heart of stone, Dorothea. You have feelings. How do you think it will make you feel to talk to him every day?"

"Good," I replied, looking smugly at him.

"Good, why?" he asked.

"Good because I know I'm going to hurt him."

He sighed. "Be careful. The lines between reality and fiction could become blurred and I don't want you to hurt yourself in the process."

"So you're not going to try and talk me out of it?" I asked, raising my brow.

"I'm not here to talk you out of things," he smiled. "I'm here to listen and understand. And I *know* why you're doing this, Thea. I can't make decisions for you. I can only try and help you self-reflect."

I nodded my head, taking a deep breath as I took in what he was saying. I had never had anyone see through me so easily before. Every time he opened his mouth, it was like he *knew* every reason – every thought – every motive. Even when I knew I was being impulsive, vindictive, and crazy, he didn't make me feel judged. He made me feel *seen, understood, and validated.* It was easy with him. I felt vulnerable and exposed, but safe and heard.

I looked up into his dark chocolate eyes and prayed he didn't see the emotions hiding there – deep in the pit of my stomach. *Fuck* Lira. *Fuck* Raymond. Fuck everybody who had ever hurt me. Suddenly they seemed less important. I hated myself for longing to reach forward and pull Dr. Griffin into my arms. He *understood* me. I could tell that he cared. If getting my heartbroken was what led me to be here in this moment sitting on this man's couch, I was grateful. I had never felt this way about someone before.

"Thank you for listening to me," I whispered, feeling my breath catch in my throat. "It means a lot to me that you can make sense of my chaos."

"It's only chaotic if you let it be," he laughed. "I'm happy to listen, Thea. You're not alone."

When he said it, I knew that he meant it. I knew his intentions were pure. I tried to push back the feelings building up within me, but deep down I knew that it was true.

Shit, I thought as I looked back at him. I was falling for my therapist. And I was falling *hard.*

CHAPTER 17

Week 7

D r. Douglas Griffin. I swooned whenever I'd say his name. I must have whispered it to myself hundreds of times over the last few days. I felt completely stupid about it.

I knew that he was a professional and that there was no way in hell he would ever be with me. But I wondered. I really did. I could tell by the way he looked at me and the way he said my name . . . he thought about it too. I was as certain of it as much as I was as certain that he wouldn't dare act on it. He was my therapist. I was his patient. There was no way he would ever admit it to himself. But perhaps with a little coaxing . . .

For now, I would have to think on it and weigh the pros and cons. I *of course* didn't want to be responsible for ruining someone's life, but I felt an undeniable pull between us that I knew I couldn't shake. I pushed thoughts of Dr. Griffin aside as the application from Tinder ping'd, pulling me back to reality and the task at hand. *Margot* had a date with Raymond. I had carved out time for the two of them to continue getting to know one another. I laughed out loud to myself as I pulled up the message thread.

Ray: Good morning, Beautiful. How have you been?

Margot: Well, hey you! *Heart emoji*. I'm better now that you messaged me. I've been excited to talk to you again.

Ray: Same! It's been such a crazy week with work, but I'm off for the rest of the day.

Margot: Awesome – me too!

Ray: Has your profile been blowing up with messages? I'm sure a girl like you gets messaged all day.

Margot: Nothing too crazy, LOL! Nothing's caught my attention so far. You're the only one I'm talking to on here.

Ray sent a blushing emoji. I laughed evilly to myself as I waited for him to continue.

Ray: I wasn't lying when I said I was about to delete my account. *Smiley emoji*. You're the only one I'm speaking to, also.

Idiot, I laughed.

Margot: I can't wait to get out to Kansas and meet you! I haven't been this nervous to meet someone in a long time – if ever.

Ray: Lies! No, I get what you mean! It's crazy how much we have in common! And you're absolutely beautiful, by the way.

I rolled my eyes as I pulled up the saved folder of photos I had for Margot. I picked a cute selfie of her blowing a kiss to the camera and snickered as I sent it to him.

Ray: Wow. Your eyes are STUNNING!

Margot: Oh, stop! *Blushing emoji*.

Ray: No seriously, you're very beautiful.

Margot: Well, thank you. You're quite handsome, yourself.

Ray: I didn't used to be, you know. When I was younger, I used to be really fat.

Margot: Oh really?

Ray: I got teased all of the time in school, LOL! That's probably why I've never really had a girlfriend.

Margot: Get out of here! You've never had a girlfriend? It's a huge accomplishment to lose the weight! You look *amazing*. I'm sure you were adorable, even with the extra weight.

Ray: Promise you won't laugh? *Laughing Emoji*.

Margot: Cross my heart.

I waited patiently, eating a bag of popcorn before hearing the ping of his response. I opened the photo and laughed out loud at the throwback. Ray had sent a picture that *I* had taken of him his freshman year of college. He was pushing 300 pounds. His green eyes sparkled as he grinned cheesily at the camera. His cheeks were round and pink.

Ray: Told you it was bad. *Laughing Cry emoji*.

Margot: You are so CUTE! What are you even talking about? Look at those dimples!

Ray: They're not dimples, they're fat rolls – LOL!

Margot: Well, I think they're cute.*Smiley emoji*. It must have taken a lot of work to lose all that weight.

Ray: It was definitely a challenge. I had to completely change my lifestyle. Even now, I'm still working on it. I workout every day.

Margot: That's impressive! You'll definitely have to give me some pointers.

Ray: As if you need any – you're already perfect. *Smiley emoji.*.

OH BARF, I gagged. No wonder Ray never had a girlfriend. With corny lines like those, girls would be running for the hills! I felt sorry for him, knowing he was trying his best to sound sincere. He couldn't help that he was creepy. He just oozed inexperience.

> **Margot: You're so sweet. Honestly, you seem like such a nice guy. I'm shocked you're not already taken.**

Ray: I am honestly extremely shy. *Laughing emoji*. Pretty much all of my friends are married. I focused so much on my business the last few years; the majority of the people I see are regulars!

> **Margot: That's sad! *Laughing emoji*. You really need to get out more.**

Ray: I'm low key glad I didn't, because now I'm here talking to you.

I took a deep breath, tapping my foot impatiently as I stared at the screen. I was bored. This was taking too long. I had never been the type for online dating or long-distance relationships. I felt that talking through a text thread was shallow and insincere. I wanted to hear his voice. I needed to step up my game.

> **Margot: Would it be forward of me to give you my number? I'm really curious to hear the voice behind the profile.**

I waited, biting my lip as I stared at the ellipses. I wondered if he would take the bait.

Ray: Not forward at all.

I smiled as I copied and pasted the number to my Google Voice.

My heart raced as I launched the voice changing app. This was all actually happening! I rocked back and forth with nervous energy for several minutes before my phone began to ring.

Here we go, I said as I prepared myself to answer the phone. *You've got this, Margot!*

I accepted the call and shut my eyes as I opened my mouth to speak.

"Hello?" I answered, biting my lip.

"Hi Margot," Raymond replied.

I launched myself out of my seat and jumped up and down – holding back internal squeals of delight as his voice rang in my ears. *I got him.*

"Well, hey there, Ray!" I smiled.

"It's nice to hear your voice," he responded – sounding surprisingly less nervous than I had anticipated. "I was about to offer you my number, also."

"It's better to talk than text," I replied. "Texts don't convey tone and can come across so vapid sometimes. I wanted to *really* get to know you."

"I couldn't agree more," Ray replied. "You know, I was staring at your profile all day. I was excited to get to talk to you. Has anyone ever told you that your freckles are cute?"

I laughed, shaking my head as I paced back and forth across the living room. I had never imagined I would be having a conversation like this with *Ray* of all people! I was entirely too entertained.

"I tried to cover them up for years!" I groaned. "I hated

them when I was a kid! I got teased for having them all of the time! I guess as I got older, they stopped bothering me."

"Freckles are trendy now," Ray replied.

I held in laughter as my eyes widened in disbelief. What the fuck did Ray know about freckles being trendy?

"At least, that's what I've heard," he laughed. "I know some girls who are obsessed with makeup and they tell me they even make freckle pens now. They're the new hot commodity in the beauty world!"

"You don't say!" I laughed. "That honestly makes me feel so much better! I'm flattered to know that my splotchy skin is socially acceptable now."

We laughed together and I shook my head in shock. This was insane to me!

"So why are you moving to Kansas?" Ray asked. "I mean, if I lived in Colorado, I'd never want to leave."

I sighed as I sat back down on the couch.

"My sister has cancer," I replied – making my voice sound somber. "I wanted to move out there to be closer to her. She needs me."

"Jesus, I'm sorry!" Ray responded. "That's terrible!"

"Oh, she's in remission," I replied. "We're confident she's going to be okay. But still, I feel horrible that I haven't been there for her. I really wish I could have moved out there sooner."

"That's understandable," Ray replied – his voice full of concern and empathy. "Which sister is it?"

"My younger sister, Annie," I responded.

"What kind of cancer?" he asked. "Sorry, you don't have to answer that if it's too personal."

"Oh, no – it's fine to ask!" I replied. "Breast cancer. But

they caught it early. I am confident that it won't come back."

"Wow, I'm sorry, Margot," Ray sighed. "I am happy she's doing better. I can't imagine what you're going through."

"Thank you so much," I replied, taking a deep breath. "Family is everything to me. I love my sister more than anything."

"Family means everything to me too," Ray said.

I felt like this was going really well. I wanted a sob story that Ray would latch onto. I wanted his heart to really go out to this girl. I wanted him to admire her selflessness for moving out to help her sister. I wanted him to admire her strength for being there for her in her time of need. I knew he would fall harder this way. Ray was a sucker for a sad story. It was odd because you would think that with all of that empathy, he would give a shit about me. But he didn't. And so, I reminded myself not to give a fuck and continue.

"That's something else we have in common," I smiled.

"I'm a huge mama's boy," Ray confessed, sounding bashful. "I'm not sure if it's because I am an only child or what, but my *God,* I love that woman!"

"That's so cute," I responded. "You can tell a lot about a guy based on how he treats his mother."

"My mom's my best friend," he replied.

I clenched my jaw – the words, *best friend,* sounded blasphemous on his tongue.

"That's amazing," I smiled. "Speaking of best friends – tell me about yours!"

My cheeks felt warm as I waited for him to respond.

"I have three best friends," Ray said. "Peter, Lara, and Westly."

I felt sick to my stomach – reminding myself I had to

stay in character.

"Oh yeah?" I smiled. "And how do you know them?"

"Peter and I have been friends for a lifetime!" Ray replied. "Lara's his wife. She's awesome. They're actually couple's goals. You'd love them. Westly and I have been friends since college. He's my roommate."

"That's awesome," I replied – trying to keep my voice steady. "I've been best friends with my best friend since I was in elementary school."

I seethed – still in shock that Ray had called Lara one of his best friends. That fucking slut was the reason Peter left me. I felt nauseated thinking that the two of them had actually gotten that close. Had they been good friends all along and he just never told me? I had so many questions, but had to keep my cool.

"That's a long time!" Ray responded. "What's her name?"

"Her name is Julie," I replied.

And Ray was living with Westly now? Since when did that happen? Had they been living together since I moved in with Lira? I felt dizzy, not believing that this was my reality now.

"Is she bummed you're moving to Kansas?" he asked.

"She is, but we've been long distance friends before," I sighed. "She's more like my sister. It doesn't matter how far apart we live. We will always be there for one another."

"I get what you mean," Ray replied.

No, Ray. You fucking don't.

"You'd love her," I continued. "She's, like, obsessed with coffee, so she'd be dying to visit your shop!"

"Any friend of yours is a friend of mine," he laughed.

"So, tell me something about yourself that nobody else knows, Margot."

I laughed, taking a deep breath as I thought about how to respond.

"Let's make this more interesting," I smirked. "I'll tell you two truths and one lie. You have to guess which ones are true."

"Deal," he laughed.

"Okay, let's see," I exhaled. "I'm a virgin. My favorite meal is breakfast for dinner. And I'm deathly afraid of butterflies."

Ray laughed out loud and I smiled to myself. Ray loved breakfast for dinner. He would think it's cute if Margot was afraid of butterflies and he wouldn't believe that she was a virgin. I knew him too well.

"Well, dang," Ray chuckled. "I'm going to guess that truth number one is that you love breakfast for dinner."

"Ding, ding, ding!" I grinned.

"Margot, that's awesome! I love that too! I know what our first date meal will be!"

I giggled, smiling from ear to ear. "And the next truth?" I asked.

"I'm going to guess that the next truth is that you are afraid of butterflies."

I giggled, shaking my head.

"Nope," I replied.

There was silence on his end of the line.

"There's no way you're a virgin," he responded.

"Well, you wanted me to tell you something that nobody else knows," I smiled. "Try not to judge me too harshly."

"How is that even possible?" he laughed. "Are you messing with me?"

"No," I sighed, trying to sound shy. "I'm not super religious or anything. I'm not saving myself for marriage. I just haven't met the right person yet. I just want it to be special. Hope that's not a turn off or anything."

"Wow," Ray said in awe.

I knew Ray was likely a virgin and that this would probably make Margot seem like she could be his soulmate in his eyes. I snickered internally at the thought of the look on his stupid face.

"It's not a turn off at all," Ray responded. "I have so much respect for that, Margot. Honestly, that's awesome."

I felt smug as I grinned from ear to ear.

"I told you I'm not interested in finding someone to hook up with," I sighed. "Usually you throw out the word, 'virgin', and guys see it as a challenge or run away screaming. I'm not interested in wasting my time with someone who isn't interested in building a real connection. When I give myself to someone, it will be to someone I truly love."

"You're wonderful," Ray replied. "Trust me, I'm not that type of guy. I want something genuine. I honestly am looking forward to taking my time and getting to know you."

"Good," I replied, knowing he had fallen completely into my scheme. "I'm counting on it."

CHAPTER 18

I had spent the last few days hinting to Lira that I wanted to start working out.

"I'm getting so fat," I said, pouting my lips. "I just want to get back to feeling like *me* again."

"You're beautiful," she told me. "I think you're perfect just the way you are, but I understand what it's like to have low self-esteem. If you want to start working out, then I support you 100%."

That was days ago. I giggled to myself as I pulled up Tess' business page on Facebook. She was local. She was affordable. She had five star reviews! I would pretend that I found her randomly. We had a few mutual friends on Facebook, so realistically it was plausible that I could find her on my own accord. I clicked on "Send Message" and smirked as I began to draft my message to her.

"Hi Tess!" I greeted her. "My name is Dorothea Duckworth and I came across your page from a mutual friend! I have been really wanting to get into shape this year and really like what I've read in your reviews! Are you accepting new clients?"

I sent the message and waited – watching the iPad with intensity for the chaos that I knew would soon ensue.

It didn't take long for Tess to message Lira. I smiled

with anticipation as I watched the messages begin to pour in.

Tess: Lira, 911! *Shock emoji*. Damnit, Lira – answer your phone!

I sipped on my coffee, taking a deep breath as I made myself comfortable on the couch.

Tess: Lira, please – I'm not joking. I need to talk to you!

Lira: What's wrong?

Tess: You're not going to believe this.

She sent a screen shot of my message to her and I bit my lip as I waited for Lira to answer her. I imagined the panic she felt and chuckled as I read her reply.

Lira: What the fuck! *Gasp emoji*.
Tess: Does she know? Is this a trap?

Lira: Just hold on a minute. Let me think.

Tess: This can't be a coincidence. How does she know?

Lira: Don't panic! *Angry emoji*. I can't believe this is happening to me!

Tess: Happening to *you*?! She reached out to ME!

Lira: Okay, listen, she told me she wants to start working out! I didn't realize she was going to look for a personal trainer!

Tess: We have six mutual friends on Facebook. I mean, these are people I went to college with. It's possible she found me through them.

Lira: Well, tell her you aren't accepting new clients!

There was a long break of silence and I sighed, wondering what Tess was going to say.

Lira: Seriously, just politely decline. I'm sorry for the scare, Babe. What are the chances of this happening to us, I mean seriously?! Small world!

Tess: Okay.

I rolled my eyes as I looked back down at my phone. I saw the ellipses indicating Tess was responding to me.

"Good afternoon, Dorothea!" Tess replied. "Thank you so much for reaching out to inquire. My schedule has been pretty crazy. What are your goals and what were you looking to achieve?"

Seriously, Bitch? I laughed out loud, feeling high from excitement as I replied to her.

"Honestly, I have just felt like crap about myself for a while," I said. "I was hoping to lose thirty pounds or so, this summer. It's been forever since I have set foot in a gym! I just need guidance and structure so that I can get back on track."

I waited a few minutes, feeling antsy as I wondered how this would play out. Would she honor Lira's wishes or would her curiosity get the best of her? I knew what I would do in her situation. I smiled as I read her response.

"I definitely know what that's like!" Tess replied. "I would be happy to meet with you for a consultation. We can make a game plan and discuss pricing. I have availability this afternoon for coffee if that works for you?"

"That's perfect!" I replied. "Where would you like to meet?"

A few hours went by and I sat alone at a corner table – sipping on a mocha as I scrolled through messages on my phone. My double life with Raymond had been keeping me very busy. I felt like there should be an award for people like me. It took hard work and dedication to manipulate people the way that I was! I was good at it. It was easy. It came second nature to me.

I felt a shiver run down my spine as I wondered whether or not that was a *good* thing. I only used my talents on those worthy of being fucked with. I was a loyal and caring human to everyone who was loyal and caring to me. I heard the bells of the door jingle as Tess walked into the shop and I waved politely as she looked around for me. Her blue eyes froze as she spotted me and I smiled as she made her way back to meet me.

I rose to my feet, extending my hand out to her. She grinned as she grasped my hand in hers. *Horse teeth*, I thought.

"Dorothea," she smiled, shaking my hand aggressively. "It's nice to meet you!"

"Thanks for taking the time to see me!" I smiled.

She set her backpack down on the back of her chair. "I'm just going to grab a coffee," she laughed.

"Oh, of course!" I replied. "Sorry, I would have ordered for you, but I didn't know what kind of coffee you like."

She shifted her weight nervously before heading to the counter. I felt satisfied with myself as I waited for her to return. She was nervous. Possibly even afraid. I felt like I was in some kind of secret pissing contest - where the two of us got to finally scope one another out and see what all of the fuss was about.

There was no way this bitch was hotter than me. She couldn't possibly be better in bed, either. I knew her and Lira fought like cats and dogs and surmised their relationship was toxic – so I was *dying* to know why Lira was choosing her over me. What was I missing? What was so great about this chick?

Tess had a strange nose. It was pointy and crooked – but her features were asymmetrical, so it oddly worked. Her strawberry blond hair was pulled up into a face-lifting, tight pony that did no favors for her face. She wore a white headband that framed her large and shiny forehead. She didn't wear any makeup. She had full lips, but I couldn't tell if they were *actually* full or if they protruded because of her teeth. But she *did* have really pretty eyes. They were the lightest color of blue and surrounded in envy worthy lashes. If you *only* looked at her eyes, it was easy to forget everything else. She reminded me of a more gingery and feminine Napoleon Dynamite. What on Earth was Lira thinking?

She returned to the table with some kind of iced coffee and I smiled politely as she made herself comfortable across from me.

"Sorry about that," Tess smiled. "There was bad traffic! I hate being late!"

"Oh don't even worry about it!" I responded. "Do you live far away? Did it take you long to get here?"

"About 20 minutes or so," she sighed. "It's not too bad."

"Well, I'm grateful you wanted to meet with me," I smiled.

"So you found me on Facebook?" Tess asked – pulling me out of my internal appraisal of her.

"Yes!" I responded. "I thought about getting a gym membership, but the thought of being trained in front of a bunch of strangers sounded nerve wracking to me."

"Some of those trainers are overpaid and underqualified," Tess smiled. "You definitely don't have to get a gym membership to get into shape."

I smiled nervously. I wanted her to see me as a non-threat. I wanted to appeal to her compassionate side and hoped that by meeting me in person, I would become more human to her. How would she feel, meeting the person she was secretly fucking over? Would it eat her up inside to realize I was *nice?* Would she grow a conscience? Or would she simply not give a damn and continue stealing my girlfriend?

"So how long have you been a personal trainer?" I asked before blowing into my coffee to cool it down for my next sip.

"Oh gosh, like four years or so," Tess replied. "I originally went to school for nutrition, but exercise science was so much fun! I helped some of my closest friends lose weight and thought it would be a great way to earn a living and stay in shape. Once you start getting into it, I swear it becomes fun! It's addicting."

"That's what they say," I laughed, licking my lips before smiling at her. "I used to be such a hottie before college. But the pandemic had me *struggling*, girl!"

"Don't be so hard on yourself!" she said, shaking her head at me. "You're beautiful! It won't be hard at all to lose the weight!"

I took a deep breath, smiling shyly as I looked away from her.

"I hope so," I whispered. "I'm definitely ready for a change."

Tess looked pensive as she sipped on her coffee. I wondered what types of thoughts were running through her mind about me.

"So tell me a bit about yourself," she smiled. "What do you do for fun? Have you ever had a personal trainer before?"

I leaned forward, resting my chin on my fist.

"Well, I'm super nerdy," I grinned. "I really just spend the majority of my time reading and watching movies. I've never had a personal trainer before. My girlfriend started working out this year and she looks amazing, so I figured I should probably stop being so lazy and follow suit."

"Oh you have a girlfriend?" she asked coyly.

Yeah, Tess. The same balding slut you fuck behind my back on a daily basis.

"Yes, she's great," I sighed innocently – trying to blush as I flashed a smile. "But she's way more athletic than me."

"Have you considered working out together?" she asked.

"Maybe I will once I'm in better shape," I replied. "That girl could run laps around me!"

"Well, we'll get you running laps around her in no time!" Tess laughed. "Are you a morning person or a night owl?"

I stared at her, wondering what the fuck my sleep habits had to do with anything.

"I'm a morning person," I replied.

"Well that's awesome!" Tess chirped. "You can knock out your workouts in the morning and have the rest of the day to do whatever you want. I used to do that all of the time, but it's hard for me to stop pushing snooze."

I laughed, trying my best to look like I found her funny. I could tell she was thinking hard about how to get the information out of me that she wanted. We were both playing a really good game.

"So you said you have a girlfriend?" Tess asked. "That's cool. I am a lesbian too."

"Oh, I'm bi," I laughed.

Tess raised her eyebrows at me.

"I was actually engaged to a guy before, but he cheated on me."

"Oh, I'm sorry to hear that!" Tess said, furrowing her brow.

"Men are assholes," I sighed, "but girls have their moments. Lira and I have been together for six years and we've been friends since we were teenagers. I'm honestly really lucky."

I watched as Tess ever so subtly clenched her jaw.

"What about you? Do you have a girlfriend?" I asked.

"Kind of," Tess sighed. "It's complicated."

"Oh, that sounds intriguing!" I said, batting my eyes.

Tess laughed, biting her lip. "Well it's not official, but I'm working on it."

"Oh, so it's new?" I grinned.

"No, we've been together for about five months."

I felt my blood boil as she smiled at me. So this really *had* been going on since Lira became an influencer. I still couldn't believe I had known about it for over SEVEN WEEKS.

"That's a long time to be unofficially dating someone," I said. "Commitment issues?"

"Basically," she laughed. "I'm in love with her. I want to settle down, but she's not one to be locked down easily."

"Oh, I hate that," I winced. "I dated a guy like that once. Biggest waste of my time. My advice is that if you're not getting back what you're putting in, it's not worth it."

She stared into me with her ice cold eyes and I momentarily wondered if I'd crossed the line.

"But what do I know?" I laughed, rolling my eyes. "I've been practically married for so long, I forget what it's like to date."

"What's your girlfriend like?" Tess asked, taking a sip of her drink.

"She's amazing," I smiled. "She's super girly, funny, kind-hearted . . . I'm really blessed."

Tess nodded her head – looking uncomfortable as she listened to me. I knew I needed to change the subject so that I wouldn't be laying it on her too thick.

"So, you studied nutrition?" I asked. "Can you help me with meal plans, also?"

"Oh definitely," Tess nodded. "Do you have any dietary restrictions?"

"No, I'm easy," I grinned.

"I'm thinking I can meet up with you and go over a workout plan and write up a meal plan for you also. After a few weeks, we can track your progress and switch some stuff up!"

"Perfect!" I smiled. "Is there a particular gym I should go to? I'm open to whatever."

"I'll email you a list of good ones and you can let me know which one you like best," she smiled. "We'll get you feeling better about yourself in no time! I know how it feels to feel gross about yourself and have your sex life be in a funk. Once I started exercising every day, I felt so much better!"

It took everything in me not to bust out into a fit of laughter at her little jab. *Is that the best you've got?* I wondered.

"Oh, my sex life is great!" I laughed. "I'm really lucky that my girlfriend doesn't care that I have the extra weight. I mean it's not like I'm fat. I'm just curvy. We fuck like rabbits! Sorry – too much information." I tucked a strand of hair behind my ear and bit my lip as I thought about it before looking back up at her. "I'm just doing this for me. But who knows! Maybe after I'm all skinny and sexy, things will be even better!"

Tess laughed incredulously as she stared back at me.

"But I'm super excited. I can tell already, you're going to be awesome. I'm so happy that I clicked on your page!"

"Me too," she replied, flashing her teeth at me.

Tess didn't know it yet, but by the time I was done with her – she and I would be "friends". Lira wouldn't look like the angel in white that she had Tess tricked into believing she was. Tess wasn't innocent, but she too was a victim of Lira's games. This bitch was nasty and undeniably a home wrecking whore. But I wasn't going to let her think Lira was the bigger person. She deserved to know the truth. *Lira* was the problem. It was only a matter of time before she would see.

CHAPTER 19

My heart was beating so hard, I wondered if he could hear it. I smiled politely at him as I took a seat on the comfy black couch across from him.

I wanted his attention. I wore a low cut, black blouse and high rise blue jeans with cute, black pumps. I had a layer of sheer, shiny lip gloss on my lips and smoky purple eyeshadow that made my brown eyes pop. I wondered if he noticed any of these things. I was hopeful he did.

"So how was your week, Thea?" Dr. Griffin asked as he leaned forward attentively in his seat.

My life was beginning to feel like a soap opera. I thought about all of the plots I had in motion and wondered where the best place to begin would be. I was nervous he would judge me. He hadn't so far, but I didn't know how far I could go or what the limit was to my level of crazy. I cleared my throat as I looked down at my lap nervously.

"Well, I've been slowly building my fake relationship with Ray," I sighed. I glanced up and Dr. Griffin nodded at me, not seeming phased by this revelation. "My alter ego is named Margot and I created her based on his likes and interests. It's been pretty entertaining pulling him in."

"So the two of you have been speaking frequently?" Dr. Griffin asked.

"Yes," I replied. "It started out as casual flirting and simple 'getting to know you' questions, but now it's getting deep. We talk from the time we wake up in the morning right up until we go to bed."

"And how does that make you feel?" Dr. Griffin asked.

"It's pretty exhilarating," I smiled.

"Has juggling your relationship with Ray been challenging whilst maintaining your relationship with Lira?"

"It can get dicey sometimes, but she's pretty preoccupied with her own shit," I shrugged.

"Has it been nice getting the extra attention?" Dr. Griffin asked.

I nodded my head, smiling slightly as I admired his curls. "It's nice to feel important again."

"And how has it been getting close to Ray again?" he asked. "Have you been able to compartmentalize?"

"What do you mean by that?" I asked.

"Meaning, has it been challenging separating yourself from your alter ego? When Ray makes Margot feel good, does it bother you that you're not the person he thinks she is?"

"I don't give a shit what he thinks!" I chortled. "I *want* him to fall in love with her. The harder he falls, the worse he will feel."

"So it hasn't made you feel nostalgic at all," he nodded. "That was my concern. I was worried you would get attached to him."

"Oh, so you worry about me?" I smirked.

Dr. Griffin smiled, looking away as he wrote in his notebook.

"I mean, it has brought up a lot of memories," I sighed. "I obviously was his best friend for a reason. He is funny and easy to talk to. I just remind myself of what he did to me and it keeps my head on straight. He's told Margot he's best friends with Peter, Lara, and Westly. Lara is the woman Peter left me for. So he has a new female best friend now. I have been officially replaced!"

"That must hurt," Dr. Griffin nodded.

"It really does," I sighed. "Like, how can he be best friends with someone who stole my fiancé? It's pretty fucked up."

"Was he friends with her before he stopped speaking to you?"

"I'm not even sure at this point," I shrugged. "Sometimes when I talk to him, I feel like I don't know him at all. And that is really sad to me. I used to know him so well."

"You feel abandoned," Dr. Griffin said. "It's very common for patients with BPD to have abandonment issues."

"I mean, he *did* abandon me," I huffed. "But, I recognize that normal people get over things easier than I do."

"What even *is* normal?" Dr. Griffin asked. "Don't shame yourself for feeling the way that you feel. Everyone's feelings are valid. We just have to learn how to deal with your feelings in a healthy and productive way."

"And I'm guessing you feel that catfishing him ain't it?" I laughed.

Dr. Griffin smiled, nodding his head at me.

"Also, I have some other news," I held my breath.

Dr. Griffin looked pensive as he waited for me to continue.

"I met Tess yesterday."

He raised his brows, appearing intrigued.

"I messaged her on Facebook and pretended I found

her serendipitously and asked if she would be my personal trainer."

I stared at him as I weighed his reaction. He nodded his head, but didn't look shocked or disturbed.

"And how did that conversation go?" he asked.

"It went well. We met for coffee."

His lips twisted into a smile as he shook his head at me. *Finally, some personality!*

"And how was that?" he asked, taking a sip of his coffee.

"She is obviously just as fucked up as I am," I laughed. "She met with me and agreed to be my personal trainer! We talked about working out and our girlfriends. And by girlfriends, I mean Lira. It was fucking nuts! She has some balls, I'll give her that! She and Lira have been together for five months! I made sure to talk about how happy I am in my relationship. You know – plant those seeds of doubt."

"You want her to think you and Lira are happy?" Dr. Griffin asked.

"I do," I smirked. "It's disgusting what they're doing to me. Maybe if Tess realizes that we are both being played, then Lira will end up with no one."

"So you're angrier with Lira than you are with Tess?" Dr. Griffin asked. "That's interesting. Usually it's the other way around."

"What do you mean?" I asked.

"Typically, people make excuses for their significant others and blame the other woman. It seems you focus the majority of your anger on Lira. Why do you think that is?"

"That's a good question," I sighed. "I guess because we've been friends for so long and she knew what I went through with Ray. It's just made me hate her. I think it would be a lot different if it was truly a onetime mistake. But this was intentional. This was calculated. She doesn't give a fuck about me and there's no salvaging what we had at this point."

"You have no desire to work things out with her?" Dr. Griffin confirmed.

"Not at all," I replied.

"Thea, you have inserted yourself into a fake relationship with Raymond and are building a fake friendship with Tess. Both of these relationships are fueled by your thirst for revenge. I have to ask, once your revenge has been completely satisfied, how do you think you will feel in the end?"

I was quiet as I thought about this. I imagined Lira crying and alone. I imagined her begging me to stay. I imagined her face when I told her I knew it all along. I thought about Raymond crying and broken. I smiled as I looked back up into Dr. Griffin's gaze.

"I will feel happy when they're devastated."

"But that is assuming you *can* devastate them," he sighed.

I furrowed my brows. What did he mean?

"What if things don't go the way you imagine they will?" Dr. Griffin asked. "Tell me how that would make you feel."

"Well, Lira values our friendship," I said. "Losing me would devastate her."

"But what if it doesn't?" Dr. Griffin replied. "What if she just accepts that she messed up and moves on with Tess?"

"She and Tess aren't soulmates," I rolled my eyes. "They won't last. She'll come crawling back to me."

"You know this for sure?" he asked.

I glared, feeling uncomfortable as he stared at me.

"I'm pretty sure," I said, crossing my arms.

"And will you be able to move on once you have catfished Raymond? Will that give you the closure you need?"

"It will certainly make me feel better," I responded.

"You feel that others should feel the pain you feel. But you feel things so much *deeper* than other people, Thea. I just wonder if you will be satisfied at the end of this."

I shrugged my shoulders as I looked away from his penetrating gaze.

"What they did to you made you feel isolated and alone," he continued. "This exhilarates you because it gives you back a sense of control. Not only are you in control of the attention you receive, but you are in control of the justice you feel they have each earned, for harming you."

"What's the matter with wanting justice?" I asked.

"It won't change the outcome," he replied. "It won't change the thing that hurt you in the first place."

"What thing?" I asked.

"They left you," he sighed.

I took a deep breath, feeling a pang of pain in the pit of my stomach that made me uneasy. I pushed it out of my mind as I looked back up into his knowing eyes.

"So, Doug, tell me," I said, turning to face him. "Are you this good of a listener in all of your relationships?"

He smiled, laughing a little as he set his pen down.

"I would like to think I am," he replied.

"Because you're *really* good at it," I answered. "You're very intuitive and very disarming. I seriously love coming and talking to you each week."

"Well, thank you, Thea," he said – seeming genuinely grateful. "That means a lot to me."

"What made you want to become a therapist in the first place?"

He blinked a few times as he looked at me. I leaned in, eager to learn more about what made him the way that he was.

"I have always wanted to help people," he responded. "I find psychology fascinating. I am a huge advocate for talking about your feelings and thoughts. I think everyone could benefit from therapy."

I nodded my head, biting my lip.

"So," Dr. Griffin smiled weakly, "aside from what you have already told me, how was the rest of your week?"

"Lira and I had sex a few days ago," I replied. "It's crazy to me that she still wants to fuck me when she knows she's going to leave."

"Does that bother you to be intimate with her?" he asked. "I can't imagine that would be easy."

"She grosses me out, but I just mentally check out," I sigh. "You know, Doug, I *really* love having sex."

He nodded his head as he jotted in his notebook. I wanted to rip the paper out of his hands and see what he was writing about me.

"Sex is very healthy," he replied.

"It's the best," I sighed. "I think it's one of the things I'm best at in life. Not to brag or anything, but I used to be a porn star."

He looked up at me, staring at me blankly as I tried to read his expression.

"You were?" he asked.

"Only for a short time," I replied. "My ex-boyfriend, Bobby was a starving artist and it helped pay the bills. It was his idea. I really didn't want to do it at first."

"That's a lot to unpack," Dr. Griffin replied with a look of empathy in his eyes.

"I've had sex with like all of my friends except for Grace and Ray. Well, Grace and I did stuff in college for attention, but it doesn't really count."

"Why do you think that is?" he asked.

"I'm not sure. I mean, I would have fucked them if they would have wanted to, but we were always just platonic."

"When you have Histrionic Personality Disorder – which you have," Dr. Griffin responded, "sex can be very important to you. You enjoy being provocative and flirtatious. You feed on being wanted and lusted after. You can be excessively sensitive to criticism or disapproval. Does this sound like you?"

I rolled my eyes, shrugging my shoulders as I stared back at him.

"So I've been told," I said. "I don't like being fit into these little boxes. Is it so bad that I feel like you really get close to a person once you've made them cum? I mean, that's as intimate as it gets."

I felt wet, imagining how this conversation was making him feel. Did I make him nervous?

"You equate sex to emotional value," Dr. Griffin nodded. "Do you feel that you need to act a certain way in order for people to feel close to you?"

"You make it sound so sad and dramatic," I laughed. "Is it so hard to imagine that it's possible I just really love to fuck? And I'm so *good* at it, Dr. Griffin. You have no idea."

Dr. Griffin nodded and looked down at his notes.

"Do you have a girlfriend?" I asked.

He peered up, looking shocked for the first time as he stared back at me.

"I mean, you should," I winked. "You're super cute!"

He took a deep breath, tapping his pen nervously – looking like he had something to say to me.

"Look, I *know* you have to be professional because you're my therapist and all, but . . . I *like* you," I whispered. "Is that terrible to say?"

Dr. Griffin took a deep breath. I think he started to blush.

"Can't we just have a normal – non doctor and patient talk for a minute?" I asked. *"Please?"*

"Do you know what transference is, Thea?" Dr. Griffin asked. The energy in the room was electric as he leaned forward, lowering his voice as he spoke to me. "Transference is a normal phenomenon in which one can transpose their feelings onto someone else. It is common for a patient to *think* they are having feelings for their therapist because of the intimacy shared between them in conversation. And because you are craving the healthy relationship you lost in Lira, I believe you are transposing those feelings on me."

"I want to get to know you," I shook my head. "I'm tired of this only being one way. I get what you're saying and to some extent, it could be true, but I really do *like* you, Doug. And I think you like me too."

His throat bobbed as he sat back in his seat.

"I do like you, Thea," he replied, "but you are my patient."

"So you *do* have a girlfriend," I sighed, rolling my eyes.

"It isn't important," Dr. Griffin replied. "But don't feel ashamed or embarrassed. Your feelings are normal."

"Come on, Doug," I implored him. "Is there any part of you whatsoever that might have a little crush on me?"

He laughed, shaking his head as he looked back at me. He was gorgeous. Why was he playing hard to get?!

"Thea, I am very happy with the professional relationship we have and I would like to keep it that way," he replied. "You're a beautiful girl. You're funny, charismatic, and smart."

"But problematic," I sighed, shaking my head at him. "Is that what did it? I told you the truth about myself and my craziness scared you off?"

"You're not crazy," he sighed. "I don't judge. This is a safe space."

"I wish you'd take me out on a date," I said, biting my lip nervously as I looked back at him. "Just one date, Doug. I know I joke a lot and I have no filter, but you're different to me. You *get* me."

"It's important for you to feel understood," he nodded. "That's important in any relationship, Thea. Which is why you should work toward leaving Lira and being with someone who treats you the way you deserve."

"Fine," I groaned, rolling my eyes in frustration. "I'll back off for now. But I'm not giving up, Douglas. You're too good of a person. I don't give up easily."

"I'm aware, Thea," he laughed. "But yes – I would like to keep it professional."

I was determined to get Dr. Griffin to fall in love with me. I knew it in my bones. He was good. He was pure. He knew how love was supposed to be. And I really wanted to know what it would feel like to taste his lips.

All in good time, I told myself. Patience was a virtue I still really struggled with.

CHAPTER 20:

I needed to go to Target to get a few things I needed. I hated being unemployed, but Target was cheap and had decent clothes. I wanted to get some cute outfits to catch Doug's attention.

I was finishing my coffee when I heard Lira make her way down the stairs.

"Thea, what's this?" she asked, holding up something in front of her, pinched between her thumb and index finger.

I cocked my head to the side, not seeing what she was holding.

"What's what?" I asked.

"THIS!" She said, walking closer to me.

I squinted my eyes as she held her hand up to my face. She was dangling long strands of blond hair in front of me.

I wanted to die of laughter, but kept my face stoic as I stared at Tedra's strands of hair in her hand.

"Hair?" I replied, playing stupid.

"Okay, but whose hair is it?" She demanded. "And WHY is it on my pillow?"

I raised my brows, looking offended as I crossed my arms across my chest.

"Seriously?" I asked. "How the heck should I know?"

Lira huffed, looking puzzled. "It's just really weird. Neither one of us are blond."

"So, you automatically assume I'm bringing someone home?" I chortled.

"No, I'm sorry," Lira muttered. "It's just . . . what is this?"

"I don't know," I wrinkled my nose. "Who are YOU hanging out with?!"

Lira rolled her eyes as she flicked the strands of hair into the trashcan.

"It's just really fucking weird."

"Anything you want to tell me?" I asked, raising the mug to my lips.

Go on, Babe. I'm all ears.

"Oh yes!" She shook her head. "Besides, I don't like blonds."

Just strawberry blonds with large foreheads. Got it.

"Where are you going?" she asked me.

"I just need to go to the store," I replied. "Do you need anything from Target?"

"Don't spend too much money," Lira replied, leaning back against the counter. "I don't want you to spend all of your savings before you find a job."

I stared at her in stunned silence. She had never tried to tell me what to do with my money before. I couldn't believe she had the nerve to begin now.

"I mean, obviously, do whatever!" She continued. "I just know it's been a while since you've worked and I,"

"I'm fine, Lira," I spat. "I have plenty of money in savings. Focus on your own finances. You have less money than me and you work."

Lira's eyes widened in shock as I placed my empty mug on the counter.

"Thea, I . . ."

"I'm going to head out now," I said.

"I didn't mean to upset you, Thea. I'm sorry."

"It's fine," I shrugged. Be back later."

I fumed as I got into my car. I was going to put piss in her body spray the second I got the opportunity. This bitch was really starting to get on my last nerve.

Target was one of my few happy places. I took my time picking out a few cute outfits and some pretty lipsticks that I couldn't wait to wear at my next therapy sessions. I was lost in daydreams of painting Doug's face with my lip prints when my thoughts were interrupted by the voice of the clerk checking me out at the register.

"Dorothea?" he asked.

I looked up and locked eyes with the man bagging my items.

"Dorothea Duckworth?"

I furrowed my brow, not recognizing the man standing in front of me. Did I know this person?

"It's me . . . Logan," he said.

I felt my breath hitch in my throat as my brain processed what I was hearing.

The only Logan I knew was the Logan who bullied me in elementary school. This man was short and round with a receding hairline and the now unmistakable blue eyes that I remembered staring into for hours on end.

"Logan?" I whispered.

"Wow!" he said, shaking his head. "I can't believe it's really you!"

My mouth went dry as he looked me up and down.

"Thea," he said, rubbing the back of his neck, "I have thought about you so many times throughout the years."

"You have?" I asked.

"Yes," he replied. "When we were kids . . . I was so fucking cruel to you. I am so sorry for everything. I know it was a lifetime ago, but I want you to know that I feel so horrible for how I treated you."

I couldn't believe what I was hearing. I shifted weight awkwardly from one foot to the other as I stared back at him. I suddenly felt like I wanted to cry as he reached forward and placed his hand on my arm.

"I know it probably doesn't matter now, but I'm so sorry, Thea. I was a stupid kid. I just wanted to be cool. I have no idea why I treated you that way. You were such a nice person and you didn't deserve it."

"I lied about you to get you into juvie," I whispered.

Logan laughed softly, shaking his head. "I deserved it."

I swallowed hard as he handed me my bag of things. "You look amazing, Thea. I am happy I got to run into you. I always wondered what happened to you."

I was speechless. I literally had no words.

"Have a nice day," he smiled.

I nodded as I started to walk away. I paused and looked back at him.

"Logan," I said. He turned around to face me. "Thank you. For apologizing. I'm sorry for what I did too."

"I'm not," he shrugged. "I was a little asshole and needed to be taught a lesson. I pretty much forced you to do it."

I smiled back at him before turning and walking toward the door. *Wow.* I really couldn't wait to talk about this with Dr. Griffin!

I barely made it 20 feet from the registers. I was lost in my thoughts when I slammed into someone walking out of the Starbucks.

"SHIT!" he said, as iced coffee splashed all over me.

My mouth gaped open as I looked up to see that the person who had just doused me was none other than my fucking therapist!

"Oh my God, Thea?" Doug said with surprise on his face.

I felt blood rush to my cheeks as he began frantically grabbing napkins from the countertop behind him.

"I am *so* sorry! I didn't see you there!"

I stared in stunned silence as he handed me a wad of napkins.

"It's okay," I responded, completely dumbstruck. "I was just thinking about you actually."

Dr. Griffin furrowed his brow as I began to dab my shirt.

"Do you need a new coffee?" I asked.

"Oh, it's okay! I didn't spill it all," he laughed. "Plus, it was my fault. I'm the one who ran into you."

"Well, do you have a minute?" I asked. "Something fucking crazy just happened to me."

Dr. Griffin paused momentarily, looking like he was thinking about whether or not he should say no. He looked at his watch and then nodded. "I have a few minutes," he replied. "Shall we?"

He motioned back to the tables in the Starbucks and I nodded as I followed him inside.

We took a seat at the table and I felt dizzy as I noticed

how absolutely hot he looked in his casual attire. He was wearing a white t shirt and jeans. His hair was more messy than usual. He still smelled amazing though. I blushed as I appraised him.

"You look fucking sexy today," I admitted, biting my lip.

Doug rolled his eyes, shaking his head at me as he took a sip of his coffee. "Behave," he laughed.

"I just ran into my fucking elementary school bully," I whispered. "This kid literally ruined my life when I was younger and he was my cashier!"

"Oh really?" Dr. Griffin responded, looking surprised. "Are you OK? How did that go?"

"He apologized to me," I responded. I was still in shock from it. "I didn't even recognize him! He said he felt horrible about how he treated me!"

"That's amazing!" Doug beamed. "I bet that was wonderful to hear!"

"It really was!" I said, shaking my head. "Oddly cathartic. Healing. I didn't even know I needed to hear that. But, I'm . . . really happy about this!"

"That's fantastic, Thea!" he smiled.

"That's how it should be!" I said, shaking my head in wonder. "When someone hurts you, they *should* apologize to you! I have spent so many years hating that guy. Now that he apologized, I'm over it! See! I'm a totally reasonable person! I am very forgiving when people are sincere with me!"

Dr. Griffin nodded as he took another drink of his coffee.

"Now, if Ray could just do the same thing."

"Don't hold your breath," Doug shook his head.

I glared at him, trying not to feel offended.

"What?" he said, raising his brows. "I'm just keeping it

real."

"Can't you just lie to me?" I huffed.

"I'm off the clock," he winked.

I felt fluttery as I locked eyes with him. "Does this mean I can ask you out on a date now?" I smirked.

Doug softly laughed, shaking his head at me. "See, this is why I shouldn't have agreed to talk to you outside of the office."

"You love it," I grinned.

"You're trouble," he laughed, leaning back in his seat. "I'm happy you got closure from your bully. We will have to talk about it more *in the office*. You know . . . when your shirt isn't soaking wet and see through."

I felt fire in my cheeks as I looked down. He was right. My shirt was *absolutely* see through. My nipples were hard. *Oh my God, was he looking?!*

"Go clean yourself up," he whispered, rising from his seat.

"Jesus," I muttered. "I'm sorry."

"I'm the one who spilled on you!" He said, shaking his head. "*I'm* sorry!"

"Do you, like, want to hug it out or?"

"Absolutely not," he laughed. "GO HOME, Dorothea!"

"Cool," I nodded.

He placed his hand on my shoulder. "It was nice to see you. I'm happy you got closure. It doesn't always happen. Small wins, am I right?!"

I nodded my head, still feeling lightheaded from the realization that my therapist saw my tits through my wet shirt.

"Have a good day, Thea."

"You too," I smiled. "Thanks for getting me wet."

"Stop," he scolded me.

Today was a really fucking good day.

CHAPTER 21

Week 8

My relationship with Raymond had been progressing nicely. It truly felt like a budding romance – a new and exciting love. It was the type of love that made you giddy and dizzy with anticipation. It was the type of love where you felt like you just couldn't get enough of the other person. We talked so much, it was almost excessive. Long distance relationships have a way of making you feel so emotionally close to a person. The intimacy shared in conversation really elevates emotions and creates a longing that can't be replicated in face-to-face dating.

When you fall in love with a person's words . . . with a person's voice . . . the buildup to finally meeting them face-to-face can be *overwhelming*. Falling in love with a person's heart and soul before having any physical connection can make the first time you experience a physical connection *perfection*.

Raymond had never been in love before. He had never felt those fluttery butterflies in your stomach that take flight when the person you think about all day makes you blush. He had never experienced the rush of missing someone you had never met in person. He had never felt that feeling of surrender when you truly give your heart to another. He was feeling it now. In all of my years of knowing Raymond, I had *never* seen a side of him like this. He was melting like chocolate . . . coming undone like an unraveling sweater . . . floating on a cloud. He was *mine*. I finally *had him.* He was a fly and I was a Venus Fly Trap. He didn't know it yet, but his days of bliss were numbered. And I was only getting started.

"I can't stop thinking about you," Ray whispered – the tone in his voice hopeless and devoted like a little, baby puppy.

"I know what you mean," I replied, smiling as the foreign sound of my voice from the app sounded equally smitten. "It's crazy to me how I can feel so connected to someone I haven't even met yet."

"I've never felt this way about *anybody,*" Ray said. "It's insane how you just *get* me, Margot. It honestly feels like I've known you for years."

Because you have, Bitch. Because you have.

"I feel the same way."

"My mom's going to love you," he laughed. "She's always wanted a daughter. She's been giving me shit for YEARS because I've never brought anyone home to her."

Ray's mom was like a second mother to me. Every time I walked into her home, she had some kind of cookies or cupcakes or muffins waiting for me. She gave the best hugs and smelled like clean laundry. I loved her more than anything. After Ray disowned me, she blocked me on all social media accounts. The shock and pain from the *cruelty* of it still made me cry when I thought about her.

"I can't wait to meet her," I sighed. "I hope she likes me."

"She's going to love you – don't you even worry!" he laughed.

"What was the weather like in Kansas today?" I asked.

"Windy and hot," he replied. "I would much rather be in Colorado with you."

"Well, we will definitely have to make a trip out here together," I smiled. "Especially in the winter! I want to get you out on these slopes!"

"It'll be a disaster!" Ray chuckled. "I'll just embarrass myself! I'll be *that* person that they will have to drag down the mountain. I'm not sure I'll be able to keep up with you!"

"I'll teach you – it'll be fun!"

I didn't know the first thing about skiing or snowboarding. I had only gone a couple of times in my life, but knew it was something Ray had always wanted to learn. I pictured him trying to impress Margot with his dedication to learn. I knew he thought his clumsiness would make him endearing to her and that the experience would bond them and bring them closer together. How sad for him that he actually believed this was happening.

"If you say so," Ray laughed. "I trust you. I'm confident you'll be a good teacher."

"Only if you don't distract me," I giggled. "It's going to be pretty difficult to concentrate on anything when you're staring at me with those gorgeous green eyes."

I often had to mute my phone to laugh out loud when I said things. Thinking about saying these things to Ray was ridiculous! Raymond was never the ooey gooey type when it came to feelings. I knew he was a softy at heart and likely had a sensitive side, but I was shocked how quickly he went there with Margot. He lived for the compliments – for the flirting and the lovey dovey bullshit you would read about in young adult/romance novels. He was totally whipped over me. I mean, *Margot.*

"You're one to talk," he said. "Have you looked in the mirror? Your eyes are *breathtaking.* They look like the ocean."

I laughed, biting my lip.

"I wish you were here right now," I said. "I want to know

what it feels like to hold you."

Dying! I was dying inside! I felt lightheaded and giddy as I imagined Ray swooning on the other end of the phone. What a fucking idiot!

"I think about that all of the time," he whispered back. "I think about what our first kiss will be like. Margot, I can't wait to touch you."

"I'm so nervous," I sighed. "I just know that it's going to be the most magical first kiss I've ever had in my life. Even thinking about it, makes my cheeks turn red."

"I can't even think straight," Raymond responded. "I feel like a little kid – it's crazy! I am so nervous! Stupid nervous! But I know it's going to be worth it. Once I get you, I'm never letting you go."

"You already have me," I said, doing my best impression of Bella Swan. "I knew it the first time I talked to you. I'm yours, Ray."

When Ray and I were kids, I knew he had a crush on me. He told a couple of people, but I never acknowledged it to his face. I didn't look at him like that. He was like a little brother to me. In our younger years, he was fat and short and super shy. I dated tall and slim guys with leather jackets and slicked back hair. He wasn't on my radar.

When I had my heart broken for the first time, there was a weird period of time where I thought I might have a crush on Ray. Puberty had been kind to him and he had really been there for me in ways no man had before. I started wondering if maybe I had overlooked him when I had the chance. I was afraid to tell him how I felt and ruin a potentially wonderful friendship. But one winter night after drinking too many spiked eggnogs, I admitted I thought I had feelings for him. I had never been more swiftly shut down in my life.

"You're like a sister to me, Thea," he told me. "I don't like

you like that. It's never going to happen."

I realized a few weeks later that I didn't even have a crush on him after all. I only *thought* I did because he was the only nice guy I had ever been around. My standards were trash and I allowed guys to treat me like shit.

Ray was nice and I wasn't used to being treated well by the guys around me, so I set the bar higher and upped my standards. I wanted someone to treat me like Ray did – but romantically. I wanted to be with someone who would treat me right. For that, I would always be thankful for Ray. But I never forgot the sting of rejection when he shut me down that winter night. Who did he think he was, saying no to me? For years, he could only *dream* that someone like me would give him the time of day! It was embarrassing. I thought about this now as he wrapped himself around Margot's finger. *It's never going to happen, my ass! Who gets the last laugh now?*

"Margot," he said. "I can't wait to meet you."

"Will your roommate be okay with me staying with you when I visit?" I asked. "I can stay with my sister too, of course! I'm not trying to be too presumptuous."

"Oh, of *course* you'll be staying with me!" Ray chortled. "Westly's awesome. You'll really like him. He won't mind at all."

"I just wanted to make sure."

"I want to fall asleep next to you," Ray said. "I can't wait to hold you in my arms."

"It's going to be everything," I responded. "I feel like a soda can that's been shaken up with all of this pent up longing I have for you!"

"You drive me crazy," he whispered. "It's going to feel so surreal to have you lying next to me. When can I meet you, Margot? I really want to see you."

I took a deep breath, thinking about how to answer. I hadn't yet put all of the pieces together and needed to solidify some plans. I had a general idea of how my brilliant revenge would go, but I wanted more time.

"I was thinking of going out there in a few months," I responded.

"A few months?" Ray asked – sounding disappointed. "I don't want to wait that long."

"I know, but work's been crazy," I sighed. "Give me about six to eight weeks and I will have my two week vacation time ready to go. I'll be all yours."

"A whole two weeks?" Ray asked – sounding cheerier. "Okay, that will be worth it. God, I'm so excited!"

"Me too," I agreed. "I really hope you like me as much in person!"

I smirked to myself as I took a picture of my tits and sent it to him. I bit my lip as I waited for him to see.

"Holy *shit*, Margot, GOD DAMN!" Ray exclaimed.

My heart pounded in my chest at the thrill of it all. I was getting off on this – on getting him excited. I knew that it was actually *me* and not Margot in the nude. The sting of rejection from years ago made me want to laugh in his face now. What a fucking imbecile. *Reject this, Bitch.*

"You like what you see?" I asked.

"They're so much bigger than I imagined!" he replied.

"It's just the angle," I lied.

"They're exquisite," Ray muttered. "Seriously – you're perfect, Margot. Those are the most beautiful breasts I've ever seen."

Oh stop it! You're welcome, asshole.

"Thank you," I blushed. "I've never sent nudes to

anyone before. But I'm really falling for you."

"I'm falling for you too," he whispered.

My phone ping'd with a notification that I received a picture and my heart sped up as I opened the attachment. I gaped in disbelief at the rock hard cock in Raymond's hand.

"Jesus Christ," I said as I stared into the phone.

"That's what you do to me," Ray murmured.

I had to mute the phone. I couldn't believe this was actually happening! I was staring at a picture of Raymond's actual dick!

"Wow," I held back laughter.

"It's all yours now."

"I'm blushing so hard right now," I replied.

"Me too," he responded. "I've never sent a dick pic before. I don't want you to feel pressured or anything though, Baby! I know you're a virgin and I completely respect that."

I rolled my eyes as I smiled into the phone.

"I know you do Ray, and I love that about you," I sighed. "Jesus, your dick is so big. I hope it fits!"

There was silence on the other end of the phone as I waited for him to reply. I muted the phone because I was cackling – imagining the shock and lustful thoughts running through his mind. I had this mother fucker thinking he was going to pop my cherry! It was too much to take!

"W-what?" Ray stuttered.

"I just mean, I hope it won't be too painful," I whispered. "I know it won't happen right away. I still want to take my time and enjoy every moment with you, but if things keep going the way that they're going, then I know I'm going to want you, Ray."

I held back giggles as I listened to the silence between us

on the phone.

"I want you to be my first," I clarified.

We had only been talking to each other for a few weeks. Given, we had spoken almost all day, every day during this time and so feelings had been accelerated. I knew that this was real for Raymond. I knew I had him whipped more than he had ever been in his entire life. I still didn't know if he was a virgin or not. I held my breath as I waited for him to reply to me.

"I want you to be my first, too," he replied.

My eyes widened into giant saucers as I sat up and gaped into the phone. So he really *was* a virgin!

"Wait," I said, "Are you saying?"

"Yes. I didn't want to tell you because I was nervous, but I want to tell you everything, Margot. I've never felt this way before. I don't know what it is about you, but I'm all in. I'm falling in love with you."

"I'm falling in love with you too, Ray," I tried not to squeal into the phone.

I felt like I was in some kind of parallel universe. This was absolutely crazy! I had my best friend convinced I was some innocent princess handing over her heart and pussy to him on a golden platter! I had him sending pictures of his erection and professing his love to me! It felt like Christmas! I couldn't wait to give him the biggest blue balls of the century with a broken heart to match! This mother fucker had it coming!

Seriously, what kind of idiot falls in love with someone in this day and age, that they hadn't even video called yet? I had told him my service was extremely spotty in the mountains - and was *stunned* when he actually bought it! Was he really that trusting and naïve? Because I was really good at photo shop, I was able to send a picture of Margot holding up a sign on top of a mountain and changed the sign to say, "XOXO

Ray". I had dedicated that 14er to him. This was entirely too easy. My best friend was falling in love with me!

"Two months can't come soon enough," Ray sighed – pulling me back down to reality. "I can't wait until you get here, Margot. I've been dreaming of someone like you."

"I know what you mean," I replied. "I have been dreaming of this for a really long time too."

CHAPTER 22

"This is a really bad idea," Tedra sighed as she stepped down from the ladder.

I smiled excitedly as I admired her handiwork. A dozen perfectly hidden cameras were scattered throughout the home – all connected to an app on my phone that allowed me to monitor the activity taking place within the walls. Tedra grimaced as I paced around in delight – making sure that each camera was perfectly camouflaged and undetectable to the untrained eye. I was over the moon.

"This isn't exactly legal, you know," Tedra warned me as she crossed her arms across her chest. "You have to swear on your life that if this comes back to bite you in the ass, you did NOT get these installed by me."

"I promise, I promise!" I rolled my eyes before pulling her in for a hug. "You're *amazing*, Tedra! Did I ever tell you how much I just adore and appreciate you?"

"You're mildly terrifying," she laughed, shaking her head. "Seriously, what is the point of doing all of this? You already know what's going to happen."

"I need to see it with my own eyes," I responded.

"This is such a bad idea," she muttered – taking a deep breath as she admired the final result. "The sooner you take these down, the better. *Seriously*, Thea. Just let me know when you want my help uninstalling."

"I'm good for now, thanks," I grinned.

"Whatever you say," Tedra sighed.

I had told Lira I was going out of town for a few days for a girl's trip with Grace (on her dime). This was untrue of course, and I was getting ready to spend a much needed and well-deserved staycation at Grace's house. I wanted to know what Lira would do when presented with an opportunity to have the house to herself. I wanted to believe she wouldn't bring that strawberry blond pony into our bedroom. I needed to know how bad she'd betray me. This was the ultimate test.

Tedra kissed me on the forehead before heading for the door.

"Sometimes ignorance is better," she whispered, looking down at me with sympathy. "I just don't want to see you get hurt."

"She already hurt me," I said to her. "That ship sailed a long time ago."

"Just don't say I didn't warn you," Tedra replied.

I packed a small suitcase and waited for Lira to come home. I felt jittery and sick as she walked into the door. She smiled at me as she made her way across the living room to pull me into her arms. I wrapped my arms around her, breathing in her sweet scent as she looked up into my eyes.

"Do you really have to go?" Lira pouted. "I hate sleeping without you – you *know* this!"

"It's only a few days," I smiled, rolling my eyes. "You'll be fine! Just binge watch Game of Thrones or find something else to get addicted to while I'm away!"

"I'm gonna have to come up with something!" she chuckled. "But you'll text me and call me as often as you can, right?"

"Obviously," I replied.

She huffed, nodding her head as she looked away from me.

"Well, I love you, Baby," she said before pulling me in for a kiss.

"I love you too," I said as I stared into the darkness of her eyes.

The entire drive to Grace's house, I thought about the weeks leading up to this. I had been dedicated to therapy and had been trying to keep my crazy in check. Sure, there were some mishaps along the way and yes, I had some unresolved issues I knew I had to deal with . . . but I was behaving myself. I was no longer planning on becoming an axe murderer. I had kept my murderous urges at bay and trusted the process. I was going to find a way to get payback, but I was currently more preoccupied with my vengeance on Ray. Lira was going to get what was coming to her. I had no doubt about that. I needed to do this to test her. I wanted to know how far she would go to disrespect me. Fucking around with Tess behind my back was one thing. Doing it in our house would be another. I needed to have a reason – any reason – not to wish death upon her. I was tired of hating her so vehemently. I wanted some relief.

I pulled into Grace's garage and waved at her husband, Greg as I got out of the car. He gave me a knowing look as he nodded at me before puffing on his cigar. Grace and Greg told each other everything. No doubt, she filled him in on my crazy scheme to spy on Lira for a few days while I hid out in their house like a maniac. What I loved about Greg was that he wouldn't give me any shit about it. He'd simply carry on with his life as usual, knowing that his wife had a crazy woman for a best friend. I walked into their kitchen and smiled as Grace looked up from where she sat at the table – already armed with a bottle of wine and two glasses on hand.

"I can't believe you're actually doing this," she said,

shaking her head as she gazed at me with her bewildered blue eyes.

I nodded my head as I pulled up a seat next to her. She poured me a glass of wine.

"So how have things been with you, aside from this bullshit?" she laughed at me. "How's your mom and dad doing? Shelly and Nathan?"

"They're all doing fine, I guess," I sighed. "I haven't seen them in a few weeks. I try to avoid family functions as much as possible now. My dad's gotten meaner in his old age."

"Your dad has always been and always will be an asshole," Grace sighed. "But Shelly's cool. You'll have to tell her I say hi the next time you see her."

"I definitely will," I replied.

"Who knows? Maybe Lira will catch you spying on her and you'll end up getting arrested. You might have to go to trial and Shelly could be the judge! I swear, your life could be a movie, Thea. I'm just sitting on the sidelines watching it like a car wreck in slow motion!"

"Anything's possible," I laughed as I raised the glass to my lips.

Grace always knew how to make me laugh, even when I was in the shittiest of moods. She had a presence about her that just felt like home to me. Maybe it was because I had been friends with her since I was a little girl, or maybe it was just because she *knew* me – but I felt completely safe when I was with her. I could relax and just be myself.

I hadn't told her about my catfishing Raymond though. That was something I didn't want to share with anyone other than Dr. Griffin. This revenge meant everything to me and I couldn't have anything fucking it up. I didn't want Grace to think less of me. I knew that what I was doing would be wrong in her eyes.

Raymond used to be one of her best friends. I didn't want the joy of my vengeance tainted by the judgement that would come from Grace knowing the full truth. The Raymond plan was mine and mine alone. But Lira . . . I would share this with Grace. I was ready to have moral support while I tested Lira for the very first and last time.

"I can't believe you're still putting up with this bullshit," Grace mumbled as she stared into the side of my face. "Please tell me that if this bitch brings her girlfriend into your house that we're going over there to put her stuff on the lawn?"

"Be patient!" I sighed as I took a big gulp of my wine.

"This is the craziest thing you've ever done, Thea," Grace laughed at me. "I can't believe I'm enabling this behavior."

"You're not enabling me, you just love me and go along with it," I smiled. "And that's what best friends do, Grace – and why I love you so very much!"

"You're lucky I love you," she sighed, watching as I opened up the app on my phone that monitored the cameras. "I really hope this doesn't go down the way that I think it will."

"Me too," I whispered, feeling queasy as I wondered whether or not I even believed there was hope for her anymore.

I launched the application and we waited. About an hour and a bottle of wine later, Tess arrived.

I turned up the volume and watched with Grace as Lira pulled Tess into her arms at the doorway. She looked around nervously before shutting the door behind her.

"I can't believe we get the place to ourselves for three whole days!" Tess smiled, pulling Lira in for a kiss.

"Fucking slut!" Grace gasped, gaping at the screen.

"Shh!" I swatted Grace's arm.

"I know, it's going to be so nice to wake up next to you,"

Lira smiled.

I felt my blood boil as they made their way into the kitchen.

"Can I get you anything to drink? Coffee? Wine? Water? Beer?" Lira asked.

"Some wine would be great," Tess said, licking her lips.

Lira made her way to the fridge and pulled out a bottle of sweet Moscato. Tess crept up behind her and pulled her hair over her shoulder before gently kissing the nape of Lira's neck.

"So how was your day, Baby?" she whispered as Lira poured them each a glass of wine.

Lira turned to face her and handed her a wine glass, clinking hers against Tess' in a cheers.

"Recorded a few videos and did a few live streams," she sighed, "but my day was exciting because I kept looking forward to finally getting the chance to be alone with you."

"That's fucked up," Grace whispered. "This is fucking crazy!"

"I told you," I responded.

"I've been thinking about you all day," Tess said as she set her wine glass down. "Today's actually been hard on me."

"Why?" Lira asked with concern on her face.

"I've just had mixed feelings," Tess sighed. "Like, it's nice I get this time with you, but it's just a reminder of what we could have if you just manned up and finally left Thea."

"I told you to be patient," Lira replied, grasping Tess' hands in hers. "I won't make you wait much longer. It kills me too, Tess."

Tess shook her head. "I just want to start my life with you, you know?"

"I want that too," Lira replied.

"This is so much more messed up than I thought it would be," Grace whispered as she looked over at me. "Like, how is this even happening? How are you okay right now?"

"I'm used to it," I replied.

"Dorothea, this is INSANE!" she huffed. "You're still seeing your therapist, right? What does he have to say about all of this?"

"He wants me to leave Lira and be with someone who treats me the way I deserve," I shrugged. "But he recognizes that it's a process for me. He mostly just listens."

"You need to get the fuck out of there," Grace said, shaking her head. "Your girlfriend is the most manipulate cheater on the face of this planet!"

"Do you know how long I've dreamt of this moment?" Tess asked, pulling our attention back to screen.

"What moment?" Lira smirked.

"The moment I get to fuck you in your girlfriend's bed," Tess grinned.

Grace's eyes bulged out of her sockets as she looked between me and the screen. I felt my blood boil as they made their way out of the kitchen and into the hallway. The screen changed to different cameras as they migrated up the stairs and into the bedroom. This was actually happening.

"This is so entirely fucked," Grace exclaimed – her jaw on the floor. "We're not actually going to watch this, are we, Thea?"

"I am," I said through gritted teeth. "You don't have to though, if you don't want to."

"Oh my God," she shook her head, looking sympathetically at me before returning her gaze to the screen with worry.

Lira leapt into Tess' arms, wrapping her legs around her waist as Tess carried her across the bedroom to the bed. Lira pulled Tess' ponytail out, running her fingers through her hair as the two of them kissed. I felt sick to my stomach as

I watched Tess fling Lira onto the bed. The mouth-breathing leviathan mounted Lira as Lira pulled her shirt over her head.

"Tell me you love me more than her," Tess panted as she pulled Lira's pants down.

"I love you so much more," Lira exhaled, biting her lip as she stared up at her.

Tess buried her face between Lira's legs and I watched as Lira arched her back and moaned out in ecstasy. I poured myself another glass of wine as Tess continued to fuck her and I watched as Grace stared in absolute shock at the screen.

"God, don't stop, Tess!" Lira whimpered as she rocked her hips into Tess' face.

It was the slurping for me. The slurping and smacking of Horsey's lips on Lira's pussy started sending shivers up my spine. I longed to reach into the screen and bitch slap her across her vertical face. Why did she have to be so noisy with it? They weren't even sexy noises. It sounded like she was struggling and fighting hard to breathe.

"I'm going to cum," Lira moaned before locking her legs around Tess' neck.

"I hope she smothers her," I muttered as I took a sip of my wine.

Grace laughed out loud, still staring at the footage in shock.

"What a fucking whore," Grace whispered, shaking her head.

"Both of them," I nodded.

I turned off the application and took a deep breath as I turned to face Grace.

"I don't even have words, Thea," Grace said, staring at me with pity.

It was that look of pity that I detested. I would be happy

if I never had to see that look from anybody again. I didn't want anyone to feel sorry for me. Lira was a slut. She wasn't worthy of my heart. I didn't want anyone thinking she had broken it. My heart wasn't hers to break. She didn't deserve the satisfaction. Not after everything she and I had been through together. This was treachery. She was a snake.

"Don't feel sorry for me," I sniffed. "I'm fine."

"How can you be fine, honey?" she asked me. "You loved her so much."

"I don't love her anymore," I said, setting my glass down. "The person I thought I loved wouldn't do this to me. You see how fucking conniving she is? She's a fucking actress! I don't know if a shred of what we shared was real."

"I'm so sorry," Grace whispered, placing her hand on my knee.

"Don't be sorry, Grace," I laughed. "I'm honestly glad this happened. I can't believe I actually thought about marrying this bitch. Can you believe I was actually thinking we would one day get *married*?"

Grace looked away from me as I held back my tears.

"I'm not even sad anymore. I'm just angry," I said. "I ruined my friendship with one of my very best friends for someone capable of doing this."

"You couldn't have possibly known this would happen," Grace whispered. "This isn't your fault."

"It doesn't matter whose fault it is," I sighed. "What's done is done at this point."

"You need to leave her," Grace responded.

"She needs to pay for what she's done to me."

"Let the trash take itself out," Grace sighed. "You're better off without her, Thea. And look at the girl she's cheating on you with. She's not even cute."

"She's hideous," I nodded.

"Lira doesn't deserve you, Thea."

"I know she doesn't," I replied.

Grace took a deep breath, drumming her fingernails on the table as she thought about what to say to me. But there was nothing she could say. She had been friends with me long enough to know she wouldn't be able to change my mind. I knew I needed out of this relationship. But I knew that Lira shouldn't be able to get away with this scot-free.

"I made the bed for you in the guestroom," Grace sighed. "Please try to get some sleep tonight. And please don't do this to yourself again. That was horrible, Thea. I'm so sorry."

"Thanks for letting me stay here," I responded as I finished my glass of wine. "I just really need these couple of days to clear my head."

I would come up with my revenge for Lira. After what I had witnessed, there was no more Mr. Nice Guy. I had been too easy on her. I had gone soft. This was a mistake I would not make again. I looked forward to discussing this in therapy.

CHAPTER 23

Grace and Greg were off to work and I laid in bed, staring at the ceiling. The events from the night prior replayed over and over and over again in my mind like a bad movie. I realized there had been a part of me – a miniscule little part – that had hoped Lira wouldn't bring Tess into our home.

I was very good at pushing feelings of sadness aside. Anger was usually my go to emotion. In the past, I had let sadness consume me until I existed only in the pits of despair – unreachable to any shred of happiness around me. After being broken one too many times, I learned a coping mechanism that worked. That coping mechanism was called rage. Sometimes in the quiet moments when I allowed myself to slow down and sit alone with my thoughts, those feelings of sadness would come. I felt them in this moment as I stared at the ceiling, wondering what I did to make Lira stop loving me.

I thought of Dr. Griffin and felt a lump in my throat. Why couldn't I find someone like him? Why couldn't I be in a relationship with someone who made me feel seen and heard? I felt tears sting my eyes as I thought about it. I didn't want someone *like* Dr. Griffin. I wanted the *actual* Dr. Griffin. He would never make me feel this way. He would never stab me in the back. I sensed this about him. Something deep in my soul knew it to be true.

There was a time when I convinced myself that Lira was the one. In hindsight, I probably should have never crossed the line from friendship into more with her. Before being with me, she had never been in love before. She had claimed I was her first real love.

This appealed to me. It made me feel special and proud. Because we had a solid friendship, I assumed it would only make our relationship stronger. But what if Lira didn't understand what love was? What if it was only lust and she realized after meeting Tess what real love was? What if she felt like she had made a terrible mistake by being with me?

I wanted to vomit. I fell in love with her because I loved her so much when we were friends. But what if that was all we were ever meant to be? The person I was meant to be with would never lie to me and lead me on the way Lira had been. The person I was meant to be with would cherish me. I would be their only one. Lira was a liar. Lira was cold. No love of mine could do what she had done.

My phone started ringing and I jumped – snapping out of my depressing daydreams. I stared at my phone and smiled when I saw who was calling me. *Raymond.* My bad mood instantly disappeared as I focused on the task at hand. I had a role to play and a job to do. Fuck Lira and fuck her stupid girlfriend. I would deal with them later. For now, I had bigger fish to fry.

I launched the voice changing app and connected it to my google voice before taking a seat in front of the mirror. I liked to watch myself perform. I took a deep breath and tried to calm my breathing as I accepted the call.

"Baby!" I squealed – smiling widely into the telephone.

"Hi, Gorgeous!" Ray beamed.

Hearing his voice made me instantly feel better. There was something so calming about knowing I was well on my way to making him cry. No human on the face of the Earth had hurt me more than Ray had. I wasn't even sure this revenge would be enough. I wanted him crippled with heartache. I wanted him broken and damaged. I wanted him to lie awake at night and pray to understand why. I hoped he would suffer. And I hoped that by suffering, he would think of what he did to me.

"I was wondering when I would hear from you," I smiled. "How's your day been?"

"It's better now that I'm talking to you," he flirtatiously replied. "Work's been pretty crazy today! It's been a really weird day."

"Weird how?" I asked – my curiosity peaked.

"Well . . ." Ray said, trailing off before going silent.

"What's up?" I asked, wondering why he was acting strange.

"It's nothing," he sighed, sounding like he was holding something back.

I stared at myself in the mirror, feeling perplexed as I tried to read the tone of his voice. He was stressed out. Annoyed possibly? Something was definitely wrong. I wondered what it could be.

"Talk to me, Babe," I responded. "Is something wrong?"

"It's a long story," he sighed.

"Well lucky for you, I have nothing but time." I grinned.

There was a long pause before Ray took a deep breath.

"Okay," he began. "So my ex best friend's dad came to see me at work today. He took me to lunch and bought me a beer."

It felt like the air was sucked out of my lungs as I listened to his words. His ex best friend's dad? Was he talking about me? Was he talking about *my* father?

"Oh?" I asked, feeling my heart rate increase.

"Yeah, it was weird," he sighed. "It was nice to spend time with him though. He was like a second dad to me."

"Who was your ex best friend?" I asked, a little too eagerly.

My mind raced as I waited for his response. I felt rage boiling under the surface. Why was my dad taking him out to lunch? He knew what Ray had done to me.

"Her name was Dorothea," Ray replied.

I felt sick at his use of the word, *was.* What? Was I dead to him now? Was that why he was talking about me in the past tense? I felt light headed as he continued to talk.

"She was one of my closest friends for many years. I haven't spoken to her in several years though."

"Why not?" I asked – trying to steady my voice as I felt anxiety taking its hold on me.

"She's a fucking crazy bitch," he laughed.

My mouth opened as I stared into my reflection. I tried to speak, but no words would come out of my mouth.

"I almost took out a restraining order on her a couple of times because she just wouldn't leave me alone."

"What do you *mean*?" I asked.

"It's stupid Margot," he sighed. "It's really old news, but seeing her dad just stirred some stuff up for me today."

"I see," I said, still feeling dizzy. "So why did you guys stop being friends?"

"Well there were lots of reasons," he sighed. "She dated a few of my best friends – Peter and Westly. She was awful to them. It made things super awkward for me."

"Elaborate," I said, gritting my teeth.

"Well, her and Peter were together in college and she was super controlling and obsessive. After they broke up, she harassed him and his girlfriend for *years*."

I couldn't believe this was happening.

I felt overcome with hatred and anger as I listened to the blasphemy spilling from his lips. Controlling and obsessive? I didn't harass them for years! Peter cheated on me with Lara! He was the one who fucked *me* over! I tried to make amends with him a few times throughout the years for Ray's sake, as I knew that he and Ray were still best friends and I didn't want there to be any bad blood between us! This picture he was painting of me to Margot was completely false!

"It was crazy," he sighed. "I was always there for this girl, but she *always* caused problems."

"Caused problems how?" I asked.

"Well, when I introduced her to my best friend, Westly, I told her that if she ever cheated on him, I'd never speak to her again. Thea was kind of a slut. She fell in love easily and slept around a lot. I was worried she would hurt my friend and didn't want to be responsible for introducing him to someone like that, you know?"

"So why did you introduce them?" I asked, feeling rage silently build up inside.

"Westly had a huge crush on her and she was one of my best friends! I wanted to believe she could settle down and get her shit together. Westly is a *really* good guy, Margot. He's one of the best people I know. And she did him *dirty*. She cheated on him with this *girlfriend* of hers behind his back. She really hurt him. It was fucked up."

I felt my heart threaten to burst from my ribcage as I listened to him.

"I gave her a chance to tell me the truth and she straight up lied to my face about it. She was such a slut. I felt horrible for Westly. She was nothing but drama. The only reason I stayed friends with her for as long as I did was because she was dating my friend."

"That's pretty harsh," I said, cringing as the words escaped my mouth.

"You'd just have to know her," Ray laughed. "But we haven't been friends for years now. Ending our friendship was worse than *any* breakup I had ever seen. She went crazy! I had to block her on social media and change my phone number. She tried to reach out to my friends and family to get me to talk to her too. She just couldn't get the picture and wouldn't leave me alone. It was creepy. I mean next level stalker," He laughed. "She was obsessive and creepy! You would *think* she was my girlfriend or something by the way she behaved!" he laughed with disgust. "Even now, she's still obsessed with me! She just sent me a hand written letter asking me to talk to her. I don't know. She has issues."

"Wow," I responded, unable to formulate words.

"I know," he chuckled. "Sorry, I know that was quite the rant! She's a psycho, but her dad is cool. He apologized to me on her behalf. Her own dad even acknowledged that she's crazy."

"Why did her dad want to see you?" I asked, not believing my ears.

"Because Thea and I were friends for so long, I was like a son to him. He just missed me and wanted to shoot the shit. He mostly just wanted to apologize to me for his daughter throwing away one of the only real friendships she's ever had and one of the only stable relationships – meaning Westly. Yeah. She's a train wreck. But, it is what it is."

I felt sick to my stomach as he finished. The blood

rushed to my head and my ears started to ring as I sat in silence.

"That's really sad," I responded. "It sounds like a really painful experience."

"Nah," he laughed. "I don't care. She's the one who was sad. I was over our friendship long before she was."

"Why didn't you tell her sooner?" I asked, feeling tears sting my eyes.

"I don't know," he said, sounding contemplative. "I'm trying to think of a good analogy. So, imagine you have a drug addict or a drunk sister. You love them because they're your sister, but they embarrass you and you know they'll never change. You try to help them many times over the years, but they never want to help themselves. Pretty soon you can only stomach being close to them on holidays. Then even holidays become too much. That's what it was like being friends with Thea. She has mental illness. I'm not exactly sure what, but being around her is exhausting. After a while, I was just over it, you know?"

There was silence as I didn't know what to say.

"Or maybe you don't," he sighed. "It's hard to understand if you've never dealt with someone toxic. You're lucky if you don't know what I mean."

"I get it," I replied. "I'm sorry you had to deal with that."

I thought about defending myself. I thought about playing devil's advocate and attempting to get into his head about how cruel he was being. I knew in that moment though, that it would be no use. It wouldn't matter. He made having a mental illness sound like a death sentence – as if dealing with someone who struggled emotionally was a burden and a total waste of time.

In five minutes, he had answered all of my burning questions. He didn't *care* about me. He wasn't a real friend. He made me sound like the villain in scenarios where *I* had been the one who had been wronged. He had no empathy. He made me sound crazy. He painted a picture of someone that I wasn't. I didn't mean anything to him. There was no point in trying to talk to him. And I didn't want to blow my cover.

He downplayed the bond I thought we shared. He made me feel disposable. He made me feel like trash. My own father betrayed me. I stared into the mirror, holding back tears as I realized I was completely alone. Raymond was gone. My best friend didn't exist anymore. Maybe the friendship was all in my head.

"It's water under the bridge now," he sighed. "Sorry, I get really fired up when I talk about her. I'm just glad to have her out of my life."

"Sounds like it," I laughed.

"I'm just glad that the only girl in my life now is *sane*," he chuckled. "I love you, Margot. Thanks for letting me rant."

"I love you," I responded as I choked back tears. "You can vent to me any time."

I basically blacked out for the rest of the conversation – going through the motions as I listened to his day. My heart was broken. I didn't know how I would ever recover from this. Maybe Tedra was right and sometimes ignorance was better. Knowing what I knew now and realizing I meant nothing to him made me feel hopeless. The callousness in his voice was a knife that cut me open and left me to bleed out. My hands were shaking as I texted Dr. Griffin after getting off of the phone with him.

"I know we aren't supposed to meet for a few days, but I need you," I trembled as I texted him. "Please, can I come see you?"

I was breaking. The walls were tumbling down. I curled up into the fetal position on the bed and started crying. An animalistic wail escaped my body as I exorcised the demons of my despair.

"Meet me at my office," Dr. Griffin responded. "I'm here."

CHAPTER 24

I sat on the couch across from him and wondered if I had made the wrong decision. Surely there would be consequences for doing what I was about to do. Divulging my deepest, darkest secrets and desires felt like a betrayal to myself. What was I hoping to accomplish? I fidgeted uncomfortably on the sofa as I gazed at the clock hanging on the wall above him and wondered if it was too late to turn back. He leaned forward in his chair and studied me as I tried to come up with an excuse to leave.

"Why are you here, Dorothea?" he asked.

I cleared my throat, looking up into his dark brown eyes. The weight of his question crushed me, but I felt the words bubbling in my throat like a steaming hot kettle of water ready to overflow.

"I think I'm a psychopath," I said to him – holding my breath as I watched my words sink in.

His reaction was unexpected. He didn't seem surprised; he didn't seem moved. He nodded his head, acknowledging me as I waited for him to make the next move.

"And why do you think you're a psychopath?" he asked – seeming genuine in his want to know.

But only a fool would tell the truth now and so I stared at him blankly - wishing I could tell him that I'd planned on killing my partner for weeks now, but that I just couldn't bring myself to do it. I wondered if he could help me. I wondered if he could change my mind. I wondered if I was beyond saving. I wondered if I was out of my mind. But mostly, I wondered if he noticed the new perfume I was wearing and wondered if it turned him on. I looked back up at the clock and instantly regretted coming. I knew we both had better things to do on a Friday anyway.

I held back tears as I looked into his dark chocolate eyes. He looked concerned as he waited for me to respond to him. I had spent the entirety of my drive spiraling into insanity.

The conversation with Raymond had me on the brink of a mental breakdown. All of my senses had gone out the window. I felt murderous again. Everyone who had done me wrong deserved to die now, in my eyes.

I knew I needed help. I knew I was going crazy. I didn't want Dr. Griffin to feel sorry for me or look down on me, though. I felt shame and sorrow as I made the decision to attempt to let my guard down.

"I might cry tonight," I said, feeling the lump in my throat.

"That's okay," Dr. Griffin replied, pushing a box of tissues across his desk at me. "It's okay to show emotion, Thea. I encourage you to let whatever is ailing you out."

"I want him to die!" I yelled, letting the tears come.

Dr. Griffin stared at me as I started sobbing uncontrollably in my seat.

"I want them all to die! Lira, Peter, Westly, Raymond, my father – they could all suck on anthrax for all I care!"

I gasped for air as I cried on the sofa. I clenched my hands into fists, shaking my head as I replayed Raymond's words in my mind again.

"What happened?" Dr. Griffin asked me.

"Raymond told Margot about me!" I sobbed. "If you could have *heard* the way he talked about me, Douglas – it was *hideous*! He painted me out to be this fucking lunatic that's completely obsessed with him! He blamed the end of our friendship on me! He said I ruined my relationships and that I was a psycho! He compared me to a drunk or a drug addict and said that he was only friends with me as long as he was because I was dating one of his friends! I can't!"

I bellowed in sorrow as I sunk deeper into the cushions, finally looking up into Dr. Griffin's face.

"He doesn't give a fuck about me, Doug! He never did! And I've been mourning the loss of our friendship for YEARS! I am NOTHING to him! NOTHING! And my own FATHER is taking him out to lunch and buying him beers and telling him how much he misses him and that I fucked up in life by losing him! Meanwhile, Lira and Tess are fucking playing house like I'm not even a real person! It's like I don't even exist! All of these people I thought cared about me don't give a fuck about me! I want them gone! I need them gone! I think something's wrong with me, Dr. Griffin. I really do wish they would all die!"

I tried to slow my breathing as I blew my nose into a tissue. This was humiliating. I was coming completely undone.

"It's okay, Thea," Dr. Griffin responded, pulling my attention back to him. "What you are feeling is normal. It's normal to feel anger when you have been betrayed."

"This goes beyond anger though," I replied, laughing as I cried at him. "I just told you I wanted them to die!"

"You're angry," Dr. Griffin nodded. "That doesn't mean there's something wrong with you."

"I'm a fucking psychopath!" I exclaimed, shaking my head at him. "Even Raymond called me a psycho! Seriously,

I'm done pretending it isn't probably true!"

"You're not a psychopath, Thea," Dr. Griffin said as he leaned forward to look at me. "I have been seeing you for weeks now and I can assure you that you are not a psychopath. You don't meet the criteria."

"*Bullshit*," I sneered.

"Do tell me how you think you know more about psychology than I do," he replied. "No, humor me."

"I have been fucking with my girlfriend and spying on her life like a crazy person! I have created an alter ego to get revenge on my ex best friend. I'm manipulating people! I fantasize about killing them!"

"You're not actually capable of murder though. You may have a string of schemes in play, but you aren't plotting any murders. You're *angry*. The root of this anger is *pain*," he replied. "And you know who doesn't experience this level of devastation you are experiencing right now, Thea? People like Bundy. That's because you are an empathetic person. And empathetic people aren't psychopaths."

I felt the tears streaming down my face as I stared at him in bewilderment. Was he for real or was he underestimating me? Was I a psycho or not? Now I was just confused.

"Raymond's an asshole and you'd be wise to stop talking to him," Dr. Griffin replied. "Just because he didn't value your friendship, doesn't mean you have no worth. You put so much stake in what these people think about you."

"So, you think I care too much?" I cried, feeling frustrated and angry as I stared back at him.

"I didn't say that," Dr. Griffin replied. "Your feelings are valid, but you are subjecting yourself to pain when you put yourself in these risky situations. You won't ever get over these people if you don't let them go."

"I know," I sobbed, putting my head in my hands. "I can't believe they're doing this to me though! I thought they loved me!"

"I know it's painful," Dr. Griffin continued. "But you don't have to keep doing what you're doing, Thea. You can choose to let them go."

"I don't want to let them go!" I screamed.

There was silence as Dr. Griffin stared at me. I heard the ticks of the clock as he jotted in his notebook.

"Did you hear what you just admitted?" he asked, looking up at me through his dark rimmed glasses. "That was a powerful breakthrough, Thea. Do you even realize what you just unpacked?"

My lip quivered as I stared back at him. I felt like a shell of a human. I felt empty and lost.

"You don't *want* to let them go," he repeated. "Why?"

"I don't know," I whispered.

"You *do* know," he responded as he rose from his desk.

He walked to the sofa and handed me the box of tissues. I felt my heart quicken as he sat down beside me.

"Dig deeper," he encouraged me, staring at me with intensity. "Why don't you want to let them go?"

"I don't want to," I cried, feeling my voice break. "I just want my life back."

"You can't get your life back," he responded. "*This* is your life now, Thea."

"I thought they loved me," I whispered, feeling completely alone.

"Why don't you want to let them go?"

"I will miss them," I responded, feeling swallowed by the sadness growing in the pit of my stomach.

"You don't want to let them go because you will miss them," he nodded. "So, you're afraid of being alone?"

I took a deep breath, shaking my head at him.

"You make it sound so dramatic like I'm so desperate for company, I choose this," I huffed. "But it's so much more complicated than that!"

"It's messy and difficult," he nodded. "I *understand* you. But you have to realize that you're clinging to toxicity because you're afraid of letting go. And you're afraid of letting go because you will miss them. You will miss them because without them, you would feel alone. But wouldn't being without them feel better than this, Thea?"

He placed his hand on top of mine and I caught on fire. I held my breath as I looked up into his eyes.

"They don't deserve you. Do you hear me? You are better off without them. The sooner you release yourself from this torture, the sooner you'll start to feel better. You don't need Lira. She isn't good to you. You don't need Ray. He's not your friend. You don't need to put up with your father's behavior. It's not your fault. Revenge won't make you feel better. It might for a little bit, but *trust* me. The best revenge and the best thing you could do for yourself is to live your life *without* them. Thriving. Happy. The opposite of love isn't hatred. It's indifference. If you really wanted revenge, you would forget them. And that's honestly what they deserve."

I took a deep breath as I listened to him. My heart started slowing and I felt my shoulders relax. This man was making sense.

"Thanks, Doug," I sniffled, dabbing the tissue under my eyes. "I know you're probably right."

He exhaled, seeming lost in thought before he pulled his hand away. The tension between us was overwhelming. How could he not want to take me out on a date?

"How are you feeling?" he asked me. "You seem calmer."

"I'm feeling much better, thanks," I replied.

He nodded before rising from the sofa and returning to his seat at the desk across from me. I felt butterflies in my stomach as I stared into his gorgeous face. I wondered if he felt it.

"So, what did you mean when you said earlier that Lira and Tess are playing house?" Dr. Griffin asked me.

"Oh yeah," I cringed, looking away from him. "I told Lira I was going out of town and put up hidden cameras. I've been staying with Grace and watching her and Tess fuck in our bed."

"Oh Thea," Dr. Griffin shook his head. "What am I going to do with you?"

"I know," I laughed. "I'm telling you – I'm fucking crazy."

"You realize you should break up with her," he said as he stared into me. "It isn't healthy to live this way."

"I know," I sighed.

"Not to mention, the camera thing isn't very ethical," he chuckled.

"I know. I can be impulsive sometimes."

"We can work on that," he replied. "So, talk to me about your father. We haven't talked about him much."

I sighed as I leaned back into the sofa. Of course he'd want to hear all about my daddy issues.

"My dad and I don't get along," I replied. "I have never been a good daughter in his eyes. He's constantly reminding me I'm a disappointment and a complete and total failure. He makes me feel stupid."

"That must hurt," Dr. Griffin replied.

"It does," I nodded. "I'm pretty used to it by now, though."

"How does he behave to the others in your family?" he asked.

"He's controlling and bossy and egotistical all of the time. But my sister has a career he approves of and my mom does her wifely duties. I'm just a rebel piece of shit in his eyes."

"So, he likes to control you?" Dr. Griffin asked.

"I can't be controlled," I shrugged.

"And this causes tension?" he responded.

"I am incapable of doing anything right by him," I exhaled. "Honestly, his love is conditional. And I've never been good at earning his affection. I stopped trying a long time ago."

"That sounds exhausting," Dr. Griffin nodded. "I can only imagine how this has effected your self-worth."

"I've always wished he would like me," I muttered. "It's really hard knowing that your own father genuinely doesn't like you."

"You're used to being in close relationships where you feel you don't measure up," he nodded. "Does that contribute to how you behave in other relationships like the ones with Lira and Ray?"

I shrugged my shoulders, not knowing what to think of it.

"When you have Borderline Personality Disorder, it affects the way you feel and think about yourself. This causes problems functioning in day-to-day life. You can have difficulties managing emotions and behavior and have patterns of unstable relationships," he said. "With BPD, you can have a fear of abandonment that becomes overwhelming. You can have difficulty tolerating being alone. But inappropriate anger and mood swings may push the people closest to you away and get in the way of the very thing you crave so very much. Loving relationships that last."

I nodded my head, looking away from him.

"Environmental factors can contribute or cause BPD. Did you know that?" Dr. Griffin asked.

I shook my head.

"People who experience trauma in early childhood such as neglect from a parent for example," he said. "People with BPD are 13 times more likely to report childhood trauma than people without mental health issues."

"I had a good childhood for the most part," I whispered. "My father was very hard on me, but he tried to give me the best chance at having the best possible life."

"What does that mean?" he asked me.

"He didn't set me up for failure and, yet, I failed him anyway."

"So, he set you up to live according to standards he set for you and not for standards you set for yourself," he sighed.

"And as I recently told you, I was also bullied horribly my fifth-grade year and spent the majority of that year suicidal," I whispered.

"That's a lot for any child to handle," Dr. Griffin replied. "You're very hard on yourself, Thea, but you have a lot of trauma to dig into. Emotional abuse and emotional neglect are traumatic. No doubt, they have contributed to why you behave the way you do today."

I took a deep breath, nodding as I looked up at him.

"You're not a psycho, Thea. You're not crazy. You're hurt and you're pissed off. You act irrationally and that's something we can work toward changing. But please, be kinder to yourself. You're going through a lot right now."

"I'm so glad I came to see you tonight," I sighed. "I really did feel like I was losing my mind."

"I'm sorry you're going through this," he nodded. "But you can always call me, Dorothea. Any time."

I longed to jump across his desk and hug him. I wondered if that would be considered unethical. Regardless of what I was or was not allowed to do, one thing was clear. Dr. Griffin recognized that I had been traumatized. And he was right – I had to deal with it. But he was still wrong about one thing. I would feel a lot better and sleep a lot sounder at night after Lira and Ray answered for the crimes they had committed against me.

CHAPTER 25

Week 9

I arrived home from my fake vacation and waited for Lira to return from work. I had been reading messages between her and Tess on the iPad all day and tried to mentally prepare myself for seeing her again. The last few days had been very hard for me. It was becoming emotionally taxing to stay in this relationship with her. This morning had been particularly rough. Lira had broken down into tears when she had to say goodbye to Tess.

"It's just been so nice having this time with you," she told her. "I wish it could always be like this."

I felt numb as I heard her car pull into the driveway. I looked out the window and watched as she gathered her things. The crown of her head was white beneath the sunlight, as the thinning strands of her hair blew in the wind. I took a deep breath and made my way to the dining room table where I sat down to wait for her.

I heard the fumbling of keys as Lira made her way inside. She opened the door and looked down at me from where she stood and a flicker of pain danced in her eyes. It was barely detectable. A blip. A momentary weakness of her defenses being down before she put her mask back on. She smiled at me then, as she made her way to the table to greet me.

"You're back already!" she said as she leaned down to hug me.

"I am," I replied as I felt her stiff arms wrap around me.

Something was different. The energy between us felt forced and strained as she pulled away and looked at me. This was a first. I looked up at her, wondering what she was thinking about as she pulled up a chair to sit beside me.

"How are you?" she asked as she turned her chair to face me.

"I'm fine thanks, how are you?" I replied.

She pursed her lips as she tugged at a loose string on the sleeve of her shirt.

"I'm actually not feeling very well," she said, looking back at me. "I'm sure you have noticed that my hair is still falling out. I'm going to the doctor's tomorrow to make sure my hormones and everything are in check. I've been really depressed about it."

I nodded my head as she ran her fingers through her hair to show me the scattered patches of bald spots on her head. I made a mental note to throw the tainted shampoo out, before she caught on that it was me.

"Oh, Babe, I'm sorry," I said, looking sympathetically at her. "It's really not that bad though."

"It's horrible," she said, shaking her head. "I am going to have to start wearing hats. I lost a couple of jobs to other models because it's becoming obvious. I just don't understand what the fuck is going on."

"You're probably stressed out," I sighed. "Is there anything going on with you? Any reason why this could be happening?"

There was silence between us before she looked down

into her lap. I felt my heart rate increase.

"Thea," she whispered.

Shit. Was this happening? Was she finally done playing her games? Had she reached her breaking point? Was she finally going to tell me about Tess? I felt my face heat up as she looked back up into my eyes.

"What is it?" I asked, watching her shift nervously in her seat.

I held my breath. Did Tess finally get to her? Had this little time they spent together been *that* monumental that she was ready to actually leave me? Her brown eyes glistened with tears as she opened her mouth to speak.

"Never mind," she muttered, looking away again.

"Lira, *talk to me,*" I pleaded with her. "I *know* you. I *know* when something is bothering you. You've clearly been upset about something for a while. What is it? You *know* you can talk to me."

Lira's eyes welled up with tears. I reached forward and held her hands in mine.

"You can tell me anything," I whispered. "Please, Lira. Just talk to me."

Just be honest with me, Bitch, I thought as I waited for her to answer me. I was giving her the opportunity! If there was ever a moment to tell me – *now would be it!*

Lira's hands were shaking as she gazed up at me. Tears were streaming down her cheeks. I felt breathless as I stared into her eyes, waiting for her to tell me.

"I'm just in a funk," she whispered before raising my hand to her lips – kissing my fingers softly. "I'm sorry that I'm worrying you. I'm just really stressed out and sad about my hair. I think you were right about it being work. Starting a new career has been really hard and maybe I'm not cut out for this.

I'll talk to my doctor about it when I go in."

I felt deflated as she stared back at me. I pulled my hands away and nodded my head at her.

"I just want to make sure you're okay," I responded. "I'm sorry this is happening to you. Hopefully the doctor can help you figure it out."

She sighed, nodding her head at me. She rose from her seat and I felt queasy. I didn't understand what was going through her head or what had happened between us to get us to the point we were at now. I felt like we were strangers. I wished I had never been with her. I was sad.

"I have a headache," she sighed. "I think I'm going to try and take a nap."

"Okay. I'm going to go workout," I responded.

She nodded her head, smiling at me, before turning for the bedroom.

I hadn't mentioned to Lira I had gotten a personal trainer. I had told Tess I wanted to keep it a secret and surprise her with my progress. Tess was very accommodating. She offered to let me workout with her in her personal gym at her own home! I texted Tess to meet up with me when Lira finally took her nap.

Tess' home was beautiful. She clearly came from money as there was *no* way a personal trainer could afford to live like this. She lived on a nice chunk of property with a lovely view of the city. Her house had blue shutters and a white picket fence.

How fucking quaint, I thought to myself as I rang her doorbell. *Must be nice to have things handed to you – including girlfriends who belong to someone else.*

Tess smiled as she opened the door for me. She looked sweaty - like she had just finished running. Her hair was pulled up into a ponytail, slicked back by a black headband.

She was wearing grey joggers and a hot pink sports bra. I looked her up and down as she stepped aside to let me in.

"Okay, Sporty Spice," I said as I walked past her. "You didn't tell me I had to dress like *that*."

Tess laughed at me – flashing her chompers as she checked out what I was wearing.

"I don't really have workout clothes," I laughed as she judged my baggy t shirt and sweat pants. "I figured this would do for now."

"Oh, you're totally fine," she chuckled as she motioned her head for me to follow her.

She led me down the stairs and for a moment, I wondered if I had been outsmarted. Was there a chance that Tess was crazier than me? Was I going to end up killed in her basement? I kept a healthy distance from her as we descended and she smiled as we turned the corner to her home gym.

"I know it's not much, but this is where we'll start!" she smiled.

I gazed around at her studio. It was really nice. She had an elliptical, a stationary bike, a treadmill, *and* a rower. She had a whole fucking free weights station and some machine that looked like it came straight out of an overpriced infomercial!

Was Tess actually rich or something? Was she one of those trainers for the stars? Was one of her clients Bieber? My eyes widened as I looked around at the mirrored room in wonder.

"Impressive," I said, turning to face her. "Are you a sugarbaby or something?"

Tess burst out into laughter, looking down at me in amusement.

"You're funny!" she shook her head at me. "No, my parents are lawyers. This is actually their house."

"You live with your parents?" I asked.

"It's temporary," she smiled.

"Well, they have a lovely home," I replied. "I could *never* live with my parents again. My dad's a douchebag."

"I'm sorry to hear that," Tess responded as I set my bag down. "Do you get along with your mom?"

"My mom's wonderful," I sighed. "She just has shitty taste in men. But hey, I can't complain I guess! Without him, I wouldn't be here!"

Tess laughed, seeming genuinely amused as she listened to me. I knew I could turn on the charm when I had to. I had been told by many people that I was funny. I don't know why I had this odd urge to gain her approval.

I don't know if it was because Lira was fucking me over or if it was because I had given her the chance to tell me and she had just lied to my face – but I wanted Tess to like me. I wanted it for my ego. I wanted to see the cracks in their perfect little relationship.

"So, I made you a meal plan," Tess said as she pulled up her phone. "I can email you the details, but it includes a grocery list and recipes for the week. I made it pretty easy. If there's anything you don't like on there, just let me know."

"That's amazing!" I smiled, batting my eyes at her. "Thanks."

"Yeah, it's high protein and low carb," Tess grinned.

"Can you help me make sure my tits and my ass don't shrink?" I asked, trying to sound innocently seductive as I cupped a tit in my hand. "These puppies are my greatest asset. I still want to be thick."

Tess gaped at me in shock as she looked at me. Her pasty little cheeks turned pink as I stared back at her.

"Oh, yeah . . . we can do lots of squats and stuff to build

up muscle. And you're built like an hourglass, so even if you do lose weight, you won't lose your classic shape."

"I mean I know I'm chubby, but I still want fat in the right places," I smirked.

Tess laughed nervously as I sat down on an exercise machine.

"What the hell is this thing?" I asked as I reached for the bar above me.

"Oh, here," Tess said as she adjusted the weight lower for me. "You can use this to work the muscles in your back," she replied to me.

"Can you show me?" I asked.

I gripped the handles and she stood behind me, placing her hands on the outside of mine on the bar.

"So, you're going to want to have a steady core and keep your back straight as you pull this down," she said, guiding the bar down as I pulled it toward me. "You want to stop the bar right about here." She stopped the bar as I pulled it beneath my chin and near my chest. "Tell me if this feels too light or too heavy for you."

"It feels good," I smiled at her as I pulled the bar down myself to show her. "You're a good teacher."

Tess stared awkwardly at me as I continued doing reps of this. I wondered if she thought I was hotter than Lira.

"So, how are things between you and your lady?" I asked as I smiled back at her. "Is she still playing hard to get?"

Tess was quiet for a moment as she thought about how to reply to me.

"We have our good and bad days," she sighed. "Honestly, sometimes I'm just over it."

"I know what you mean," I replied. "My girlfriend and I

have days like that too."

"You do?" she asked, a little too eagerly.

I stood up as I lifted the bar to finish the workout.

"Oh yeah," I nodded. "I mean, every couple has their issues. It's just about how you handle those issues together. Relationships are hard work!"

"They really are," she nodded. "I just feel like I'm the one putting in all of the work sometimes."

"Same," I sighed. "I think that's one of the most annoying things about my relationship. So I can totally relate to you!"

"Haven't you been with your girlfriend for a really long time?" she asked.

"Yes. We were friends for years before we started seeing one another," I replied. "Don't get me wrong – she's wonderful! But sometimes it can be really stressful with her addiction."

"Addiction?" she asked, raising her eyebrows at me.

I looked down morosely as I took an exaggerated deep breath.

"I really shouldn't talk about it," I sighed. "I'm sorry – I talk too much."

"No, it's totally OK!" Tess said, sounding concerned. "The gym is a safe space!"

I looked up at her nervously before tucking a strand of hair behind my ear.

"Well you probably don't want to hear about my relationship issues," I laughed.

"Oh no, please share!" she replied. "It's nice to talk about a relationship other than my own for once!"

"It's just hard sometimes," I sighed. "I love my girlfriend more than anything. I'm not going to give up on her or abandon her. We've come too far."

"What do you mean?" Tess asked, staring at me with intensity.

"Well, part of the reason I want to lose weight is so that I can keep Lira's attention," I pouted. "She's a recovering sex addict and has a propensity to cheat, so I do what I can to keep her interested."

"What do you mean?" Tess asked as she gaped at me. "She's a *sex addict*?"

"Ohhhh yeah," I chuckled. "We have to go to sex addict anonymous meetings and therapy regularly. Every single person she has ever been with has left her because of it. But I love her. I have stuck through it with her."

I wanted to die of laughter as Tess penetrated me with her stunned blue eyes.

"That sounds difficult," Tess responded, looking pale. "So she's cheated on you before?"

"Hundreds of times!" I replied. "Oh yeah, the last time she relapsed, I walked in on her fucking three guys in our living room. It was insanity! It was a legitimate train!"

Tess' jaw dropped on the floor.

"Choo choo!" I said, pretending to pull the train horn. "Sorry, I make jokes when I'm nervous."

"Wow," Tess replied.

"Yeah, but she's been really good for the last year and a half," I sighed. "We go to our meetings and therapy sessions weekly and it's really helped. She's made so much progress. God, she would KILL me if she knew I told anyone this! Sometimes I just want to get it out though, you know? I love her so much. She's the love of my life and I just *know* she's the one. That just means I have to be able to deal with her tendency to fuck the occasional side bitch or two or three once in a while, unfortunately!"

I couldn't believe I was able to keep a straight face as I smiled thankfully at her before walking over to the free weights. Tess looked like she had just been slapped in the face with a 12 inch dick. She stood frozen where I left her for several seconds before following me.

"So what's next?" I smiled. "Cardio?"

CHAPTER 26

Things had been pleasantly progressing with Raymond and Margot. It felt like I was juggling two full-fledged relationships with the amount of secrecy and deceit that consumed my life now. I was grateful that Lira was preoccupied with scandal of her own, and often wondered how oblivious she would have to be to not realize I was having an affair.

I didn't even try to hide it, really. I was constantly on my phone messaging him! This made me hate Lira even more. Her inattentiveness to the situation only solidified for me that she had more important things to worry about than her own fucking relationship! It made me sick. The silver lining was that over the last few days, Tess had seriously begun to back off. I was monitoring their conversations on the iPad and Tess was becoming less and less talkative. She blamed it on her busy schedule and family troubles, but I knew better.

Tess actually *believed* my little white lie about Lira being a sex addict! I giggled to myself as I saw Lira throw herself into one sided conversations with Tess in desperation. Poor Lira. She wasn't getting the attention she so pathetically craved. Oh well! I had more important things to worry about. My long distance relationship with Raymond was taking up the majority of my time.

Lira was working late. For once she wasn't lying, as Tess

had been too busy to hang out. So, I opted for a chill night in and made some cornbread and chili as I got ready for my phone date with Ray. I sat on the couch and got comfortable as the phone started to ring and pulled up the voice changing app on my phone. Playing the role of Margot had become thrilling to me. I was confident that my plot for revenge would work and that I had Raymond exactly where I wanted him. Soon, the bastard would know what it was like to be abandoned. He should be *thankful* it was only by someone he was in love with. Being abandoned by a close friend was a million times worse! I took a deep breath and tried to relax as I picked up the phone.

"Hey, Babe!" I said with enthusiasm as I picked up the phone to greet him.

"Hey, Lover!" Ray responded. "I raced home as quickly as I could! I couldn't wait to talk to you!"

"Ugh, I know what you mean!" I swooned. "I have been thinking about you nonstop all day!"

"Today's been rough," he agreed. "Luckily, the truck was super slammed today for this catering event, so I didn't have much time to sit around and stare at the clock. I like when we're busy because it feels like the days go by faster – and the faster my days go by, the sooner I get to come home and talk to my baby!"

"Aw, you're sweet!" I laughed, trying to sound like I was blushing.

Barf. One of the most challenging aspects of this whole little charade was trying to pretend like I was *actually* in love with him. I'll admit, going into it, I didn't think it would be that hard. The phone creates several degrees of separation, but I underestimated how awkward it would be. I had known only one side of Ray my entire life. Because I didn't *actually* look at him that way, it felt strange to act like I did. Admittedly, I got off on deceiving him, though. Because he had shut me down once in the past, it felt like a boost to my ego to know he was in love with me now! It made me want to laugh.

I would sooner date horse faced Tess than stoop down to Ray's level. Raymond was so beneath me now. He wasn't even interesting in a relationship. He was too romantic and lovey dovey.

I tried to remind myself that he didn't know any better and was acting so hopeless because Margot was his first love.

Even better. It would make the heartache that much more painful and humiliating for him.

"So what are you up to tonight?" Ray asked me, pulling me out of my inner monologue.

"Just hanging out and cooking some dinner," I smiled. "It's kind of cold out tonight, so I decided to make some chili and cornbread."

"That sounds delicious!" Ray approved. "I was going to just order a pizza. I don't want to get off of this couch for the rest of the evening."

"I know what you mean," I laughed. "It's just me and Sunshine curled up for the rest of the night! At least I have the dog to cuddle with me."

"I can't wait to cuddle with you," he whispered.

I chuckled to myself as I rolled my eyes. *It's never gonna happen, bitch.*

"Margot, I miss you," he sighed. "It's crazy how you can miss someone you've never physically met. But it's driving me crazy. I can't wait so see you."

"I know it," I sighed. "I am going to smother you in kisses! It will be tragic. We'll be *that* couple that people can't stand to be around! I don't know how you're going to get me off of you!"

"I can't wait for that," Ray groaned. "It's all I think about. I started sleeping with a pillow because I wish I had you in my arms."

I muted the phone and laughed out loud at this. *What a little girl!*

"I love you, Baby," I whispered. "I have never felt this way about anyone in my life. I am so happy I gave online dating a try."

"Best decision I ever made," Ray laughed. "I can't imagine my life without you now!"

Fucking pathetic!

"Margot," Ray whispered – his voice trailing off before silence filled my ears.

"Yes?" I asked, smiling into the phone.

"Babe . . . can we try something?"

I raised my eyebrow as I waited for him to elaborate.

"Try something?" I asked.

"Don't laugh," he chuckled. "I know it might sound crazy, but . . ."

"What is it?" I laughed.

There was silence again. Why was he acting so weird? My heart rate increased as I imagined what he was going to ask me. Hopefully he wasn't going to ask to video chat again. That was the *one* thing that would for *sure* blow my cover.

"Babe, I know that we're virgins and I'm not trying to pressure you into anything – I swear I'm not," he said, "but I was hoping we could try something."

Oh God. What?

"What? What do you want to try?" I asked.

Ray was heavy breathing into the phone and I stared – mortified – into the wall before me.

"Have you ever had phone sex?" he asked me.

Oh my God. This couldn't really be happening.

"I haven't, but I would with you," he sighed. "I just want to hear you," he whispered. "I want to be intimate with you, Margot. I've never felt this way before. I want to feel close to you."

"Okay . . ." I replied, feeling my cheeks turn pink as I cringed into the sofa. "What do I have to do?"

"Do you ever touch yourself?"

I laughed quietly, shaking my head at the ridiculousness of the situation.

"I do," I replied.

"Well, can we do it at the same time?" Ray asked.

I took a deep breath, exhaling dramatically into the phone. I couldn't believe this was actually happening. What the fuck was I going to do now?

"Okay," I bit my lip. "I've never done this before, but I want to feel close to you too."

"Okay, great," Ray replied – sounding like he was smiling from ear to ear. "I was worried it would be too much for you."

"Oh no, I want you," I replied. "I'm so excited right now. Are we really going to do this?"

"Yes," he sighed. "I'm already hard."

JESUS.

"Okay," I replied. "Just give me a second to get more comfortable."

I laid down on the couch and stared at the ceiling. Now was the time to really go for that Oscar! There was no way in *hell* I was actually going to flick the bean with Ray on the phone! I had faked it thousands of times with other people. This would be no different. *I could do this*, I told myself. *Just pretend he's Lira! You fake it with her all of the time!*

"Baby, I'm touching myself," Ray exhaled.

My eyes widened as I listened in shock to the change in his tone.

"Mmm," he exhaled. "I'm sliding my hand up and down my dick, slowly. I'm taking my time with it. I'm pretending you're lying down next to me – watching me move my hand up and down every ridge of my dick."

My mouth gaped open as I held back a blurt of laughter. *Wow, he was really getting into it!*

"Oh yeah?" I sighed into the receiver. "You like when I watch you?"

"If only you could see how bad I want it," he whispered. "I'm going a little faster now. It feels so good."

"I want you to feel good," I whispered. "I'm touching myself too. I'm so wet."

"Oh God," he breathed.

"I'm thinking about you while I rub my clit," I whispered – trying to sound as breathy and helpless as possible. "I wish you were on top of me right now."

"Margot, uh," he groaned. "I am imagining your mouth around me . . ."

"I bet you have such a huge dick," I exhaled.

"It's pretty big," he replied.

I could hear wet stroking in the background as I responded.

"Well, we'll have to go slow so that I don't gag on it."

I muted the phone and laughed hysterically to myself as Ray reacted into the phone.

"Jesus Christ, Margot," he muttered. "Don't talk like that! You'll make me cum too quickly!"

"Don't do that," I taunted. "I want you to cum *with* me. Wouldn't you like that? To hear me moaning in your ear?"

"Oh God," his voice trembled.

"Ohh," I moaned into the phone. "That feels so good, Baby . . ."

"God, I love you," he groaned into the phone. "Margot, I'm going to make love to you. I'm going to give you everything."

"I want it," I exhaled. "I need you, Baby, I'm so close . . ."

"God, I'm jacking off so hard right now," his voice quivered. "I'm going to cum so hard, Baby . . . it feels so fucking good."

"I want you inside of me," I moaned back at him. "I'm going to cum, Ray. I'm going to cum . . ."

"Margot!" he grunted as I heard him ejaculate into his hand.

I faked my own climax as I filled up a bowl of chili – laughing internally as Ray came down from his high.

I giggled into the phone coyly as he laughed also in return.

"Wow, that was amazing," he panted. "You sound so cute when you moan."

"You sound amazing," I smiled. "It felt so real, Ray. I imagined you were actually right here with me!"

"I know, it's insane!" he laughed. "Margot, I can't do this anymore. I really need to see you."

"I know," I laughed as I sat back down at the couch with my dinner. "I can't wait until I can finally see you in person."

"No, I'm dead serious," he said.

There was momentary silence. I furrowed my brow as he continued.

"I know you said you've been saving up vacation time to come to Kansas, but I honestly don't want to wait that long. I was going to wait and surprise you, but I can't hold it in any longer. Baby, I'm coming to Colorado to see you!"

Shit.

I gripped the phone in my hand as I tried to remain calm. Why the fuck was he being so impatient? Was I *really* that good that I had him pussy whipped enough to travel out of state for me so soon?

I felt dizzy as anxiety started taking over me. I could *NOT* have Raymond visiting Colorado now. I wasn't ready for this! I needed to *be there* to see his face when he realized Margot didn't love him! What the fuck was I going to do now?

"Baby," I said as I rose from the couch to pace back and forth. "I would love nothing more than to have you come visiting me, but my schedule is so crazy right now with work ..."

There was silence for a moment before Ray responded to me.

"Why are you acting like that?" he whispered. "That was *not* the reaction I was expecting from you at all. I thought you would be thrilled to see me."

SHIT, SHIT, SHIT!

"Honey, I am!" I exclaimed. "You just caught me off guard, that's all! I just want the first time we meet to be perfect! I don't want to have to be working while you're in town! That will kill me! I'll get fired, Ray! I won't be able to concentrate knowing you're in town!"

Ray chuckled, seeming to relax a bit. I felt my heart throbbing in my chest as I tried to come up with a solution for this. I had hoped to fuck with him a few months longer. Was he really being serious?

"Don't worry about it, Margot," he sighed. "I can just bring my laptop and sit in your section all day. It will be okay, Babe! And you can still take your vacation time to come visit me in Kansas! I just can't wait any longer. I LOVE YOU, Margot. I need to meet you face to face."

I shut my eyes, silently cursing before looking up to see a photo of Lira and I at her aunt's cabin. A wave of calm came over me as I realized what I had to do.

"Okay," I replied, taking a deep breath. "Do you think you can come in 2 weeks, or would that be too soon?"

I held my breath, hoping and praying he would be able to wait that long.

"Absolutely!" Ray responded. "That actually works perfect for me!"

I sighed, shaking my head as I sat back down on the couch. This was NOT how I imagined things would go with him. But the timing was perfect, so I would just have to make do. Lira and I were set to go to Colorado in two weeks' time to visit her aunt and go camping. I would be in Colorado anyway, so would have to find the time to drive to Aspen to set Ray up for the finale.

"Well, it's settled then," I smiled. "Let's make a plan and discuss the details!"

CHAPTER 27

I followed Dr. Griffin into his office and smiled as he shut the door behind me. I had waited all week to stare into those almond brown eyes of his. The energy between us felt palpable as he took his seat across from me at his desk.

I wondered if it was all in my head and if it really was just "transference", or whatever he had referred to when he tried to justify why I felt the way I felt about him. I really didn't want to believe that was true. I had spent weeks with this man and though I knew very little about him, I could *sense* the connection. And he basically knew everything there was to know about me! You can't fake chemistry and that was something I knew that we had. It was heavy in the air like a fog that swirled around us. I couldn't be imagining it. I was vulnerable with him. Cut open and on display. I tried to shrug it off, but this wasn't playful anymore for me. This was real. I felt like I could actually fall in love with him.

"So how was your week, Thea?" he asked, showcasing his perfect smile.

I played with the corner of my sweater as I thought about how to begin the session with him.

"It was pretty eventful," I smirked, feeling guilty as my eyes locked in with his.

"Eventful how?" he asked, as he clicked the back of his

pen.

"First of all, I want to thank you for meeting with me last minute last week," I sighed. "It meant a lot to me that you took time out of your evening to help me. I was a mess and you really helped calm me down."

He looked at me – a wrinkle forming between the center of his brows, as he nodded his curly tendriled head.

"No need to thank me," he responded. "That's what I'm here for. I'm happy I was able to help. Please don't hesitate to reach out if you ever feel like that again."

I nodded my head, feeling annoyed at his response. I hated when he talked to me like that. Sometimes he spoke to me so void of emotion and formal that it made me forget the moments we shared that I *knew* were real.

"Yeah," I continued. "Well anyway, things went further south with Lira this week."

He scribbled in his notebook as he listened to me – the muscles beneath his cardigan flexing as he wrote.

"I pretended to come back from my trip and she was acting super weird with me. I thought for sure that she was going to tell me about her and Tess, but it didn't happen."

"What made you think she was going to tell you about her and Tess?" he asked.

"Well, she looked guilty as fuck and seemed super depressed for once," I sighed. "I knew she was depressed because I read her text messages and she and Tess had had this *amazing* time together when I was away. She was sad it was over. So when I came home, she pulled up a seat next to me and got super emotional. I thought she was going to finally tell me."

"But she didn't?" he asked.

"Nope. She vented about how depressed she was about

her hair falling out," I giggled. "I gave her the golden opportunity to talk to me, but she didn't open up. I even said, 'You can tell me anything, Lira. I *know* you. I *know* when something's wrong. Please just talk to me'. But she hesitated and instead, went on this tangent about how she's stressed at work and stressed that she's going bald."

"That must have hurt," Dr. Griffin replied. "How did that make you feel when she dismissed you like that?"

"I felt hurt," I admitted. "I was hoping she would be honest to me for once in her life. I had this tiny shred of hope that she would be a good person and come clean to me. But she didn't."

"I can understand how that would hurt you," he nodded. "Have you considered initiating the conversation with her? Have you thought about just asking her if she is unhappy?"

I felt uncomfortable as I thought about it. I shifted nervously in my seat.

"You seem bothered by that question," Dr. Griffin said, leaning forward. "Talk to me about that."

"I just don't like thinking about it," I responded. "I get anxiety when I think about ever having that conversation."

"What about talking to her makes you anxious?" he asked.

"I don't know, it's just a fucked up situation," I sighed. "What am I supposed to even say? 'Hey Lira, I have been spying on you like a psychopath for the last nine weeks and I know you're having an affair with a personal trainer. *My personal trainer.* Oh yeah, your mistress is my personal trainer. And, by the way, I'm the reason your hair is falling out!'"

Dr. Griffin watched me as I shook my head in annoyance. There was no easy way to go about leaving Lira. Not without exposing myself for the crazy person I was.

"So you worry about her learning you have been hiding your knowledge of this affair from her," he said as he stared back at me. "That's interesting."

"Why is that interesting?" I asked, feeling perplexed. "Shoot it to me straight, Douglas. I don't like when you speak in riddles."

"It's just interesting that what keeps you from confronting Lira about her lies and manipulation is the fact that you have been lying and manipulating her in return. Why do you care what she thinks at this point?"

"I don't know!" I huffed. "I just don't want her to tell everyone I'm crazy."

"You worry she will tell people you're crazy," he nodded, writing again in his stupid notebook. "But doesn't that all seem small in comparison to what she has been doing to you?"

"Not really when you think about it," I replied. "I mean, I've taken it pretty far, haven't I? I have literally flushed her grandmother's ashes down the drain and put Nair in her shampoo."

"You don't have to tell her that," Dr. Griffin responded. "You can simply tell her you know about her affair with Tess and leave it at that."

"What if she denies it?" I asked.

"It won't matter. She knows what she did. If you leave her, she's bound to admit it to you eventually. And even if she doesn't, it doesn't matter if you want to leave her."

I sighed, crossing my arms across my chest.

"Also, I met with Tess again and convinced her Lira is a sex addict."

Dr. Griffin raised his eyebrows as he stared back at me.

"Yeah," I chuckled. "It was pretty petty of me, but you know . . . you win some, you lose some."

"I see," he sighed. "So if I am understanding you correctly, Tess is your personal trainer. She has no suspicions that you are onto her?"

"I'm not certain," I shrugged. "If she suspects, she isn't 100% convinced because she keeps meeting with me."

"And I take it Lira has no knowledge of these meetings?" he asked.

"No she does not," I replied. "She would be livid with Tess if she knew what she was doing. So I very much doubt Tess will ever tell her."

"So Tess is lying to her," Dr. Griffin said as he reached for his coffee mug. "That adds another level of deceit to the situation."

"Right!" I exclaimed. "Like seriously, they are so wrong for each other! If I was in love and having an affair, I wouldn't hang out with my girlfriend's girlfriend! Isn't that fucking shady?"

"That's actually something I could see you doing," Dr. Griffin smirked.

I rolled my eyes, shaking my head at him.

"Thanks, Doug," I sighed. "That's beyond the point I'm trying to make though."

"What point are you trying to make?" he smiled.

"Tess is lying to Lira. Lira's lying to me. I'm lying to everyone. Everybody's fucking liars! But I have a reason to lie, you know what I mean? Anyway, I pretended to vent about my relationship problems with Lira to Tess and told Tess that our relationship was challenging because Lira suffered from sex addiction. I actually have Tess believing Lira is unfaithful in all of her relationships - and that she struggles keeping her vag in her pants because she's just so addicted to sex!"

I laughed out loud before biting my lip.

"That's clever," Dr. Griffin responded. "It makes you feel in control to sway Tess' views on Lira. You also satisfy your need for vengeance when you paint Lira in a negative light to Tess. Maybe Tess will break up with Lira because she fears she's incapable of being faithful. I see where you were going with that."

"Yeah," I nodded.

"But then what?" Dr. Griffin asked me.

"What do you mean?" I replied.

"So Tess dumps Lira and Lira is sad. What do you hope will be Lira's next move? Do you think Lira will leave you if that happens?"

"I don't know," I replied, feeling perplexed as he stared back at me.

"Who's to say Lira doesn't just try to work things out with you? If Tess leaves her, she might be sad, but not enough to break up with you, Thea. Do you really want to be her consolation prize?"

I gaped at him, feeling flushed as he sat back in his seat, raising the mug to his lips.

"I haven't thought that far ahead," I replied, annoyed.

"Things to ponder," he said before taking a sip of his drink.

"Well," I crossed my arms, "aside from all of that drama – I had phone sex with Raymond this week also."

Dr. Griffin choked as he swallowed his coffee. He quickly set his mug down and wiped his mouth. I tried to read his expression, but he was wearing the world's best poker face, so I couldn't tell if it made him jealous. I hoped it did.

I took a deep breath and smiled before continuing, "Yeah, he and I were chatting and he said he wanted to try something new, so we ended up fucking around on the phone."

Dr. Griffin raised his eyebrows, putting pen to paper. "You had sex with him then?"

"Well, kinda," I smiled. "Not really. You can relax, Doug. I didn't cum."

He stared at me, pursing his lips as he wrote more in his notebook.

"So what happened then?" he asked me.

"I just played along," I sighed. "He wanked one off while I talked dirty to him. I faked it and got him there. It was weird. But this shit has been really progressing with him, you know? It was crazy! I have him so whipped over me that he's actually going to Colorado to meet Margot in a few weeks!"

Dr. Griffin narrowed his eyebrows. "And how is that going to work?"

"Well, thank God I'm going camping here soon with Lira! We go to Colorado every year and that's why I used Colorado as Margot's place of residence in the first place! I know a lot about Colorado, so I could make it sound believable, you know? Anyway, when I go out there with Lira, I'm going to have to make a detour at some point to break things off with Ray."

"And how do you plan on doing that?" Dr. Griffin asked me.

"A magician doesn't reveal all of their tricks!" I smirked. "I have some things to workout still, but in the meantime – this is crazy! I actually did it, Dr. Griffin! I actually have Ray where I want him! God, it's just . . . victory tastes so sweet!"

I smiled ear to ear as I gazed out of the window in ecstasy. I was so proud of what I had accomplished in my fake relationship with Ray.

"So, will this bring you the closure you need?" Dr. Griffin asked me.

I looked back at him, tilting my head to the side.

"Meaning, once you have hurt him, will you be able to move on from the pain his abandonment has caused you?"

"I think so," I sighed. "I hope so."

"You have no plans of carrying on talking to him once this has been accomplished? You won't concoct another persona and mess with him some more down the road?"

"No, this should be enough," I replied.

"You will feel like justice has been delivered?"

"Yes," I smiled.

"So what can you do to accomplish the same thing with Lira?"

I took a deep breath, fidgeting uncomfortably in my seat.

"Doug, I feel like I can talk to you about anything, so I'm just going to be real with you," I sighed. "I didn't want to tell you before, but for a while there, I was really thinking about killing Lira."

Dr. Griffin stared at me, raising his eyebrows. I didn't want to let myself believe he would tell on me. I knew he really liked me. I needed to be able to fully open up to him. I was hopeful my intuition was right.

"I know, it's pretty shocking," I continued. "But listen, you changed my mind, ok? I realize that's not the healthiest way to deal with my emotions, so I have stopped fantasizing about killing her."

There was silence as Dr. Griffin stared back at me. I felt shivers up my spine as I momentarily wondered if I had just really fucked up.

"So you fantasized about killing Lira?" he asked. "In these fantasies, how would you carry this out?"

"I never got that far," I huffed, running my fingers through my hair. "I would imagine drowning her or smothering her. Strangling her or running her over with my car. Shooting her or electrocuting her. The possibilities were really endless! But I didn't know how to get away with it or how to hide a body, so I really never acted on it. I mean, the Nair shit was the only thing I have ever done to physically hurt her. And that to me was so harmless in comparison, you know?"

Dr. Griffin stared at me as I tugged on the sleeve of my sweater.

"I know, it's fucked up," I sighed, feeling guilty. "I don't like that I had thoughts like that, you know? I just really hate her sometimes."

"It's interesting to me that you have thought about killing Lira, but you haven't expressed ever wanting to kill Ray," he replied.

I opened my mouth, but didn't know how to respond to him.

"Do you know why that is?" he asked.

"I've never really thought about it before," I responded.

"Well, may I attempt to guess?" Dr. Griffin replied.

"Sure . . ." I answered, hoping he could explain it to me since I didn't understand it myself.

"You know what I think, Thea?" he asked me. "I don't think you are a murderous person at all. I don't think you were ever going to kill Lira."

I rolled my eyes, thinking it was cute that he thought so. But I kept listening to him to give him the benefit of the doubt.

"I think that that you have this idea of justice in your mind, as we have already established. Raymond abandoned you. He left you. He ended your friendship without any explanation."

I felt uncomfortable as Dr. Griffin spoke to me – the reminder of what Ray did feeling like punches to my gut.

"In your mind, justice would be to hurt him the way he hurt you," Dr. Griffin said, clicking his pen. "You love Ray and wish you were still friends with him. You just want him to know what it feels like to be hurt the way he hurt you. That to you, seems fair."

"Yeah," I nodded.

"But with Lira, it's more complicated," he sighed. "Lira cheated on you. Fine. That hurts. But that isn't the core of your issue with her."

"Okay," I replied, trying to understand.

"The cheating alone, you could probably deal with. It's the fact that you chose her over Ray. Whether subconscious or not, it doesn't matter. Ray told you what would happen if you cheated on Westly. And you did it anyway. You cheated on Westly with Lira and Ray left you. So when it *really* comes down to it, Thea . . . you chose Lira over Ray."

"Whatever, fine," I huffed, staring at him to elaborate.

"So, how can you get vengeance on Lira, really? In your mind, the crime is too great. The pain you feel from the loss of your friendship with Raymond is so devastating. It's made you want to die."

I felt tears sting my eyes as I listened to him.

"You know that Raymond will never forgive you. That's a hole you will have in your heart forever. So your first instinct is to make her feel the same pain you feel. And since losing Ray has made you feel so desolate, your natural reaction is to want her to feel that pain."

Tears fell down my face as he leaned forward in his seat.

"She betrayed you in such an unforgivable way in your

BRIANABEIJO

eyes. You can't get back what she has taken from you. So that is why I think you fantasized about killing her, Thea. No amount of revenge would suffice in your eyes. Unless Ray were to forgive you and be your friend of course, which you have made clear isn't a possibility . . . there's nothing Lira could do to fix it. So in your mind, she deserves to die."

I placed my head in my hands and started crying – hating myself for knowing that he was right. Was I really that pathetic of a person that I let someone hurt me so deeply I couldn't let myself ever get over it? Did Ray really have that much power over me? Why? I loved Lira. I wanted to be with her. He was right – on some level, I must have known what I was risking with Ray. It just made me feel so betrayed that she took that for granted. After what I lost, I was just disposable to her? I couldn't live with that. It made me crazy.

"You're right," I sobbed, looking back up at him. "I hate that you're right, but you are."

"But you're not a bad person, Thea," Dr. Griffin replied, pushing the box of tissues toward me. "You feel this way because of your Borderline Personality Disorder. But you're not a murderer. You aren't actually going to hurt her, Thea. It's okay that you have had those thoughts and feelings. I am *proud* of you for being brave enough to tell me."

"I don't want to feel this way," I cried. "I want to be able to get over it."

"Well you wanting to get over it and embracing that is the first step," Dr. Griffin replied. "Soon you will be done with your vengeance on Raymond. Hopefully that will give you what you need to let him go. We can work on finding a more healthy solution than murder for Lira."

I laughed, wiping the tears from my cheeks as he smiled at me.

"God, I'm sorry," I laughed through my tears. "I know I

probably sound bat shit crazy to you, but I really don't want to be this terrible person."

"You just need to learn to control your impulses," Dr. Griffin replied. "One step at a time, Thea. You will eventually leave Lira. Or you won't. Maybe you will want to stay with her. That's up to you. But either way, you will learn to communicate with her in a healthy way and face your problems head on instead of hiding behind plots and schemes to make you feel like you have the power. Sometimes having the power means letting go of what is hurting you."

"Thank you," I sniffled. "You're right."

He smiled sympathetically as he sat back in his seat.

"Give me your phone," I sighed, looking up at him.

"Pardon me?" he asked, furrowing his brow.

"Your phone. Let me have it for a sec," I sighed.

He hesitated for a moment before opening the drawer in his desk and pulling out his cell phone. He unlocked it before handing it to me.

"Here," I said as I took his phone from him.

He stared at me in bewilderment as I sent him a link from my phone and then clicked to accept it on his. I smiled before handing his phone back to him.

"What did you just do?" he asked curiously.

"I shared my location with you," I sighed. "I want you to be my emergency contact in case anything ever happens to me. And well, now you'll always know where I am in case you want to hang out or something."

"Thea," he said, taking a deep breath.

"I'm just saying!" I said, throwing my hands up in the air.

"I'm your therapist, not your friend," he replied. "I'm

flattered, but we aren't going to hang out outside of this."

"Why do you have to be so pessimistic, Doc?" I rolled my eyes. "It's okay, Doug. I *know* you like me."

"I do," he exhaled. "But that doesn't change anything."

"For now," I smirked. "Anyway, if you ever want to meet up with me, you can just look on your iPhone and you'll see where I am!"

"We will work on your boundaries," he smiled.

"I told you, I have feelings for you," I smiled. "It's a little late for boundaries, don't you think?"

"Oh Thea," he shook his head. "WHAT am I going to do with you?"

CHAPTER 28

Week 10

I t was wine night with Grace and I was excited to get some stuff off of my chest.

The last several days had been interesting between Lira and me. Tess had told Lira she was going out of town to visit a friend. Their relationship seemed really strained and Lira knew something was up, but Tess wasn't offering any information. This didn't surprise me. I knew that Tess wasn't going to admit to Lira that she had been seeing me and admit that she had been lying to her, so the obvious solution in her eyes was to push Lira away.

She wasn't fighting with Lira or acting like anything in particular was *wrong*. She was just acting cold and distant. This had obvious effects on Lira's mental health.

Lira had spent the last few days moping around when she was home – clearly depressed. When I would ask her what was bothering her, she would insist it was just normal depression from losing her hair. I had replaced the bottle of tainted shampoo with good shampoo and knew her hair would finally start to recover. She was waiting to hear back from her doctors on her hormone levels, but they too seemed convinced that the hair loss was stress induced.

I tried not to feel bad, but I *was* starting to feel guilty. I figured the distance from Tess would suffice for now, and figured Tess' cold shoulder would be punishment enough. I needed to put all of my focus into our upcoming trip to Colorado. I didn't want anything foiling my plan.

I waved to Greg as I walked through their garage and into their kitchen where Grace was assembling a charcuterie board of fruit, meat, and cheese. She smiled up at me as I gave her a cheek-to-cheek kiss before taking a seat at the table. She swiftly joined me with snacks and wine glasses in hand.

"I am so glad it's Friday," Grace smiled as she took a seat at the table. "I have been looking forward to this *all day*!"

"God, me too," I groaned as I poured myself a generous glass of Riesling. "I've been dying to tell you all about what's been going on with Lira! I hope you're ready for the tea."

"Spill it, Girl," Grace replied, placing her chin on her hand attentively. "I can only imagine what's been going on with you."

I laughed, shaking my head at the craziness of it all. I had longed to tell Grace everything, but was so nervous about what she would think. Letting my therapist see how crazy I am, was one thing. Letting my best friend see it, was another. I wanted her to like me. I didn't want her to actually be concerned. I took a sip of my wine before I began to fill her in.

I told her all about the week prior with Lira and admitted I had been meeting up with Tess. Her eyes widened as I told her all about Lira's fake sex addiction and about how Tess had been slowly putting distance between her and Lira. I felt my heart start to race as I made the last-minute decision to confide in her what I had done to Lira's shampoo. I avoided eye contact as I told her what I had done that day with her grandmother's ashes. I felt my cheeks warm with shame as I felt Grace's horrified eyes on me. I took giant sips of my wine between sentences, feeling out of breath as anxiety consumed me.

I wanted to open up to her. I wasn't telling her about Ray, but I at least wanted to be able to talk to her about Lira. I finished my story and winced before finally looking up into Grace's shocked stare.

"Please say something," I said after several seconds of agonizing silence passed us by.

"What the fuck . . ." Grace gasped, her mouth open like a fish as she looked through me. "Just give me a minute. That's a lot to take in."

"I know." I flinched, pouring myself another glass of wine.

I felt dizzy as I watched Grace process the information. I wondered if I had finally fucked our friendship up and made a terrible mistake.

"Dorothea, so much of what you just said is so messed up," she said, looking serious. "Please tell me you've been talking to your therapist about this."

"I have," I nodded, taking a deep breath.

"You're not going to keep doing these psychotic things to Lira, right?" she asked me, desperate for confirmation that I was human. *"Promise me* you're not going to keep doing things like that."

"I promise," I croaked. "I already told you, I replaced her shampoo."

"Do you hear how fucking crazy this is?" she exclaimed, seeming somewhat angry. "Thea, you can't just hurt people like that for hurting you!"

"She's cheating on me!"

"It doesn't matter," she gaped. "That doesn't give you the right to do the shit you have done."

"I know," I groaned. "Please don't be upset with me, Grace. I'm going to therapy. I'm getting help."

"I'm not mad, I'm disappointed," she sighed, "and honestly a little afraid. This isn't normal behavior, Thea. What does your therapist think?"

I took a deep breath as I gazed back into her judgmental blue eyes.

"He thinks I'm doing this as a way to get control back and deliver vengeance for what she did to me with Ray."

"What the fuck is that supposed to mean?" Grace wrinkled her nose.

"Meaning, because I chose to be with her when I *knew* Ray would be mad at me, I blame her for the loss of my friendship with Ray. Because she's leaving me for Tess, I feel like I sacrificed my friendship with Ray for no reason. It's complicated. He gets it. He is going to help me work on healthier ways to cope with my anger and depression."

"Well, I really hope so," she shook her head at me, "because what you just told me is terrifying. I pray Lira never finds out what you did to her. You could actually get in a lot of trouble for doing what you did. And her grandmother's ashes, Thea! JESUS! That's just horrible!"

"Okay, okay," I huffed. "I know already. You don't need to make me feel even more bad about it."

"Someone needs to be the voice of reason," she laughed incredulously. "Seriously, you need to have a conscience, Thea. I mean, fuck! What are you going to do to me if I ever piss you off?"

"Don't piss me off and we'll never find out," I joked.

Grace glared at me as she took a sip of her wine.

"I'm kidding," I sighed. "Obviously. I went a little bit nuts there for a minute. I feel bad about it, okay?"

"Okay, you need to break up with Lira," Grace replied, looking serious. "Play time is over, don't you think? You need break things off with her and get the fuck out of that house."

"I will," I promised. "Eventually."

Grace opened her mouth, staring at me in disbelief. "Dorothea, what the fuck are you waiting for?"

"I don't know," I sighed. "It's just not the right time with the Colorado trip. I'll do it when I get back."

"Wow," Grace shook her head at me. "You are something else."

"It's not that easy, okay?" I cried. "I just need a couple more weeks to get my shit in order."

"You better leave her soon," Grace responded. "Honestly, Thea – I'm being serious. You need to leave her if you care at all about what I think of you. This behavior is really unhealthy and I'm not going to sit back and watch my best friend fall into lunacy! You need to snap out of it. Lira's a fucking cheater. Cut your losses. Get out with what little dignity you have left!"

I glared at her, trying to hold my tongue as I envisioned slapping her across her mouth. Why was she so against me? Dr. Griffin didn't make me feel this way! I thought Grace was my best friend! Maybe opening up to her was a bad idea after all.

"I'm sorry, I know that's harsh – but I love you," Grace sighed. "I'm your best friend, so you know I'm going to tell you how it is. I'm worried about you, Thea. I'm sorry she hurt you, but this is next level. Just please start making plans to leave her and STOP this insanity!"

"Okay," I replied, taking another sip of my wine.

"Okay," she sighed, reaching across the table and placing her hand on mine. "So, you're still in therapy? That's good."

"Yeah, he's great," I muttered, taking a deep breath. "I actually think I need to stop seeing him soon, though."

"Why?" Grace asked, looking puzzled.

"It's complicated," I sighed, looking back at her.

"Complicated? How?" she replied.

I shook my head before looking away from her.

"Oh, for the love of God, Thea . . . *no*," Grace groaned.

"I have feelings for him," I sighed, gazing back at her. "I don't know how to explain it, Grace. I'm really falling for him. I think it's probably a good idea to stop seeing him professionally if I want to be able to have a relationship with him out in the real world."

"You need to wake the fuck up," she said with seriousness in her tone. "Dorothea, he's your fucking *therapist*. There is no way he's going to go out with you! Do you have any idea how unethical that is? He could lose his license! Do you want him to get in trouble because of you? What is the matter with you, Thea? You can't go out with your *shrink*! That's an abuse of power! No therapist is going to throw away their career for you!"

She laughed before chugging her glass of wine. I stared at her in silence as she poured herself another drink.

"You need a new therapist – that much we can agree on," she said. "You need to find an ugly old person who you won't want to fuck after opening up to them! You don't even really like this person, Thea. You only *think* you do! It's because you can tell him all of your secrets and he doesn't tell you what's up the way that I do! Of course, you're going to have feelings for someone like that! But don't get it twisted my friend, he's just doing his *job*. He gets *paid* to listen to you. Please don't do anything stupid, Thea. I don't want to see you get hurt. Jesus Christ, only *you* would fall in love with your therapist!"

"It's not like that," I responded, trying not to let her see how hurt I was. "You don't even *know* him."

"Oh my God, and do you?" she chortled. "I mean seriously, tell me, Thea! Because if he's a professional then you don't know him at all!"

I clenched my hands into fists beneath the table.

"What do you know about him?" she pressed. "Seriously, what's his favorite color? When's his birthday? What's his favorite book?"

"I don't know," I muttered, feeling flushed.

"What kind of music does he like? Does he have any siblings? What are his hobbies? Does he like sports?"

I clenched my jaw as she poured me another glass of wine.

"You don't know any of these things, do you? It's okay that you don't, Dorothea! You're not supposed to! He's not your friend, honey. He's not your boyfriend. He's your doctor. He's your sounding board. It's his *job* to know everything about you and make you feel validated and heard. But don't confuse that with feelings. That is a sure-fire way to get yourself heartbroken."

"Okay, I fucking get it!" I yelled, feeling tears sting my eyes as I looked back at her. "I don't know why the fuck I even came here tonight! I thought you were my best friend! I thought I could tell you *anything* and *everything*! But you have made me feel so fucking stupid tonight – did you know that? I am humiliated right now! Like, how the fuck am I supposed to feel after you talked to me like that?"

"I'm just trying to help you," Grace replied sympathetically. "I'm sorry, Love, but I am. I'm not trying to hurt you. I would never want to hurt you! I'm trying to protect you because I don't want you to do anything crazy . . ."

"A little late for that, don't you think?" I laughed.

"Oh, come on," she sighed, grabbing my hand. "I'm sorry, honey. I'm sorry. You can tell me anything, okay? You're going through a lot. I know that. I just don't want you to do anything you'll regret."

"Okay," I sniffled.

Bitch, I regret coming here and confiding in you.

"You're right, Grace. I'm sorry."

"I'm sorry too," she sighed. "I'm happy you told me about all of this. That's a lot to take in, but I get it now. I just hope you leave Lira as soon as possible so that you can move on with your life. And I hope you stop having feelings for your therapist or find a new one so that you don't put yourselves in an awkward position. I say this all with love. Because I *love* you, Thea. You're my best friend."

"You're my best friend too," I whispered as I wiped a tear from my eye.

Well, that was educational, I told myself. Never again would I let Grace see my crazy! She was right about one thing though. I didn't know anything about Dr. Griffin. And I didn't like that. I would rectify that as soon as possible. This relationship was totally one sided and I would *not* stand for that any longer.

CHAPTER 29

It had been a few days since my uncomfortable conversation with Grace. It had been a week since I had seen Dr. Griffin. Now as I followed him into his office, I felt focused and ready. A lot of what Grace had pointed out was true. This relationship was one-sided. I didn't give a fuck that he was my therapist anymore! I was falling in love with him. I needed to have a real conversation with him and get to the bottom of this! I needed to know if he had feelings for me too.

I took a seat on the sofa, feeling nervous as he made himself comfortable across from me. I stared into his inquisitive eyes as he ran his fingers through his curly hair. He relaxed his shoulders, looking pensive and thoughtful as he stared back at me. *God, he was perfect.* I gulped, taking a deep breath as I felt my leg shake from nervousness.

"How are you tonight, Thea?" he asked me, looking puzzled as he watched me fidget anxiously in my seat. "Is everything all right?"

"Not really," I responded, trying to sit still as I stared back at him with anticipation. "I don't really think tonight will be so much of a therapy session as it will be an actual conversation."

"What do you mean?" he asked, furrowing his brow.

I exhaled, biting my lip as he gazed at me. Why did this

have to be so hard?

"I need to talk to you," I sighed.

"Okay, well I'm here," he responded, looking concerned.

"No, you don't get it," I huffed.

"Well help me out, Thea," he shook his head at me. "Something's obviously bothering you. What's on your mind?"

"You are!" I responded. "You are. All of the time."

He frowned. "Thea, we've talked about this before," he sighed.

"It's fucking bullshit," I laughed, shaking my head at him. "Seriously, just stop. I get it. You're my therapist! You have to be professional! You've made your point. But can you just be real with me for a second? Do you have feelings for me?"

Dr. Griffin raised his eyebrows, looking shocked as he stared back at me.

"Dorothea, I'm your therapist," he reiterated. "I don't have feelings for my clients. I care about you. Just not in that way . . ."

"You're lying," I responded, shaking my head in irritation. "Doug, I'm done with this bullshit! Honestly, I am! I'm falling in love with you! I don't care if that makes you uncomfortable and I'm not ashamed to admit it. I am falling head over heels in love with you!"

I stood up from the sofa and started pacing back and forth as he stared up at me – his jaw on the floor.

"Do you have any idea how exhausting it is walking around pretending like I don't want you?" I continued, playing with my hair nervously as I walked around his room with anxiety. "I go home at night and think about being with you. If I honestly felt like you didn't possibly feel the same way,

I wouldn't be talking to you right now, but I *feel* it, Douglas! And I *know* you're a good doctor and that's why you aren't admitting it to me! But seriously, what the fuck, Doug? You know everything about me. And I don't know anything about you! What's your favorite color?"

I stopped in front of his desk and placed my hands on the edges as I leaned down to look at him.

"Is it blue? Is it red? Is it black like your dark little heart? Just tell me!"

He closed his mouth, taking a deep breath as he stared back up at me.

"Thea, please sit down and we can talk about this."

"Please tell me," I pleaded.

"It's red," he answered. "Please sit down."

"Do you have any siblings?" I asked, pacing back and forth again.

He sighed, pinching the bridge of his nose as he looked away from me.

"Well?" I repeated.

"I have an older sister," he responded.

"We have that in common!" I chirped. "What kind of music do you like?"

"Sit down, Thea," he said, staring up at me.

"You seem like an indie kinda guy. Folk perhaps? Do you like Coldplay? You look like the kind of dude who listens to Coldplay."

"Seriously?" he responded. "Can you sit down and actually talk to me and not *at* me for a minute?"

"Talk *at* you," I laughed. "Oh, I'm sorry! Does this make you uncomfortable? Maybe you don't like talking about yourself because you're afraid to open up to me!"

"Thea, STOP!" he yelled – his voice hard as stone. "Do you think it's cute, this little thing you're doing? Do you think this is the type of conversation I *want* to have with you?"

"Well what type of conversation *do* you want?" I spat as I took a step closer to his desk. "The kind where I pour my heart out to you and you give me nothing in return?"

"I'm your doctor. You're my patient," he responded – the corners of his mouth twitching as he whispered the words.

"I don't believe you," I replied as I reached over and traced my fingertips down his cheek.

He flinched away from me – his eyes widening as he stared up at me.

"Tell me you don't have feelings for me," I whispered, feeling my heart beating faster. "Look me in the eyes and tell me you don't."

He swallowed as he stared back at me – penetrating me with his chocolate eyes.

"What you are experiencing is called Transference," he responded. "You don't really love me, Thea. You don't."

"I do," I nodded, stepping away from him. "I do and you know it."

I walked back to the sofa and sat down as I glared back at him. He looked angry and hurt and concerned all at once. I didn't understand why he wasn't opening up to me.

"I'll leave Lira," I whispered as I gazed into his eyes. "I'll leave her. I will. I'll break up with her right this second if I can have you."

"Thea, I'm sorry," he whispered, running his fingers through his scruff. "I know this must be hard for you and I'd be happy to unpack this with you another time, but,"

"Why are you trying to push me away?" I interrupted with tears in my eyes. "You *get* me, Dr. Griffin! You get me like no one has! And I want to get to know you! I want to talk to you, to listen to you . . . to hold you and hug you and kiss you! I want to fall asleep next to you at night. I don't have to be your patient anymore. I can quit right now. I'll quit if you will tell me you have feelings for me!"

"I don't" he responded, his tone grave. "I'm sorry, but I don't look at you that way, Thea."

"You're a liar," I said as I tried not to cry.

I felt my lip tremble as I looked away. Dr. Griffin took a deep breath and after moments of silence, rose from his seat and walked over to me. He sat next to me on the couch and I felt his eyes burning on the side of my face.

"I'm not trying to hurt you," he whispered. "I care about you very much. I want to help you get better, Thea. I want to continue being your therapist. Please don't ruin our working relationship. Please just stop. Let this go. You don't really love me, I promise you. You only believe that you do. But in time, you will see this is a good thing. It's good to express your true emotions. We can work on doing the same thing in your other relationships."

"Fuck my other relationships," I laughed, looking back at him. "I'm good at reading energy and I feel the energy between me and you. I want to be with you, Doug. Please."

I reached my hand toward his face, but he quickly rose from the sofa and walked back to his seat.

"You need to stop this," he said, shaking his head at me. "We need to establish boundaries. If you want to continue seeing me, then you need to be professional."

"Shut the fuck up," I rolled my eyes before staring back at him. "Did you hear anything I just said? I told you I'm falling in love with you, Dr. Griffin! I told you I'd leave Lira to be with you! Can you stop with the shrink act for one minute and have an *actual* conversation with me?"

"It's not an act!" he replied in exasperation. "Are you fucking serious? This is my *job*, Thea! Do you want me to get fired?"

"Is that why you're playing hard to get?" I smirked.

He took a deep breath, seething as he stared at me. I held eye contact with him as I stood up – raising my dress over my head.

"What the fuck are you doing?" he asked, looking horrified as I threw my dress down on the ground.

"Just stop," I whispered as I laid down on the couch.

"Have you lost your mind?" he asked through clenched teeth. "Put your fucking clothes back on."

"Shh," I whispered as I pulled my panties down.

"Thea, this isn't funny," Dr. Griffin scolded. He stared at me with a mixture of anger and horror as I spread my legs open for him to see.

"Just shut the fuck up, Doug," I whispered as I began to rub my clit. "Shut the fuck up, please."

I closed my eyes and exhaled as I started rubbing my clit. The room was silent as I touched myself, breathing heavily as I relaxed into the cushions of the soft, black sofa.

"Sometimes at night, I go home and do this after our sessions," I whispered, biting my lip as I felt myself getting wetter. "I think about you on top of me and it really gets me ready."

I quickened my pace before beginning to finger myself. I felt the heat between my legs grow as I opened my eyes and looked back at him. He stared at me straight faced as I continued to pleasure myself.

"I want you inside me," I whispered, feeling my nipples get hard beneath his gaze. "I want to feel you push yourself inside me as you tell me you love me too."

I whimpered, feeling overcome by the sensations taking over me as Dr. Griffin stared at me like a statue.

"I want to really fuck you, Doug," I moaned, massaging my g-spot as I looked into his eyes. "I want to get on top of you and own you completely. I want you to know how bad I want it as you watch me right now. I want you inside me. I want you to cum inside me . . ."

I moaned quietly as I arched my back, fucking my hand as he watched me.

"I love that you're my doctor," I moaned. "It turns me on. Ohhh," I bit my lip, feeling my legs shake as he stared at me. "I love it, it feels so good, but you'd feel better. Don't you wish you could be balls deep in me right now – just *knowing* I'm your patient and *knowing* how vulnerable you make me? I'm yours you know, Doug. Ohh. I love you . . ."

Doug's throat bobbed as he watched me get myself closer. I whimpered softly as I maintained eye contact with him.

"You can come over here and finish this, yourself," I whispered. "Don't you want to? Don't you want me?"

He glared, shaking his head no as my vision began to blur.

"Come lick it," I begged. "Please, baby . . . please . . ."

I couldn't hold it anymore. I felt my legs tremble as I reached the best orgasm of my life – coming completely undone in front of him as I whimpered his name.

"Doug," I moaned softly, biting my lip as I looked back at him with watery eyes. "Doug."

I closed my eyes and panted for a moment, feeling my whole body flush with the orgasm that had just ripped through me. I had never experienced anything more erotic in my entire life! I felt alive as he watched me! It made me cum harder knowing that he was there.

I finally slowed my breathing enough to relax and sat up – looking over at him as I reached for my dress on the floor.

"Are you finished?" he asked through gritted teeth as I dressed myself in front of him.

"I think we both know that I am," I sighed.

"Do you feel better now?" he asked me, pursing his lips.

"You know I feel good," I smiled.

"You can *never* do that again, Dorothea – do you understand me?" he whispered. "I'm fucking serious. I hope you got that out of your system. If you *ever* pull something like this again, we're through."

"Whatever," I said, shrugging my shoulders.

"I'm not fucking around," he whispered. "You need to be fucking professional."

"I'm going to be out of town next week," I sighed as I fixed my hair in the mirror. "I'm going to Colorado with Lira, if you remember. So, we can skip next week and I'll see you when I get back?"

I turned to face him and he glared as he watched me.

"Is that okay with you?" I asked, smiling shyly.

"Never again, Thea," he repeated. "I'm not fucking with you."

"Fine," I whispered. "Just please think about me while I'm gone, okay? Think about how the fuck you were able to just try and convince yourself you don't have feelings for me. I know you didn't fuck me just now, but I was making love to you in my mind."

I blew him a kiss as I picked up my purse.

"Have a safe trip," Dr. Griffin muttered – still shooting daggers at me from where he sat.

"I'll miss you, Doug," I smiled before walking out the door.

I don't care what the fuck he told himself. That would go down in history as the single hottest moment of that man's life. He'd be masturbating to the thought of me until the day he died. I knew he'd miss me. He was just in denial.

CHAPTER 30

Week 11

D oug was all I could think about the entire drive to Colorado. I was convinced he was in love with me. I also wasn't stupid and understood his hesitancy in admitting it to me, considering his career was on the line. But our connection was something special. Maybe he just needed time! I couldn't believe I actually got naked and masturbated in the middle of our session, but desperate times call for desperate measures. I was hoping he enjoyed it as much as I did.

It was about a nine-hour drive from Salina, Kansas to Basalt, Colorado where Lira's aunt Helga lived. We had been visiting her every summer for the last several years and always looked forward to our mini road trip and mountain adventures.

Helga was a retired scientist and outdoor enthusiast. She didn't have any kids and never got married, so spoiled her nieces and nephews as if they were her own children. Lira was her favorite. Helga would always encourage us to try new and exciting things while we were there, and so we would typically spend a night or two at her cabin and a night or two branching off on our own.

There was a lot to do in the area. Basalt was a

vacationer's dream and it was no wonder Helga loved living there. It was an outdoor enthusiast's paradise. Tucked between the wondrous Sopris and Basalt mountains, there were countless activities to behold. There were hiking and mountain biking trails through thousands of acres of mountain wilderness. You could go fishing at the confluence of the Frying Pan River and the Roaring Fork River. You could go white water rafting and kayaking from west of Aspen, CO to Basalt – or go on a relaxing float trip down the lower 12-mile part of the Roaring Fork from Basalt to Carbondale, CO. There were lakes where you could go windsurfing, sailing, and skiing. Because Basalt was nestled between Glenwood Springs and Aspen, you could easily access the White River National Forest, which blankets Basalt on each side. Paddle boarding, hiking, biking, fishing, running, cycling . . . the possibilities were endless! The best part of all of this? Basalt was only *half an hour* away from Aspen, where Raymond believed Margot lived.

Everything was in order. I had spent almost the entirety of my night on the phone with Ray and planned on meeting him at a little café in downtown Aspen in two days' time. I just needed to figure out a way to dodge Lira. I didn't imagine it would be too hard. The drive from Salina to Basalt was lovely. Lira and I barely spoke to one another!

We were both fans of true crime and thrust ourselves into a couple podcasts about serial killers. You would be surprised how quick a little road trip can go when you spend it enthralled in murder and mystery.

We arrived at Helga's right around 5:00 PM MT. She waved at us from atop her enormous porch and smiled as her crazy corgi, Cobalt, bolted down the stairs in a fit of barking to greet us. Lira giggled as she turned off the car and launched the door open to meet him.

"Cobalt!" she squealed as he defied gravity and soared

into the driver's seat.

He licked her face enthusiastically as she smothered him in kisses before looking over at me with leeriness. Cobalt didn't love me as much as Lira and I could never understand why. I always showered him in attention, but he would always be so judgmental toward me – always watching from a close distance, but never close enough to let me love on him. With Lira, it was a different story. She was his moon and stars. I practically felt like the third wheel whenever we'd visit, as he would take up half of the bed to sleep next to her. It was funny, but it secretly hurt my feelings. I wondered what it was about me that he didn't fully embrace.

"I missed you so much, Buddy!" Lira crooned as she cupped his face in her hands.

His butt wiggled as he gazed into her. I rolled my eyes as I stepped out of the car, making my way around to the trunk to gather our things.

"Did you girls have a nice drive?" Helga called down to us as Lira exited the car with Cobalt in tow.

"It was beautiful!" Lira smiled. "Everything's so lush and beautiful over here! It's nothing like this in Kansas!"

"Kansas is the litterbox of America," Helga replied as Cobalt bolted up the steps to return to her. "Nothing out there but bugs, dirt, and bad weather! I don't know how I managed to live there as long as I did."

"Way to rub it in," I replied, smiling as we walked up the stairs to greet her.

"Oh Thea, come here," she grinned as she pulled me into a hug.

Helga had wild, long, curly hair of silver and grey that she wore half up/half down – pinned with a French barrette. Her eyes looked a smidgen too big – magnified by her round glasses that took over her face. She smelled like peppermint and essential oils and always gave the best hugs.

"I missed you," she said, squeezing me tight. "You seem healthy. Glad Lira's feeding you well out there."

I felt my cheeks flush as I pulled away from her. She pulled Lira in for a hug before kissing her on the cheek.

"Why do you only visit your old aunt once a year, Dear? You know you can come by whenever you want!"

"I know, it's just so hectic with work and everything," Lira laughed. "We wish we could come more often though! We always love visiting you!"

"Well, I have fish in the oven – so we'll have a nice supper tonight! I actually caught the bastard myself, this morning!"

"You did not," Lira laughed, her eyes widening.

"Not too bad for an old lady, huh?" Helga winked.

We followed her inside where we made our way to the kitchen, pulling up stools to the island where Helga began to finish chopping vegetables. She pulled a few bottles of beer out of the fridge, sliding them over to us before tossing the vegetables into a skillet of oil.

"So how are things out there, you two? How are you liking your new job, Lira? Are you and Thea talking about marriage yet?"

I fidgeted awkwardly as Lira laughed, looking over at me momentarily before reaching for my hand.

"Work's going really good! It's been pretty challenging working for myself! Photographers can be assholes, but I guess that just comes with the territory. And no talks of marriage yet!" Lira laughed.

"Well, you're not getting any younger!" Helga narrowed her eyes. "It's not like you two haven't been together for a thousand years, anyway! Might as well make it official."

"Way to put us on the spot," I laughed, smirking at Lira in amusement.

Lira laughed uncomfortably before taking a gulp of her beer.

"What about you, Thea? Work going good?"

I fidgeted awkwardly in my seat. "I'm currently looking for a new job. I wasn't happy at the publishing house. I'm more worried about Lira, though, honestly. Her stress levels have been through the roof!"

Lira gripped my hand, digging her nails into me as Helga gazed at her from across the island.

"What do you mean?" she asked.

"Tell her, Babe," I pouted. "Maybe she has some advice or tricks to make things better."

"Thea," Lira uttered between gritted teeth.

"Her hair's been falling out," I sighed. "I think it's alopecia."

"Oh, you don't say?" Helga said, tilting her head down to study Lira's scalp.

"It's embarrassing," Lira huffed. "But I'm taking vitamins and I went to the doctor. Everything seems to be normal, so I hope it's nothing serious."

"It's probably all of the shit that's in the water," Helga said as she shuffled the pan to redistribute the vegetables. "I'd start drinking bottled water and stop eating and drinking any of that crap with ingredients you can't pronounce! Go organic!"

"Yeah, that's a good idea," Lira sighed, smiling as she tucked a strand of hair behind her ear. "It's just humiliating. My hair has always been so healthy and beautiful. Losing it's been really humbling – I'll tell you what."

"It'll grow back, Dear." Helga replied. "Thea will love

you no matter how bald you get, won't you, Thea?"

I nodded as I took a swig of my beer.

"You're still beautiful, Lira. Don't focus on it too much. Stress can do crazy things to the human body."

"So, I've been told," Lira sighed. "But it's affecting my modeling shoots, so I can't exactly relax about it. I can't let this ruin my job."

"Oh honey," Helga frowned. "Just shave your head. It will be edgy. Photographers will eat that up."

"I would never," Lira laughed.

"So, you two are going camping tomorrow, is that right?" Helga asked as she peaked into the oven.

"We're really going to be roughing it!" I smirked. "None of that campground bullshit. We're hiking into the wilderness. I even got bear spray!"

"That's smart," Helga laughed. "Wildlife is everywhere out here this time of year. You two should have a great time! You still plan on spending a few days with me afterward, though, right?"

"Absolutely!" Lira grinned. "The only reason we're going tomorrow is because tomorrow's the nicest day this week!"

"It will still be pretty chilly at night, so I hope you girls brought plenty of blankets and warm clothes. If not, I can load you up with some of my stuff."

"No, we've got it," I smiled. "Lira even got this fancy tent on Amazon."

"Lira setting up a tent? Now that's something I wish I could see," Helga laughed.

I giggled as the two of us looked at Lira in amusement. She rolled her eyes, shaking her head at us as we teased her.

"Whatever, I'm not outdoorsy – so what!" she huffed. "I still appreciate the beauty of it all. I can't help it if I prefer having running water."

"Your mother babied the shit out of you," Helga chuckled. "If you were raised by me, you would have learned to *love* rolling around in the dirt. It's good for ya! Builds character and immunity! All of these kids get sick so easily these days because their parents don't let them eat dirt. People are so sheltered!"

"I agree," I laughed. "It should be fun though! I have been researching some cool areas for us to go. We'll be somewhere in The National Forest.

"Well, keep your phones on you and battery powered chargers," Helga warned. "I don't want you getting lost out there."

"We're on it!" Lira smiled. "I'm honestly excited to get out of the city and just be alone under the stars. It will be nice to connect with nature."

"I'm sure you'll have a lovely time," Helga smiled. "Dinner's just about ready! I hope you're hungry. This guy put up quite the fight!"

We laughed as we head for the table. Visiting Helga always felt like coming home.

The evening with Helga went wonderfully. We ate dinner, played cards, and talked about life together. We ate dessert out on the porch and watched the sunset – basking in the warm summer air. When it was time for bed, we parted ways. Helga made her way upstairs. She always had the basement made out for us. Cobalt followed us downstairs, struggling to jump up onto the mattress with his stubby legs. Lira picked him up and kissed him on the nose before setting him down on her pillow. He glared begrudgingly at me as I lifted the covers to get into bed.

"I need to talk to you," Lira whispered, just as I was about to turn off the lamp on the nightstand.

I froze, staring into her big brown eyes as she stared at me. She took a deep breath, gripping the blanket as she began to speak.

"Thea, I'm not happy anymore," she said to me.

I stared at her, unable to believe if I had heard her correctly. Did those words really just come out of her mouth?!

"What?" I whispered.

"I know you're not stupid," she shook her head. "I mean, I know you have probably sensed I've been distant. I feel horrible about this, Thea, but I haven't been happy for a really long time."

I gulped, sitting in silence as she looked up at me with tears in her eyes.

"Can you please say something?" she asked me.

"I don't know what to say," I responded. "Can you please elaborate?"

"What do you want me to say to you?" she whispered. "It's been eating me up inside, but I can't just go around pretending anymore!"

"Pretending what?" I asked, feeling my heart beat faster.

"That everything's okay!" she responded. "I don't know what to do about it because I love you, Thea! You're my best friend in the whole wide world, but that passion between us has been fizzling."

"And why do you think that is?" I asked, glaring at her.

"I don't know . . ." she replied, her voice trailing off. "I think we both just got sucked into our own lives, you know? The romance has just suffered."

"I'm feeling pretty blind-sided right now," I whispered,

pursing my lips. "Because you haven't given me any reason to think you've been unhappy. If you have been so unhappy, then why is this the first time I'm hearing about it?"

"I was scared," she said, her lip trembling. "I didn't want to lose you."

"But you do now?" I replied. "Why? Why now?"

"No," she sighed, wiping her face before reaching for my hand. "I still don't want to lose you."

I huffed in exasperation as I stared back at her.

"What do you want, Lira?" I asked. "Is there someone else or something? Just say what you fucking mean! Use your fucking words!"

"There's no one else," she said, scooting closer to me. "I don't want to break up, Thea. I just need to be honest with you."

I stared at her in bewilderment as she gazed at me. She wasn't going to tell me about Tess? Was this because Tess had backed off from her? Suddenly she wanted to work things out with me?

"I think you and I can fix things," she said – her voice shaking as she tried to catch her breath. "I think relationships take hard work and I haven't been putting in the effort you deserve. I don't want to give up on us just because we've gone through a rough spot."

"You're the one who's been going through a rough spot," I said to her, shaking my head in annoyance. "You've been leading me to believe everything is fine, so don't try to put this on me!"

"Okay, you're right!" she replied, looking hopeless as she gazed at me with desperation. "I don't want to just be friends with you, Thea! I need *passion*! I need to feel lusted after and longed for! I want to feel sexy, not cute! I want there to be excitement in our relationship, not routine! I want to feel alive again!"

"Are you having a mid-life crisis?" I asked, shaking my head. "What? So I don't treat you slutty enough?"

"We used to have sex in public places!" she sighed, slapping her hands into the blankets at her sides. "We used to text cute and sexy things to each other all day, every day! Now it seems like all we talk about is what we're going to have for dinner! That's so fucking boring to me, Thea! I'm BORED! There, I said it! You fucking bore me!"

I gaped at her, not knowing if I should laugh or cry.

"Well, then," I said, looking away. "Thanks for the clarification."

"I'm sorry," she whispered. "I don't want to feel this way, Dorothea. I don't! Please . . ." she reached over and placed my face in her hands, turning me to look at her. "I haven't been fair to you. I haven't been communicating. But I want to fight for this relationship. I want the chance to try."

I felt dizzy as she stroked my cheek with her thumb.

"Can we please try and fix our relationship? I don't want to give up on us, Thea. Please forgive me for not communicating with you. I'm so fucking sorry! I *promise* you I won't lie to you again! Can we *please* try and make things better? I know this feels like it's coming out of nowhere, so I understand if you're hurt and pissed off, but I just need to feel wanted, Thea! I want this week to be a fresh start for us! *Please* can we do this? Please don't give up on me!"

I didn't know what to say. This was certainly a curve ball. Sure, Lira was still a fucking liar and omitting her entire affair with Tess, but was that important in the big picture? She was coming to me with her concerns and seemed sincere in her want to make things better. Was this whole thing with Tess just a fluke she needed to get out of her system in order to feel desired? Had I neglected her somehow? Was I a *bad* girlfriend? Is this why this happened? Did I push her into another woman's arms? My mind raced as she stared into me with her desperate brown eyes – just waiting for an answer.

"I want to start over," she whispered. "I want to make things better between us."

"So no more lies," I said, holding my breath as I looked back at her. "If we do this . . . if we give this a real shot, I need to know you're not going to keep hiding things from me. You need to talk to me when you're upset about something. You need to be able to communicate with me."

"I promise," she insisted, kissing my hands as tears streamed down her cheeks. "I haven't been good to you, Thea. I know I haven't. I haven't been honest."

No shit, asshole.

"And you think things can be different now?" I asked.

"Yes," she whispered. "I'm ready to really make this my number one priority."

I took a deep breath, not knowing what to think. I had spent weeks hating this bitch. I had actually considered ending her life at one point because she was betraying me. I lost one of my best friends because of her!

What if she was being honest? What if she was ready to change her whorish ways and actually step up in this relationship? Didn't I owe it to myself to give her a chance? Shouldn't I at least try?

"Dorothea, I love you," she said, biting her lip. "Even though that love has shifted, I know I can get it back if we can just connect again. It's not too late. I want to spend my life with you. I want us to be close again."

I swallowed hard, looking away from her. This was *not* how I thought this was going to go. Maybe now that horse tooth Tess was out of the picture, she realized what she was giving up. I nodded my head as I looked back at her.

"If I ever find out that you're lying to me like this again, this is over," I whispered. "I mean it, Lira. No more games."

She stared at me in shock. I wondered if she guessed that I knew she was keeping more from me. It didn't matter. I would give her another chance. Only one last chance. For some fucked up reason, I believed everything she was saying.

"No more lies," she assured me. "I'm ready to dedicate myself to this completely."

"Okay," I said, nodding my head. "Then it's settled."

She smiled before leaning in slowly to kiss me. Cobalt growled as I pushed him aside, pulling her into me. She wanted to feel wanted? Was that really what all of this was about?

I felt angry and frustrated as I thought about how I had managed to fail her. I always prided myself with how good I was in bed. Was I really that fucking *boring*? I felt sick as her words echoed in my mind. I would show her how exciting things could be.

I fucked Lira like it was our first time. I prayed Helga was a heavy sleeper because I pulled out all of the stops for this one. I couldn't have my girlfriend feeling unsatisfied. I felt like an idiot now that I knew what the deal was. It was an easy fix. I had her shaking and panting and quivering, helplessly beneath me. I didn't stop until she squirted on my face – unable to handle anymore.

She cried afterward as I held her in my arms, kissing my cheeks softly as she told me over and over again how sorry she was. I told her it would be okay. I told myself it would be okay too. But something deep in my stomach haunted me as she drifted off to sleep. We had just had some of the hottest sex of my life, but something was missing. No matter how hard I tried, when I came, I only thought of Doug's face.

CHAPTER 31

I woke up early in the morning as the sun was coming up. I gently woke Lira, telling her I wanted to take the car to get some last-minute camping supplies and get a quick workout in. She dazedly told me that was fine and asked how long I would be gone. I said a few hours, tops. I tiptoed up the stairs, staying as quiet as possible so that I wouldn't disturb Helga from her slumbers. I grabbed my purse and keys and crept out the door, feeling the chilly morning air kiss my face as I sent a text to Ray.

Margot: I can't wait any longer I need to see you *now*! Want to grab some breakfast?

The drive to Aspen was quick. Ray had arrived the night before and was staying at a hotel in town. He was excited that I had reached out to him so early, and eagerly agreed that we should meet. We had agreed to meet up at a popular diner - and I felt lightheaded and dizzy with nerves as I sat in the parking lot, staring at the building ahead.

Come on, you can do this! I told myself as I opened the trunk and reached under the spare tire for the bag of supplies I had brought with me.

I pulled out a short blond wig and squatted behind my

car, pulling my hair up into a bun before putting the wig on. I grabbed a pair of oversized sunglasses and put them on my face before checking myself out in the side mirror. I didn't look like myself. Even though I knew it had been six years, I wanted to be sure Ray wouldn't recognize me. I popped a couple of Xanax before locking the car to head inside.

The diner was busy. I was seated at a little table in the back of the restaurant with a perfect view of the rest of the floor and sipped on my coffee nervously as my phone vibrated. I nonchalantly glanced down and read the text from Ray – holding my breath as I read his words.

Ray: It's finally happening, Baby! I'm walking in the door now!

I looked up, hearing the bells on the door jingle as Raymond made his way inside. His blond curls blew in the breeze before he stepped into the doorway. He was huskier than I remembered him in person. His green eyes lit up as he scanned the restaurant for Margot's face. I looked down and texted him as discreetly as possible.

Margot: Grab a table for us. I'm almost there!

Raymond beamed as he looked down at his phone screen – smiling wider than I had ever seen him smile before as he got a booth close by. My heart was racing. I sipped on my coffee as he stared at the door – perking up with anticipation each time someone new would walk in. Fifteen minutes passed and he started to look worried. He started texting and I held my phone on my lap, feeling it vibrating as his message came in.

Ray: Is everything okay, Babe? I'm sitting at the booth

to the left when you walk in.

A couple more minutes passed and he seemed anxious – fidgeting awkwardly in his seat.

Ray: Baby, I'm worried. Am I at the right place?

I started eating my omelet, watching bemusedly as he visibly began to panic. I couldn't believe I had gotten him to drive nine hours away to meet someone he didn't even know. I couldn't *believe* I had gotten him to fall in love with said person! I almost felt sorry for him as he looked around for her. *Almost*.

My phone started vibrating. I let it go to voicemail and listened as he spoke into his phone.

"Hey Margot, it's Ray. I've been waiting here for almost a half an hour now. I hope everything's okay . . . Please call me back. I'm worried. I love you."

He hung up the phone and shook his head, furrowing his brow as he looked out the window for her. I finished my breakfast and patted my lips with my napkin before sending a text to him. I watched his eyes widen as he read it. I stared – feeling my heart flutter with excitement as he stared at his phone.

Margot: You're fucking pathetic. It's actually quite sad.

He shook his head as he frantically drafted a response.

Ray: What? What do you mean?

I took a deep breath as I made my way to Margot's fake profile. I deleted the page and then pulled up my Google Voice app. I disconnected the number associated with Margot. She would now be completely unreachable. He would find no trace of her anywhere. If he called, it would be a bad number. If he texted, it wouldn't go through. If he tried to search for her on the dating site, her profile would be deleted. It would be like she never existed at all.

He picked up the phone and shook his head in denial – staring in horrified sadness at the wall ahead of him, as he attempted to call again.

I took a sip of my coffee, feeling a little sad that it was over. It was anticlimactic. I was happy, but still left wanting more. He messed with his phone for several minutes – I assume looking for Margot's profile – before setting the phone down and staring vacantly at the empty spot across from him.

I watched with curiosity as tears began to well up in his eyes. I had never seen Ray cry before. He took a deep breath as he gazed out the window after wiping a tear from his cheek.

I wondered what Ray was thinking. I could only imagine the unanswered questions swirling around in his mind. I thought about the countless nights I had stared at my phone after reaching out to him. I thought about the missed calls and unanswered texts. I thought about the nights I cried myself to sleep, crumpled up in the fetal position after *begging* him to respond. I thought about the hand written letter where I had poured my heart out to him – telling him I just needed closure. If he could just give me closure, I would be able to move on. I thought about how he dismissed me. I thought about his conversation with Margot and how he had told her I was crazy. I thought about how he made me feel less than *nothing*. Disposable. Like trash.

I closed my tab and took one last look at him. Now, he

would get a glimpse of how it feels. He would *never* get an answer to any of his texts or phone calls. He would *never* know what happened or what went wrong. He would spend the rest of his life wondering what the fuck had just happened. He would question his reality and his sanity. He would wonder if it was ever real. He would wonder if she loved him. He would wonder what he did wrong. He would *never* get an answer though. He would *never* get the closure he would so desperately need. He would lie awake at night and think about her. He would *never* know what happened. It would haunt him. I hoped that at some point in his misery – if only for a second – he would think of me and what he did to me. The only answer he would ever receive is silence. And this comforted me as I walked out the door.

Goodbye, Raymond, I whispered to myself, as I got in my car.

I took a deep breath, feeling a weight lift off of my shoulders. I looked at myself in the rearview mirror, smiling at the blond headed reflection on the other side. I smiled as I reached into the bag and pulled out the iPad. I had been so focused on my revenge on Raymond that I had neglected checking in on everything with my girlfriend.

Girlfriend. It felt so funny the think of her that way again. I couldn't believe the conversation we had shared the night prior had actually happened. I felt so *hopeful* that things would actually change. I needed to check in and see what was going on between her and Tess now. Hopefully, that large forehead of hers would stay the fuck away now that we were working things out. I got excited as I imagined how Lira broke the news to her. My heart pounded as I pulled up their text thread.

I stared in confusion as I began to scroll. I felt a wave of nausea hit me as I read the conversation they had been having this morning. My ears started ringing as blood rushed to my head. I read faster, feeling frantic as my eyes danced across the words.

Lira: Who told you I was a sex addict? *Angry emoji*. Who in the *fuck* would even say that about me?

Tess: I already told you it doesn't matter, Babe. I realize it isn't true now. Just a jealous psycho trying to get in-between our relationship.

Lira: Well, who have you even been telling about our relationship?! This doesn't even make any sense!

Tess: I've told a couple of people, but have been careful to make sure it doesn't get back to you. I'm sorry, Lira! I just got in my head! I already told you I was sorry last night!

Lira: To think you thought I was a *sex addict*, LOL! *Laughing emoji*. Tess, you should have talked to me! I *knew* something was wrong!

Tess: Well, I meant what I said earlier. It's time, Lira. You need to leave Thea.

Lira: Okay well wait! I told you this morning when I talked to you about what happened last night - I thought we were done, Tess. I told Thea I was going to work things out with her. I need to make it look like I'm giving it another shot before breaking up with her now.

Tess: I can't believe you were going to go back to her just because you thought I was done with you. *Throwing up

emoji*. Do you know how pathetic that is, Babe?

Lira: It's complicated. I told you, we've been friends for a really long time. I told her there was no passion anymore, though. I told her we'd have to work on it.

Tess: You guys are toxic! You're not in love with her and Thea knows it. She's grasping at straws just to keep you. She's a fucking psychopath.

Lira: You don't know her! She was blind-sided.

Tess: Yeah, I'm sure. *Eye roll emoji*. Fine, do what you gotta do. But you're going to sign the lease with me next Monday for the new apartment, right?

Lira: Absolutely. *Smiley emoji*. I'll meet up with you on my lunch and we can go to the leasing office then.

Tess: Okay, perfect! I'm happy we're actually doing this, Babe. I love you. I'm ready to start my life with you.

Lira: I'm ready too. *Heart emoji*. I can't wait to see you again.

I closed the iPad and gripped the steering wheel, feeling my knuckles turn white as tears brimmed my eyes. I screamed at the top of my lungs, slamming my hands into the steering wheel. I hit it over and over again as tears poured out of my eyes.

YOU FUCKING LYING BITCH! I wailed as I picked up my

cell phone.

This was it for me! I had finally reached my breaking point! Lira had managed to get me to let her in and give her the benefit of the doubt, but she really just didn't give a flying *fuck* about me! She was manipulating me so that she wouldn't be alone!

I hyperventilated as I dialed Dr. Griffin's number. My hands trembled as the phone rang several times before reaching his voicemail. I knew I had to act quickly. I knew there wasn't much time.

"Doug, I'm sorry," I cried into the cellphone. "I tried to listen to you – I *tried*. Lira lied to me . . . she's lying! She said she wanted to work things out with me, but she's *still* going to leave me for *Tess*! I can't do this anymore, Douglas! I can't! I'm going to kill her! I'm going to fucking kill her! Go ahead and call the cops on me, I don't fucking care! Maybe I *need* to be thrown in jail! Maybe I *am* dangerous! I'm *not* going to let her do this to me again! I'm not going to let her ruin my life! I love you, Dr. Griffin! I mean it! I hope you know how much I care about you. I'm sorry if this makes you think less of me! But I'm done. I honestly want to die! If I had a gun, I'd shoot myself right now. I feel like I've lost everything! I can't lose anything else. There's nothing left. I'm going to make her pay for this. She's going to pay."

I sobbed into the receiver before hanging up the phone. I took several deep breaths, trying to calm myself down before taking the wig off. I turned the rearview mirror down and fixed my makeup before exhaling and putting the car into reverse.

Well. Time to go camping! I smiled as I pulled out of the parking lot.

I was *really* looking forward to spending some quality time with my girlfriend. I knew she was probably just *dying* to get the show on the road.

CHAPTER 32

The White River National Forest encompasses 2.3 million acres. There are 2,500 miles of trails and 1,900 miles of Forest Service System roads. There are 4 major reservoirs and 8 wildlife areas. There are countless campgrounds, but camping is also permitted outside of developed campgrounds, also known as dispersed camping. This was something I had been looking forward to and with some coaxing, I had managed to convince Lira to be adventurous and rough it with me. I wanted to get lost with her. I wanted to go deep into the woods where we could be at one with nature. I wanted us to be isolated. I wanted us secluded enough that no one would be able to hear her scream.

Camping wasn't really Lira's thing as much as it was mine. I had been going practically every summer for as long as I could remember with my family, and knew how to survive on my own with very little supplies. I could start a fire by myself. I could fish. I knew how to look out for predators – just the basic stuff. I wouldn't call myself outdoorsy by any means, but I wasn't sheltered from the outdoors the way that Lira was. For this reason, we typically camped in designated campground areas, close to many others. If Lira had it her way, we would have brought a motor home.

But, I really wanted to get a little more *daring* this time. I wanted us to hike and explore the woods. I promised her I had done it countless times before and that it would be *fun*. We were ready. I even had her looking forward to pitching a tent in the middle of the woods.

We got an early start and by late afternoon, had hiked several miles from where we had left our car. It was hard work. I let Lira rest while I got the tent set up and felt a shiver up my spine as I pulled out our dinner supplies from my backpack and took another look at the 10-inch chef knife I had carried with me.

I had spent some time sharpening it before we left and had it wrapped carefully in several layers of clothes. Lira read a book as I got the fire going – and I was relieved when she set her phone down on a stump, before heading off into the trees to use the bathroom.

I was surprised we had any service at all out here – no matter how patchy. As she disappeared into the woods, I quickly grabbed her phone and dropped it into the pot of boiling water I had going on the fire. I watched as the screen turned to black before pulling it out with tongs – drying it as quickly and frantically as I could before setting it back onto the stump where she had left it. I felt my heart begin to race as she returned, but quickly felt a wave of relief as she reached for her book and not her phone and continued reading. I prepared some easy macaroni for us – humming softly to myself as I enjoyed the beauty of the outdoors.

"Do you think there's lot of bears out here?" Lira asked as she put her book down after several minutes of blissful quiet. "I really hope they aren't out here with us. I watched a movie about some couple that got attacked by a bear while out camping."

"Lira, we're in Colorado," I replied, staring dumbfounded back at her. "It's literally *bear country*."

"Well, that doesn't make me feel any better," she shivered, holding her hands out toward the fire. "You're supposed to lie to me and tell me that we're perfectly safe out here."

"I never said we weren't safe," I smiled. "As long as we do things correctly, there should be no reason they come poking around for food. Most of the time they are more afraid of us than we are of them. Just try not to think about it. But also, respect the fact that this is *their* home. But also," I waved a can of bear spray, "just in case."

"Ugh, fine," she sighed as I handed her a bowl of macaroni. "It's just so isolated out here."

"It's awesome, isn't it?" I grinned.

"It kind of gives me the heebie jeebies."

The fire cracked and popped – the air smelling of sweet smoke as we shared our final meal. The sun was starting to lower in the sky – the trees casting grey and haunting shadows all around us as the temperature began to drop. I stared across the fire at Lira as she ate her food – gazing out into the trees to her side as I watched her.

I wondered what she was thinking about. I wondered if she was counting the seconds until she could return to Tess. I felt a calm come over me as I reached down into the backpack at my side and pulled out the iPad.

"You know, there was a time when I thought you would be the last person in the world to hurt me," I said, pulling her attention away.

Lira stared back at me in confusion as I penetrated her with my gaze.

"I really thought you loved me, you know? If someone had told me six months ago what you were capable of, I would have laughed in their face."

Lira swallowed, sitting silently as the pops and cracks of the embers in the fire filled the space between us with ambient noise.

"What are you talking about?" she finally asked, trying to look calm.

I smiled slightly before raising the iPad up to face her.

"You know, I didn't want to believe it for a long time, but I'm pretty impressed with how you've been able to pull it off," I said, watching as her eyes began to widen as she stared at the device in my hands. "I mean, to imagine the *dedication* one has to have to maintain a five-month affair. It's pretty incredible."

Lira's mouth slightly opened as I pulled up their conversation.

"And after the night we had last night, I mean – I was hopeful. I thought maybe there was a chance for us after all and that maybe some part of you was actually *human.* You can imagine how disappointing it was for me to read your conversation with Tess this morning about leaving me and signing a lease." I clicked my tongue, shaking my head as I looked back up at her. "It's really disheartening."

The fire glistened in the tears that began to pool in Lira's eyes. Her shoulders rose and fell with her exhilarated breaths as she stared at me in shock. For what felt like hours, we sat there in silence just looking into each other – waiting for one of us to speak first.

"How long have you known?" she whispered.

"Does it really matter?" I answered.

"Thea," she said, her voice shaking. "It's not what you think."

"Oh my God, it's not what I think? *Really*? Is that the best you can do?" I laughed. "Are you fucking kidding me, Lira?"

"Baby, please," she said, standing up to walk over to me.

"Stay the fuck away from me," I warned, gazing up at

her with hatred in my eyes as I took the last bite of my food.

Lira froze there, looking panicked as she gazed down at me. I took a deep breath, avoiding eye contact as I stared into the fire.

"Thea, I'm so sorry," she cried – her voice breaking as she took another step closer. "Please just talk to me – we can talk about this! I don't even know what to say! I have wanted to talk to you about this for such a long time, but I was afraid, Dorothea! I didn't know how to tell you!"

"How to tell me what?" I asked, glaring up at her as I rose to my feet. "You didn't know how to tell me you were cheating on me for months and months? Leading me on mercilessly like it was a *game?*"

"Thea, I *love* you," she choked as tears streamed down her cheeks. "I never wanted to hurt you!"

"Don't use that word," I warned her. "I don't think you know what it means."

I wondered if now would be a good time to stab her. I thought about how long it would take for the police to find me. They might already be looking for me, if Dr. Griffin alerted the authorities once he got my voicemail from this morning.

I wondered if I had a chance of fleeing to Canada. Maybe I could run away and start a new life – create a new identity somewhere.

Lira sobbed as she took another step closer to me, reaching her hands out as she pleaded with me to listen.

"Thea, please don't hate me," she cried. "I didn't mean for any of this to happen – I swear to God, I didn't! I got in way over my head and I didn't know how to talk to you because I didn't want to ruin the friendship we've had!"

"It's already ruined," I said, biting my lip. "It was ruined the moment you decided to betray me. Maybe if it was a onetime thing, I could have gotten over it. But *this*, Lira?" I said as I waved the iPad in her face. "This is unforgivable."

"I'm sorry," she sobbed as she reached for my face.

I pushed her back, watching her stumble backward as I took a step toward her.

"I gave *everything* to you," I spat, gritting my teeth. "I threw away one of the most cherished friendships I have ever had to be with you! I thought you *loved* me! I thought you were my *friend!*"

"Thea please," she wailed, shaking her head at me. "I love you so much, Thea! I am your friend!"

"You're a fucking *whore*," I yelled, feeling tears fall from my eyes. "You never *cared* about me! You don't do what you did to someone you love!"

"I never wanted to hurt you!" she cried, crouching down on the ground, placing her head in her hands. "I'm *sorry*, Thea! I don't know what to say! I was a *coward!* I didn't want to lose my best friend!"

"I fucking *hate* you, Lira," I said, bending down to say it close to her ear. "I hate you and hope you spend the rest of your life knowing you fucked up one of the best things you've ever had for some fucking fling that isn't even going to last that long!"

"Thea please don't say that!" she howled, looking up at me with her swollen brown eyes. "Please! I love you! You're my best friend!"

"You're dead to me," I said, glaring down at her as my heart began to race.

"Thea, I can explain!"

"Try me," I fumed.

Lira held her breath, pinching her eyes shut before blurting out her alleged "explanation" to me.

"I'm in love with you both, ok!"

I gaped at her, not knowing how to respond. "What?"

"I can't explain it, ok? I didn't know it was even possible, but I'm in love with two people! I want to be with you both! I haven't been able to tell Tess yet because I know she wouldn't like it and I always knew I had to talk to you about it first – but . . ."

She cried as she gazed up at me with despair.

"Wait," I laughed as I processed what was being said to me. "You wanted to talk to me about this? For what possible reason?!"

"I want to be with you both!"

I couldn't believe what the fuck I was hearing. I watched as she got up, brushing the dirt off of her pants as she ran a hand through her hair. She took a step closer to me – pleading with me to listen.

"Dorothea, I think you guys would really like each other! You're both so different, but you both give me things I need and want in a relationship! I think if you two got to know each other that you would-"

"You fucking looney Bitch!" I cackled, stepping back. "You honestly thought you could cheat on me for months and then pitch a *throuple* situation to me? What is the *matter* with you?!"

"I don't want to lose you!" she wailed.

Now was the perfect time. I should grab the knife and slit her throat. I could hike back to the car before it got too late out. I could set her corpse on fire or leave her for the bears.

"Please don't leave me," she begged, grabbing my wrists. "Please, Thea! I'll break up with Tess! My relationship with her doesn't mean as much as my relationship with you! Please! We can call her right now and I'll end everything! I'll tell her everything!"

"Are you fucking delusional?" I said, staring down at her in bewilderment. "I don't believe a fucking word that comes out of your mouth! You had your chance to leave her and you didn't! You told her you were going to play it out to make it look like you gave our relationship a shot before ending things with me! You're a fucking crazy bitch if you think there's a chance in hell that I'm staying with you now!"

"I know, but I didn't mean it! I always planned on eventually getting you two together to talk about how I feel! But now that I'm losing you, I realize what a horrible mistake I've made!" She sobbed, hiccupping as she tried to catch her breath. "I'll go to therapy – we can go to counseling! I'll do *anything*, Dorothea! I can't lose you! You're my best friend!" She threw her arms around me.

I wiggled out of her grasp, taking a step back as I clenched my hands into fists at my side.

"I don't love you anymore, Lira," I said, holding back tears. "The person I thought I loved doesn't exist."

I stared down into the darkness of her eyes and wanted to vomit. Why couldn't I be strong in this moment? Why did I have to let her see me vulnerable like this?

"I fucking hate you," I whispered, shaking my head.

Fuck this! I couldn't kill her whilst snot was dripping out of my nose and tears were streaming down my face. I needed to keep my shit together! I needed a moment to clear my head! I grabbed my backpack and shoved the iPad inside, glaring down at her before swinging it over my shoulders.

"Where are you going?" Lira asked, staring helplessly up at me as I stepped away from her.

"Shut the fuck up," I said. "I need a little space, ok? Just give me a bit to think."

"Thea, please," she begged, still gazing at me.

"I'm going for a walk," I said, wiping my cheeks. "If you love me at all, then you *won't* follow me."

I heard her continue to cry as I turned and walked away from the campsite, making my way quickly into the trees. I needed to calm down and keep my wits about me. I didn't want her to see that she had hurt me.

I didn't even know why I was crying at this point! I meant it when I said I didn't love her anymore! At this point, I think I was crying from the humiliation of it all. I couldn't believe she had tricked me into believing she was worthy of a second chance after everything she had done to me! And to think that she actually thought I would be game for three way relationship with her pony ass bitch! She really was the most fucking hideous human being on the face of this planet. I would enjoy ending her life!

After about 20 minutes of hiking through the trees, I reached a trail and paused to get a drink of water. I reached into my backpack and pulled out my water bottle, but froze as I heard the breaking of twigs in the distance.

Every hair on my body stood up as I looked out ahead of me. The sun had started to set and the barely lit trail looked desolate as my eyes searched for the source of the noise. Was it a wild animal? The sound was pretty loud. I hated that Lira had put the thought in my mind, but I began to wonder if it could be a bear.

I heard shuffling and the crunching of walking ahead of me and held my breath as a figure began to emerge up ahead. My heart was thumping in my chest as the silhouette got closer – coming into focus with each step it took. I blinked several times, wondering if I was hallucinating as the person slowly approached me.

"There you are, Thea," Dr. Griffin sighed as he walked

toward me. "Please fucking tell me that I'm not too late."

CHAPTER 33

I stood in shock as Dr. Griffin walked toward me. The dim lighting of the fading sun painted him a shadowed hue of blue. My mouth hung open as I stared at him in astonishment. How the fuck did he find me out here? What the hell was I supposed to do now?

"Douglas?" I asked as he cautiously approached.

He was wearing a black jacket, jeans and hiking boots. His curly hair wisped in tendrils over his forehead and his dark eyes were wide with expression – *fear* being the predominant look on his face. He stopped in front of me and I shook my head in complete and total confusion as he began to speak.

"Thea, you didn't . . . did you?"

"What are you doing here!?" I asked him, still unable to wrap my mind around this entire situation. "How did you find me?"

He stared dumbfounded at me as he pulled out his phone to show me his screen.

"You shared your location with me, remember?" he exhaled. "Now, answer me, please! You didn't do it, did you?"

I held my breath as I stared back at him. Of course. I had taken his phone during one of our sessions and shared my location in an attempt to be flirty and cute. What an *idiot*! I wanted to scream as he stared at me, waiting for an answer.

"Did you call the police?" I asked, looking nervously behind him. "Are they coming? Do they know I'm here?"

"No, I didn't fucking call the police!" he growled at me. "*Should* I though?! You aren't answering my question!"

"What question?!" I asked frantically as I tried to figure out what the fuck was going on.

"I got your voicemail," he said. "You said you were going to kill her. Where's Lira, Thea? What did you do?"

I huffed, rolling my eyes in annoyance as I glared up at him.

"She's fine, Doug," I whispered through gritted teeth. "She's back at the campsite. I confronted her about the affair and stormed off to clear my head. This definitely puts a damper on my plans."

"So she's all right?" he exhaled, placing his hand over his heart. "Jesus Christ, thank *God*, Thea! I got here as quickly as I could. I was so afraid I would be too late!"

I furrowed my brow in confusion as I stared up at him. He looked visibly more relaxed as he looked at me through his dark rimmed glasses.

"Wait, why the fuck are you here?" I asked, feeling confused. "I left you a voicemail telling you I was planning on murdering my girlfriend! Shouldn't you have turned me into the police or something?"

He took a deep breath as he avoided eye contact with me. I took a step toward him as I waited for an explanation.

"If you didn't call the police, then what are you doing here?" I repeated.

He looked back at me – his expression annoyed and frustrated as he pressed his glasses up the bridge of his nose.

"I was worried about you," he responded. "I took your voicemail seriously. I hopped on the first flight I could find to

Colorado and tracked you down because I didn't want you to do something fucking *stupid*. I was hoping you were just having a mental breakdown! When I saw you were in the actual *National Forest*, I started to panic!"

I huffed in exasperation as I stared back up at him.

"That doesn't make any sense!" I replied, shaking my head. "If you really thought I was going to murder somebody, wouldn't you be required to alert the authorities? Why the fuck did you get on a plane and . . ." My voice trailed off as I stared at him. His eyes shifted as he looked away in shame.

"Oh my God," I laughed – not able to believe it. "Did you come here because . . . do you . . . are you in LOVE with me?!"

He scoffed as he looked back at me, crossing his arms across his chest as he shook his head. I couldn't contain my laughter and felt myself getting dizzy as he gazed down at me.

"Don't be so presumptuous," he responded, shaking his head.

"Well, please explain!" I gasped, unable to hide my smile.

He hesitated, pressing his lips into a thin line before finally looking back at me. I watched his pupils dilate as he took a step closer.

"I care about you, Thea," he replied, his voice full of defeat and a hint of resentment. "I didn't want you to make a terrible mistake."

"You care about me?" I repeated, raising my brow.

He sighed before slowly nodding his head.

"Dorothea, this isn't ethical," he whispered. "You *have* to know that everything about this is wrong."

"Everything about what? Me telling you that I'm going to murder my girlfriend, or you following me out into the woods to make sure that I don't?"

"*All of it*," he snapped. "This whole thing crosses so many boundaries. But I knew that before coming here."

There was silence between us as I let that sink in. I heard the whisper of wind dancing through the branches of the trees and felt a shiver as the temperature began to drop. I was quickly losing daylight and didn't know what I should do now that Doug had shown up here. This certainly threw a wrench in what I had planned.

"If you came here to stop me, don't bother," I looked away from him. "If you mean what you say and really care about me, then just turn around and walk away."

"Not going to happen," he responded – his voice stone.

I glared at him, growing impatient as he took another step toward me.

"You don't have to do this, Thea," he said calmly. "You're angry and hurt, but you aren't a murderer."

"You don't know what I'm capable of," I huffed.

"I *know* you," he continued. "I know what's in your heart."

"That's a pretty weird thing for a therapist to say."

"I'm not your fucking therapist," he said, shaking his head at me. "I mean . . . I'm not your therapist anymore."

I raised my eyebrows, feeling confused as he looked down at me.

"Is this because I'm a psycho?" I asked, feeling my heartrate increase. "What? I'm too crazy for you to help anymore?"

"You're not a psycho, Thea," he replied, shaking his head at me. "If sanity were a cliff you could jump off of –into psychopathy – you wouldn't leap. But you'd certainly stand on the edge. You'd be surprised how many people dance on the precipice. But that isn't why I won't be your therapist anymore."

I stared at him, not understanding.

"Then why?" I whispered.

"Oh so *now* you play coy?" he replied as he took a step closer to me. "What happened to you being so good at reading energy?"

I felt lightheaded as he slowly reached for my hand. I gulped, locking eyes with him. He had never willingly gotten this close to me before. The way he was looking at me made me dizzy.

"I hate everything about this, Thea. I tried to fight it, but I just can't pretend anymore."

"Pretend what?" I whispered, feeling weak as I locked eyes with him.

"That I don't care too much about you," he whispered – his voice almost muted beneath the rustling of the leaves. "It isn't appropriate for me to be your therapist anymore. Not when I feel this way about you."

I couldn't believe what I was hearing as I felt him place his hands on the small of my back. He had followed me out here because he *cared about me*?! But what exactly did that mean?

"What do you mean when you say you care too much?" I asked him.

He smiled, shaking his head as he penetrated me with his knowing eyes.

"I wanted to hate you after what you did in our last session," he whispered. "I was so angry at you for trying to cross the line with me, but the more I thought about it, the more I realized that what you were saying was true. I *do* have feelings for you, Thea. It's wrong on so many levels and goes against *everything* I stand for, but it's true. When I got your voicemail, it just solidified for me how much you actually mean to me. I didn't want you to do anything and risk ruining your life over something as foolish as Lira hurting you! I can *help* you, Thea! And I want to! But I just can't in good conscience do it as your therapist anymore."

I held my breath, licking my lips as I gazed back at him.

"And why is that?" I asked him.

"Because therapists can't fall for their patients," he said – his eyes darkening as he pulled me into him.

He crushed into me and I moaned as he coiled a fist full of my hair in his fingers. I tasted his sweet breath on my tongue as his lips danced with mine. He ripped my backpack off, lifting me up off of the ground as I wrapped my legs around him. He pressed me against a tree and kissed me passionately as I ran my fingers through the curls in his hair.

I felt him hard beneath his jeans as he pressed himself against me. I kissed him eagerly as I reached for the buckle of his belt. He set me down and unzipped his pants as I pulled my own down in a frenzy. He gripped my ass firmly as he lifted my leg up around his waist in desperation.

"Look at me," he breathed as he stared into me.

I panted as he lifted me up and lowered me onto his enormously hard shaft.

I moaned, feeling completely full as he made his way inside of me. He whimpered as he thrust himself into me – fucking me greedily as he lifted me against the tree.

"I've wanted you since the first time I saw you," I panted as I stared into his eyes, feeling him hit my g spot with each thrust. "Tell me you wanted me too. . ."

"I wanted you," he panted, sucking on my bottom lip as he pummeled me.

I felt high. He was so much bigger than I had imagined

and it had been a hot minute since I had let a guy fuck me. It felt so good, I *knew* he could tell how tight I was and how much I was enjoying this.

"I jacked off when you left the office, thinking about you touching yourself on my couch. I knew I had to stop seeing you professionally. I knew I had to make you mine," he growled.

"Dr. Griffin!" I cried out, locking my legs around him as I felt my clit rub against his body with every slam he delivered. My eyes rolled in the back of my head as the bark of the tree dug into the back of my coat.

"Tell me you're mine," he said as he buried himself into me.

"I'm yours," I cried.

"You're *mine.*"

I locked eyes with him as he got me closer. I felt his dick expand and contract as he got ready to explode.

"Thea, you're so fucking tight for me – I'm going to cum soon."

"You better fill me up, Doug!" I said, biting his earlobe. "Show me who it belongs to."

"Holy fuck," he moaned. "I love you," he said, looking into my eyes.

"I love you too," I exhaled as I got ready to come undone.

He gasped my name as I felt him empty himself into me. I shuddered as I reached my own release right after – crying out in little breaths as he held me there against the trunk of the tree. He held me for several seconds before pulling out of me – setting me down gently as he tried to catch his breath.

"Wow," I gasped, shaking my head in wonder as I stared back at him.

He pulled his jeans up, shaking his head in disbelief as I zipped up my pants.

He was so fucking beautiful. I couldn't believe how completely in love with him I already was. I felt my stomach do somersaults as he looked at me.

"That was *not* how I thought this day would play out," I laughed.

"I know what you mean," he exhaled, kissing me gently on my lips as he tucked a strand of hair behind my ear. "But I'm happy this happened, Thea. I meant everything I said to you. Please forget about your revenge on Lira. Fuck her! Seriously. Forget about her and leave here with me!"

I held my breath as he looked pleadingly into my eyes.

"You're not a murderer, Dorothea. You just have dark fantasies. And I'm not a bad doctor. I just happened to fall for you! This is all really fucked up, but we can work *through* this – I promise you! Just *leave her*. Let it go. Please! Leave her and come home with me!"

I felt tears sting my eyes as he held my face in his hands.

"Be with me?" he whispered.

I nodded my head as I felt tears roll down my cheeks.

"I don't want you to hurt me," I cried as he pulled me into his chest. "I can't be hurt anymore . . ."

"I won't hurt you!" he consoled me. "I *know* what they did to you, Thea. I won't hurt you like that!"

"I can't go through this again," I sobbed.

He held me tightly as I cried into his chest. He kissed the top of my head and I slowly relaxed into him, trying to calm myself down as I listened to the sound of his heartbeat.

"It's going to be okay, Thea," he promised me. "Just go back to Lira and break things off with her. Get your things and leave with me. *Please.*"

I exhaled, wiping my cheeks as I looked up at him. His eyes were filled with concern and something unspoken as he looked down at me. I had seen that look before, but didn't know if I could trust it after everything I had been through. But I knew in this moment with sincerity that his feelings were true. It was written all over his face as he stared down at me. Love. And not the superficial kind. The kind that swallows you whole and holds you hostage. I knew he belonged to me now. And I wanted to belong to him too. I knew that in order to do that, I had to let go of my vengeance on Lira. I felt a pang of anger as I looked over my shoulder in the direction of where she awaited me.

"Be with me," he whispered. "Leave her and be in a real relationship. One without lies and deception. Leave with me and I'll love you, Thea. I'll treat you the way you deserve."

I took a deep breath, sighing before looking back at him. I smiled before pulling him into my arms – squeezing him tightly as I nodded my head.

"Just give me a bit to get back there and get all of my things," I said. "I'll meet you back here when I'm done talking to her."

"You're not going to kill her," he said – needing reassurance.

"I guess I'll let her live," I muttered as I bent down to grab my backpack.

"Then I'll be waiting here," he smiled, tracing his thumb over my lower lip.

"You mean what you said?" I asked, feeling nervous. "You really love me?"

"I'm so stupid in love with you, Dorothea. I wouldn't risk all of this for you if I wasn't. Go break up with your girlfriend so that I can be your boyfriend."

"Boyfriend." I repeated, loving how the word tasted on my lips.

"I know. It's crazy. But this is real, Thea."

I nodded my head – still whirling from everything that had just transpired.

"God, I can't believe I'm dating my *doctor*," I smirked, biting my lip as I looked back at him seductively. "That's so fucking *hot*."

"Get out of here!" he laughed, rolling his eyes at me. "Hurry back! I'll be here waiting for you."

I smiled as I swung the backpack over my shoulders and moved back into the trees. Lira really had no idea how lucky she was that I sought therapy. I made a mental note to thank Dr. Griffin for keeping me out of jail the next time he was balls deep inside of me.

CHAPTER 34

I made my way back to the campsite, smiling in a daze as I felt the remnants of his cum dripping down my leg. I would for sure have to get the day after pill. I hadn't been fucked like that in a long time – if ever! Who would have guessed that Doug was hung like a horse?

I felt my heart flutter at the memory of him telling me he loved me. I was giddy and high as I replayed it over and over again in my mind. His lips. His moans. His strong arms holding me up as he fucked me against the tree. I couldn't get over it. He said, *"You're mine."* I was completely whipped over him now!

I smelled the smoke of the campfire as I made my way back through the brush and into the clearing where Lira awaited me. She was sitting on the stump of a tree, sobbing hopelessly as I crept up behind her. I cleared my throat and watched as she looked up at me through tear-stained eyes – leaping to her feet as I approached her.

"Thea!" she wailed, throwing herself at me.

I felt myself go rigid as she wrapped her arms around me, wailing into my chest like one of those obnoxious baby doll toys that sound like they're dying when you squeeze their bellies. I pushed her away, taking a step back as she wiped the snot from her nose on the sleeve of her sweater.

"I thought you left me here," she cried. "I tried to call you, but I couldn't because something's wrong with my phone! It won't turn on! I was so afraid!"

I tried not to laugh as she held the dead hunk of metal in her hands. I took a deep breath before looking up into her swollen brown eyes.

"We're breaking up," I said as I stared down at her. "I just needed to clear my head and get some space. But I don't need time to think about this, Lira. You can be with Tess now. We're through."

Her mouth opened as she stared at me. I felt awkward as she seemingly waited for me to have something else to say.

"I'm just going to get my things and leave. I'll give you the iPad so that you can find your way back to the car."

"But we came here together," she said in disbelief, holding herself as she looked up at me. "It's dark out. You're just going to leave me here?"

"You'll be fine," I said, shrugging my shoulders. "And I'll find my own way home."

"Don't be ridiculous!" she snapped, taking a step toward me. "You're not going to leave me in the middle of nowhere! Can't you at least stay with me until morning?"

"I'm *not* going to stay with you!" I shook my head incredulously. "Seriously, count your blessings that I'm leaving, Lira! You should be *glad* that I'm going – honestly! I fucking despise you and want nothing to do with you anymore! There aren't enough miles on this Earth to satisfy the distance I want between us! I literally never want to see you again!"

"Thea, please," she sniffled, pleading as she followed me to the tent.

"Just back the fuck off and let me pack my things!" I

huffed. "I'll leave the tent and some food! You'll be okay!"

"Please just fucking talk to me!" she sobbed, grabbing my arm as I tried to walk away from her.

"Don't fucking touch me!" I screamed, pushing her back.

I pushed her hard and she stumbled, falling onto the ground in shock as she stared back up at me.

"I won't tell you again, Lira! Leave me the fuck alone!"

I reached into the tent and pulled out some of my belongings, getting ready to shove as much as I could fit into my bag.

"We can work this out, Thea," she cried, wiping the dirt off of her backside as she stood up to face me. "I told you, I'll leave Tess! We can go to counseling!"

"Honestly, Lira, it's like that saying! 'You lose them how you find them.' I should have known you would cheat on me when we started our relationship in the first place by having an affair! I'm an idiot for thinking you would be any different with me!"

"I didn't mean for this to happen!" she cried. "Do you think I *liked* lying to you? It ate me up inside! I feel like a fucking monster, ok?! I didn't know what the fuck I was supposed to do!"

"I don't know, Lira! How about closing your legs for starters? And Tess? Seriously? She is *foul*! You could have done so much better than that fucking giant foreheaded wildebeest!"

"You don't even know her!" she screamed. "If you only gave her a chance . . ."

"Lira, you don't get it," I sighed, turning to face her. "You and I are over! What do I need to say to you to get it through your head?"

"I know that you love me," she cried, shaking her head

326

in denial. "I know we can work through this. Please don't give up on me!"

"Lira, you've been in a fucking relationship for almost half a year!" I laughed. "Seriously, go fuck yourself! You're a terrible girlfriend! I'm actually convinced you're a terrible human being! I really just can't even believe I ever even cared about you! It's over! I mean it! I never want to see you again!"

Lira screamed in frustration, kicking the pot of macaroni into the fire as she pulled at her thinning hair. I laughed, taking her by surprise as she looked back at me. I shook my head in amusement as I started loading my backpack.

"How can you be fucking laughing right now?" she asked in exasperation. "Do you honestly not care at *all?!*"

"Nope," I said, as I continued getting my things together. I felt her eyes burning into me as she continued to fight with me.

"Thea, please . . ." she pleaded.

"I've known for months," I said, turning to face her. "I've known for almost 12 weeks."

She blinked several times as she stared up at me in shock. I glared at her as flames painted her face orange – the light from the fire glowing as I took a step closer.

"I've been in on your little affair for a long time now," I snickered. "At first, I was in denial. But, I read your conversations every fucking day. I really didn't want to believe it though, so you know what I did, Lira? I put a fucking bug in your car."

"You did *what?*" she whispered.

"I bugged your car," I replied. "I put cameras all over our house too! I watched you fuck Tess in our bed while I was out of town, Lira. I never even went out of town! I left for a few days to see what you would do without me! You brought your fucking whore into the home you share with me! Do you have any idea how that made me feel?"

She stared at me in stunned silence as I felt rage building from somewhere deep within.

"You know I've been seeing a therapist?" I laughed. "I felt like I was going crazy! I couldn't believe you were doing this to me! I couldn't believe you fucking played me the way that you did!"

Her mouth hung open as I stared into her. Tears poured from her eyes as I spoke through gritted teeth.

"You're a fucking whore, Lira – you know that? I mean, what kind of *monster* treats their girlfriend that way? I fucking hate you, Lira. I hate you!"

"Wait, wait, wait," Lira said – throwing her hands up in the air. "I need to process this. Why didn't you tell me you knew?!"

"Why the fuck would I?" I laughed.

"Wait," she said – confusion still on her face. "You've been spying on me?"

"That's what you're upset about?" I laughed. "For fuck's sake, Lira!"

"Why didn't you just fucking *talk to me*?" she wailed. "I don't even know what to say to you right now!"

"Say to me?!" I asked incredulously. "You're the one who has been having an affair! You know what, this is fucking stupid! I don't even know why we are talking right now, to be honest. I've gotta go. My boyfriend is waiting for me."

"Your WHAT?!" she screamed.

I smirked, taking a step closer to her.

"Oh, did you think that you were the only one having all

of the fun?"

"What the fuck are you talking about, Dorothea?"

"Just leave me alone," I huffed. "I am serious. I need to go. What do I need to tell you to make you stop groveling? How about this? I dumped your grandma's ashes down the sink weeks ago. I've spit in your food and drinks when you're not looking. I hid things that were special to you. I put Nair in your fucking shampoo!"

I cackled, shaking my head as I looked down at her. Her eyes widened in horror as she registered what I had been saying.

"I fucked my ex-girlfriend in our bed several times while you were working! It really was Tedra's hair that you found on your pillow! I've hired Tess to be my personal trainer and have met up with her a few times behind your back! She's had me in her house, Lira! I told her you were a sex addict to try to get her to leave you. You're fucking pathetic! You cheat on me with a fucking ugly ass horse faced meathead who lives in her parents' basement? Like seriously, do you have any idea how pathetic you are? Talk about a downgrade! Your children will have huge teeth and huge foreheads! That's assuming you even last that long, which I doubt because you guys are fucking awful! I give it a few months – tops – and she'll be onto someone better."

I took a deep breath, shaking my head in disgust before looking away from her. It happened so quickly; I almost didn't realize what had happened. One second, she was several feet away from me and the next, she was right next to me - grabbing my phone from the stump I had set it down on while I packed. She leapt back from me and I stared at her in worried confusion as she unlocked my phone.

"You fucking bugged my car," she whispered through gritted teeth.

I stared at her anxiously as she stepped farther back from me.

"You put hidden cameras in our house and practically stalked me? You destroyed my grandmother's ashes and had the audacity to put Nair in my shampoo?!"

"Lira," I said, taking a step closer to her. "What are you doing?"

"Stay the fuck BACK!" she screamed, holding her hand out in front of her.

I froze, feeling anxiety consume me as she stared at me with hatred in her eyes.

"You act so high and mighty, but you're a fucking *psychopath*, Thea! The things you just admitted to doing are fucking *insane*! Did you really think I'd just be ok with this? You watched me cry for weeks and weeks about my hair falling out and it was falling out because of *you*! You're a fucking sociopath, Thea! You're fucking crazy!"

"Lira, calm down," I said, taking a step closer to her.

"Stay back!" she screamed, shaking her head as she lifted my phone.

"You're done for, Dorothea! *Do you hear me*? You're going to prison by the time that I'm through with you! You invaded my privacy and destroyed my personal belongings! You maimed me and stalked me! You stalked Tess too! I'm going to tell *everybody*, Thea! I'm going to get a restraining order and I'm going to the police! I'm going to call your family! Your life is over! You're through! You're a fucking psychotic *bitch*, do you hear me?! You need to be locked up! You're fucking insane!"

"Lira, wait," I said, feeling my heart increase as she looked down at my phone.

"I'm calling the police," she cried, shaking her head at

me. "Stay the fuck away from me, Thea! You're not going to stop me!"

She turned her back and I lost touch with reality. I didn't realize I had pulled the knife out of my backpack pack until she turned away from me.

"If you press one button, I'll fucking slit your throat," I said through gritted teeth.

Lira looked back at me and froze as she registered the giant blade in my hand.

"Thea, what the fuck?" she asked, afraid. "Why do you have a fucking knife?"

"Put my phone down or I will fucking kill you! I mean it, Lira!" I screamed.

Lira stood frozen. I watched as she tried to determine whether I was bluffing. I was *not* bluffing.

"Don't make me say it again," I warned her. "Drop my fucking phone, or I swear to fucking God."

She threw my phone down and stared at me, wide eyed.

"Thea, just calm down," she whispered. "Give me the knife."

"You fucking bitch," I said, pointing the knife at her. "*You're* the one who cheated on me. *You're* the one who ruined my friendship with Ray. You think you're going to ruin my life now too?"

"Thea, stop," Lira pleaded, shaking her head. "This is getting crazy! Put the knife down! Let's talk about this."

"Shut up!!!!!!!!!" I screamed. "Shut up, shut up, shut up!!!!!!!!!"

I felt rage as I stared across at her. Who the fuck did she think she was?

"Give me the knife," Lira said, taking a step closer. "I

won't call the police, okay? We can talk about this. You're scaring me."

"I hate you," I cried, shaking my head. "You did this! Not me!"

"It's okay," she said, moving closer. "Just put the knife down."

I closed my eyes, holding back tears as I tried to calm myself down. It only took that one second of letting my guard down for Lira to lunge at me.

I screamed as Lira grabbed at the handle of the knife.

"Give me the knife, Thea!" she yelled, tugging with her entire body weight to pull it away from me. "You're fucking crazy!"

"Lira stop!" I shouted, pulling back with equal force.

I locked eyes with her as she grappled with me to let it go.

"Let it go!" she screamed.

She pushed me and I toppled back, pulling her with me.

I felt like I was out of my body as we fell to the ground. I felt the long blade plunge into her abdomen. I felt it penetrate her flesh before she started screaming. She rolled off me and I scrambled backward – my eyes wide in horror as I watched her pull the ten inch blade out of her gut.

"Thea," she said in shock as I watched her cream-colored sweater turn scarlet. The knife had gone all the way through her, leaving a gash toward the center of her stomach. She rolled on her back, panting as she pulled her hand away from her sweater – the palm of her hand was wet with blood as she began to cough.

I grabbed the knife and my phone and checked it in a panic. I felt sick to my stomach as I looked down at her. She laid on the ground and stared up at me as blood poured from her wound!

Shit!

"Lira," I whispered, as she gazed up at me in horror. She coughed and blood collected on the corners of her lips.

I stood frozen in a panic as I gazed down at her. My hands trembled as I heard a voice come from behind me in the trees.

"Thea," Dr. Griffin said.

I whipped around, looking at him in terror as his eyes moved behind me to Lira's crumpled body on the ground.

"Help . . . me . . ." Lira whispered, reaching her hand up to Doug as he stepped out into the light of the glowing flames. "Help me," she pleaded, moving her hand down to the stab wound. She sputtered up more blood as she looked up at him with desperation in her gaze. "Call 911."

Dr. Griffin pushed passed me, crouching down at her side. He lifted up her sweater and recoiled as blood pooled out of both sides of her – a puddle forming on the dirt beneath where she laid.

"Jesus Christ," he whispered in terror, staring up at me with disbelief in his eyes. "Thea, what the fuck did you do?"

I couldn't breathe. I felt suffocated as he looked up at me. I felt a rush of panic wash over me as I realized the gravity of what had happened. I stared at my phone in my hand, feeling tears sting my eyes as I contemplated what had to be done.

"Please help me," Lira gurgled, clutching Dr. Griffin's coat in her wet, bloody fingers.

He nodded his head, standing up behind her. I stared at him – not knowing what do to- as I watched him crouch down by the fire. I watched in confusion as he rose with something in his hands.

333

Lira laid on her back in the pool of blood beneath her. She was struggling to breathe as he stood behind her, clutching a boulder in his hands. At first, I didn't realize what he was doing. I felt like I was in some kind of shock as he made his way closer to her. Lira looked up then with horror in her eyes. She barely had time to let out a faint scream.

Dr. Griffin dropped the boulder. I watched as it fell on her face, crushing her skull beneath it. I flinched at the sound of crunching and splatter as it landed. I gaped in horror as Dr. Griffin and I stood silently – staring at her dead body as if we were both in trance.

After what seemed like an eternity, Doug made his way over to me. I trembled as he carefully reached for the knife in my hand.

"Thea, give this to me," he said, gently taking the knife away from me.

I was frozen – staring at her body in disbelief before looking up at him.

"You . . . you dropped a boulder on her head," I whispered.

Tears pooled in his eyes as he nodded at me.

"You stabbed her, Thea," he said – his voice catching in his throat as he looked at me. "She probably wouldn't have lived long enough for the paramedics to get here."

"It was an accident," I said – still in shock. "She's dead."

"She was going to ruin you," he whispered, grabbing my chin so that I would face him. "She was going to go to the *police*, Thea. She was going to put you in jail."

I felt lightheaded as he set the knife down before stepping closer to me. I heard the crackles and pops of the fire and the wind in the leaves as he gripped the sides of my arms.

"Thea, listen to me," he said, pulling my attention back

to him. "Everything's going to be ok – do you hear me? Now is not the time to panic!"

"She's dead," I repeated – still in denial as I glanced back behind him at the corpse on the ground.

"She is," he nodded. "And isn't that what you've wanted?"

I looked back at him – the reflection of flames dancing in his eyes as he penetrated me with his stare.

"You're not a murderer, Thea. This wasn't your fault! But, I couldn't let this destroy your life, either! I love you, Thea. Do you hear me? I love you!"

I felt tears stream down my face as I gazed back up at him.

"Everything's going to be okay," he assured me. "Just stay right here. I'm going to look for a place to get rid of the body."

He turned away from me and disappeared into the darkness beyond the campfire. The sound of his footsteps grew softer as he made his way back into the trees. I felt a calm embrace me like a warm blanket as I waited for him to come back to me. And I *knew* that he would come back to me.

I sat down next to Lira and held her hand as I waited for him to return. I didn't know how to hide a body, but I *knew* that I was ready and willing to learn. How hard could it be, after all? It's always so easy in the movies. I thought about the 2.3 million acres of the forest. People disappear every day! I took a deep breath as I looked down at her. I almost felt bad about how everything played out.

Almost.

Made in United States
North Haven, CT
28 May 2024

53045511R00185